# THE ULVERSCROFT FOUNDATION
## (registered UK charity number 264873)

was established in 1972 to provide funds for research, diagnosis and treatment of eye diseases. Examples of major projects funded by the Ulverscroft Foundation are:-

- The Children's Eye Unit at Moorfields Eye Hospital, London
- The Ulverscroft Children's Eye Unit at Great Ormond Street Hospital for Sick Children
- Funding research into eye diseases and treatment at the Department of Ophthalmology, University of Leicester
- The Ulverscroft Vision Research Group, Institute of Child Health
- Twin operating theatres at the Western Ophthalmic Hospital, London
- The Chair of Ophthalmology at the Royal Australian College of Ophthalmologists

You can help further the work of the Foundation by making a donation or leaving a legacy. Every contribution is gratefully received. If you would like to help support the Foundation or require further information, please contact:

**THE ULVERSCROFT FOUNDATION**
**The Green, Bradgate Road, Anstey**
**Leicester LE7 7FU, England**
**Tel: (0116) 236 4325**

**website: www.foundation.ulverscroft.com**

# THE LAST POST

In England, the hells and horrors of the Great War are slowly receding, but the scars remain . . . With an American tenant ensconced in the Tietjens' ancestral home of Groby, Christopher and Valentine, now domiciled together in a rural cottage, must attempt to negotiate the hazardous terrain of peactime. Whilst he immerses himself in his antique furniture business, she privately harbours deep concerns regarding the future of their unborn child. For even now, the shadow of Sylvia — Christopher's estranged wife — still looms . . .

FORD MADOX FORD

# THE LAST POST

*PARADE'S END PART 4*

*Complete and Unabridged*

# ULVERSCROFT
*Leicester*

First published in Great Britain in 1928 by
Duckworth

This Large Print Edition
published 2013

The moral right of the author has been asserted

A catalogue record for this book is available
from the British Library.

ISBN 978–1–4448–1678–5

Published by
F. A. Thorpe (Publishing)
Anstey, Leicestershire

Set by Words & Graphics Ltd.
Anstey, Leicestershire
Printed and bound in Great Britain by
T. J. International Ltd., Padstow, Cornwall

This book is printed on acid-free paper

*Oh Rokehope is a pleasant place*
*If the fause thieves would let it be*

# Part One

# 1

He lay staring at the withy binders of his thatch shelter; the grass was infinitely green; his view embraced four counties; the roof was supported by six small oak sapling-trunks, roughly trimmed and brushed from above by apple boughs. French crab-apple! The hut had no sides.

The Italian proverb says: He who allows the boughs of trees to spread above his roof invites the doctor daily. Words to that effect! He would have grinned, but that might have been seen.

For a man who never moved, his face was singularly walnut-coloured; his head, indenting the skim-milk white of the pillows should have been a gipsy's, the dark, silvered hair cut extremely close, the whole face very carefully shaven and completely immobile. The eyes moved, however, with unusual vivacity, all the life of the man being concentrated in them and their lids.

Down the path that had been cut in swathes from the knee-high grass and led from the stable to the hut, a heavy elderly peasant rolled in his gait. His over-long, hairy arms swung as if he needed an axe or a log or a full sack to make him a complete man. He was broad-beamed, in cord breeches very tight in the buttocks; he wore black leggings, an unbuttoned blue waistcoat, a striped flannel shirt, open at the perspiring neck and a square, high hat of black felt.

He said:

'Want to be shifted?'

The man in the bed closed his eyelids slowly.

''Ave a droper cider?'

The other again similarly closed his eyes. The standing man supported himself with an immense hand, gorilla-like, by one of the oaken posts.

'Best droper cider ever I tasted,' he said, ''Is Lordship give me. 'Is Lordship sester me: 'Gunning,' 'e ses . . . The day the vixen got into keeper's coop enclosure . . . '

He began and slowly completed a very long story going to prove that English noble landlords preferred foxes to pheasants. Or should! English landowners of the right kidney.

'Is Lordship would no more 'ave that vixen killed or so much as flurried, she being gravid like than . . . Dreadful work a gravid vixen can do among 'encoops with pheasant poults . . . Have to eat fer six or seven, she

4

have! All a-growing . . .    So 'is Lordship sester Gunning . . .

And then the description of the cider . . . 'Ard! Thet cider was 'arder than a miser's 'art or 'n ole maid's tongue. Body it 'ad. Strength it 'ad. Stans to reason. Ten-year cider. Not a drop was drunk in Lordship's 'ouse under ten years in cask. Killed three sheep a week fer his indoor and outdoor servants. An' three hundred pigeons. The pigeon-cotes is a hundred feet high an' the pigeons nesteses in 'oles in the inside walls. Clap-nests a 'ole wall at a go an' takes the squabs. Times is not what they was but 'is Lordship keeps on. An always will!

The man in the bed — Mark Tietjens — continued his own thoughts:

Old Gunning lumbered slowly up the path towards the stable, his hands swinging. The stable was a tile-healed, thatched affair, no real stable in the North Country sense — a place where the old mare sheltered among chickens and ducks. There was no tidiness amongst South Country folk. They hadn't it in them, though Gunning could bind a tidy thatch and trim a hedge properly. All-round man. Really an all-round man; he could do a great many things. He knew all about fox-hunting, pheasant-rearing, wood-craft, hedging, dyking, pig-rearing and the habits of

5

King Edward when shooting. Smoking endless great cigars! One finished, light another, throw away the stub . . .

Fox-hunting, the sport of kings with only twenty per cent of the danger of war! He, Mark Tietjens, had never cared for hunting; now he would never do any more; he had never cared for pheasant-shooting. He would never do any more. Not couldn't; wouldn't from henceforth . . . It annoyed him that he had not taken the trouble to ascertain what it was Iago said, before he had taken Iago's resolution . . . *From henceforth he never would speak word.* . . . Something to that effect: but you could not get that into a blank verse line.

Perhaps Iago had not been speaking blank verse when he had taken his, Mark Tietjens' resolution . . . *Took by the throat the circumcised dog and smote him* . . . . Good man, Shakespeare! All-round man in a way, too. Probably very like Gunning. Knew Queen Elizabeth's habits when hunting; also very likely how to hedge, thatch, break up a deer or a hare or a hog, and how to serve a writ and write bad French. Lodged with a French family somewhere in a Crutched Friars or the Minories. Somewhere.

The ducks were making a great noise on the pond up the hill. Old Gunning in the sunlight lumbered between the stable-wall and the raspberry canes, uphill. The garden was all uphill. Mark looked across the grass up at the hedge. When they turned his bed round he looked down on the house. Rough, grey stone.

Half round, he looked across the famous four counties; half round, the other way on, he could see up a steep grass-bank to the hedge on the main roadside. Now he was looking uphill across the tops of the hay-grass, over the raspberry canes at the hedge that Gunning was going to trim . . . Full of consideration for him, they were, all the lot of them. For ever thinking of finding possible interests for him. He did not need it. He had interests enough.

Up the pathway that was above, beyond the hedge, on a grass slope, went the Elliot children — a lanky girl of ten with very long, corn-coloured hair; a fat boy of five in a sailor's suit — unspeakably dirty. The girl too long in the legs and ankles, her hair limp . . . War-starvation in early years! Well, that was not his, Mark Tietjens', fault. He had given the nation the Transport it needed: the nation should have found the food. They had not, so the children had long thin legs and wristbones that protruded on pipe-stems. All that generation! . . . No fault of his! He had

7

managed the Transport as it should be managed. His department had. His own department, built up by himself from junior temporary clerk to senior permanent official; he had built it up, from the day of his entrance thirty years ago, to the day of his resolution never more to speak word.

Nor yet stir a finger! He had to be in this world, in this nation. Let them care for him, for he was done with them . . . He knew the sire and dam of every horse from Eclipse to Perlmutter. That was enough for him. They helped him to read all that could be read about racing. He had interests enough!

The ducks on the pond continued to make a great noise, churning the water, up the hill, boisterously with their wings, and squawking. If they had been hens there would have been something the matter — a dog chasing them. Ducks did not signify. They went mad, contagiously. Like nations or all the cattle of a county.

Gunning, lumbering past the raspberry canes, took a bud or so and squeezed the pale things between finger and thumb. Looking for traces of maggots. Pale green leaves the raspberry had: a fragile plant among the robuster rosaceæ. That was not starvation, but race. Their commissariat was efficient enough, but presumably they were not gross feeders. Gunning began to trim the hedge with sharp, brushing blows of his bagging hook. There was still far too much bramble among the quickset: in a week the hedge would be unsightly again.

They kept the hedge low so that he should be amused by passengers on the path, though they would really have preferred to let it grow high so that passers-by should not see into the orchard . . . Well, he had seen passers-by. More than they thought for! . . . What in hell was Sylvia's game? And that old ass Edward Campion's? . . . Well, he, Mark, was not going to interfere. There was undoubtedly something up . . . Marie Léonie — formerly Charlotte — knew neither of that precious couple by sight: she had certainly seen them peer down over the hedge . . .

They — it was more of their considerateness — had contrived a broad shelf on the left corner post of his shelter. So that birds should amuse him. He had always sought after larger quarry! . . . A hedge-sparrow, noiseless and quaker-grey, was ghost-like on his shelf. It flitted hiding itself deep in hedgerows. He thought of it as an American bird — or perhaps that was because there were so many Americans about there, though he never saw them . . . A voiceless nightingale, slim, long, thin-billed, almost

9

without markings as becomes a bird that seldom sees the sun, but lives in the deep twilight of deep hedges ... American because it ought to wear a scarlet letter. Nearly all he knew of Americans came from a book he had once read — about a woman like a hedge-sparrow, creeping furtive in hedge-rows and getting into trouble with a priest ... But no doubt there were other types.

This desultory, slim, obviously Puritan bird, inserted its thin bill into the dripping that Gunning had put on the shelf for the tomtits. The riotous tomtit, the great tit, the bottle-tit ... all that family love dripping. The hedge-sparrow obviously did not; the dripping on that warmish June day had become oleaginous. The hedge-sparrow, its bill all greased, mumbled its upper mandible with its lower but took no more dripping. It looked at Mark's eyes. Because these regarded it motionlessly it uttered a long warning note and flitted, noiseless, into invisibility. All hedge things ignore you whilst you move on and do not regard them. The moment you stay still and fix your eyes on them they warn the rest of the hedge and flit off. This hedge-sparrow no doubt had its young within ear-shot. Or the warning might have been just co-operative.

Marie Léonie née Riotor, was coming up

the steps and then the path. He knew that by the sound of her breathing. She stood beside him, shapeless in her long pinafore of printed cotton, holding a plate of soup and saying:

'Mon pauvre homme! Mon pauvre homme! Ce qu'ils ont fait detoi!'

She began a breathless discourse in French. She was of the large, blonde, Norman type; in the middle forties, her extremely fair hair very voluminous and noticeable. She had lived with Mark Tietjens for twenty years now, but she had always refused to speak a word of English, having an invincible scorn for both language and people of her adopted country.

Her discourse poured on. She had set the little tray with the plate of reddish-yellowish soup on a flat shelf of wood that turned out on a screw from underneath the bed; in the soup was a shining clinical thermometer that she moved and regarded from time to time, beside the plate a glass syringe, graduated. She said that *Ils* — They — had combined to render her soup of vegetables uneatable. They would not give her *navets de Paris* but round ones, like buttons; they contrived that the carrots should be *pourris* at their bottom ends; the leeks were of the consistency of wood. They were determined that he should not have vegetable soup because they wanted

11

him to have meat juice. They were anthropophagi. Nothing but meat, meat, meat! That girl! . . .

She had always in the Grey's Inn Road had Paris turnips from Jacopo's in Old Compton Street. There was no reason why you should not grow *navets de Paris* in this soil. The Paris turnip was barrel-shaped, round, round, round like an adorable little pig till it turned into its funny little tail. That was a turnip to amuse you; to change and employ your thoughts. *Ils* — he and she — were incapable of having their thoughts changed by a turnip.

Between sentences she ejaculated from time to time:

'My poor man! What they have made of you?'

Her volubility flowed over Mark like a rush of water over a grating, only a phrase or so now and then coming to his attention. It was not unpleasant; he liked his woman. She had a cat that she made abstain from meat on a Friday. In the Gray's Inn Road that had been easier, in a large room decorated with innumerable miniatures and silhouettes representing members of the Riotor family and its branches. Mme Riotor *mere* and Mme Riotor *grand'mere* too had been miniature painters and Marie Léonie possessed some

12

astonishingly white statuary by the distinguished sculptor Casimir-Bar, a life-long friend of her family who had only never been decorated because of a conspiracy. So he had a great contempt for decorations and the decorated. Marie Léonie had been accustomed to repeat the voluminous opinions of Monsieur Casimir-Bar on the subject of decorations at great length on occasion. Since he, Mark, had been honoured by his sovereign she had less frequently recited them. She admitted that the democracy of to-day had not the sterling value that had distinguished democrats of the day of her parents, so it might be better to *caser* oneself — to find a niche amongst those whom the State distinguished.

The noise of her voice, which was deep-chested and not unpleasing, went on. Mark regarded her with the ironic indulgence that you accord to a child, but indeed, when he had been still in harness it had rested him always to come home as he had done every Thursday and Monday and not infrequently on a Wednesday when there had been no racing. It had rested him to come home from a world of incompetent imbeciles and to hear this brain comment on that world. She had views on virtue, pride, downfalls, human careers, the habits of cats, fish, the clergy,

13

diplomats, soldiers, women of easy virtue, Saint Eustachius, President Grévy, the purveyors of comestibles, custom-house officers, pharmacists, Lyons silk weavers, the keepers of boarding-houses, garotters, chocolate-manufacturers, sculptors other than M. Casimir-Bar, the lovers of married women, housemaids . . . Her mind in fact was like a cupboard, stuffed, packed with the most incongruous materials, tools, vessels, and debris. Once the door was opened you never knew what would tumble out or be followed by what. That was restful to Mark as foreign travel might have been — only he had never been abroad except when his father, before his accession to Groby, had lived in Dijon for his children's education. That was how he knew French.

Her conversation had another quality that continually amused him: she always ended it with the topic with which she had chosen to begin. Thus, to-day having chosen to begin with *navets de Paris*, with Paris turnips she would end, and it amused him to observe how on each occasion she would bring the topic back. She might be concluding a long comment on ironclads and have to get back suddenly to custards because the door-bell rang while her maid was out, but accomplish the transition she would before she answered the bell. Otherwise she was frugal, shrewd, astonishingly clean and healthy.

Whilst she was giving him his soup, inserting the glass syringe in his lips at half minute intervals which she timed by her wrist-watch, she was talking about furniture . . . *Ils* would not let her apply to the species of rabbit-hutches in the salon a varnish that she imported from Paris; Monsieur her brother-in-law had really exhibited when she had actually varnished a truly discreditable chair — had exhibited a distraction that had really filled her with amusement. It was possible that the fashion of the day was for furniture of decrepitude or gross forms. That *they* would not let her place in the salon the newly gilt arm-chair of her late mother or the sculptural group representing Niobe and some of her offspring by the late Monsieur Casimir-Bar or the over-mantel clock that was an exact reproduction in bronze of the Fountain of the Medicis in the gardens of the Luxembourg at Paris — that was a matter of taste. *Elle* might very well feel umbrage that she, Marie Léonie, should possess articles of such acknowledged prestige. For what could be more unapproachable than a Second Empire fauteuil newly gilt and maintained, she could assure the world, at such a pitch of

15

glitter as dazzled the eyes? *Elle* might very well feel umbrage when you considered that the skirt that she wore when gardening was . . . Well, in short was what it was! Nevertheless in that skirt she allowed herself to be seen by the clergyman. But why did *Il* who was admittedly a man of honour and sensibility and reputed to know all the things of this world and perhaps of the next — why did He join in the infinitely stupid conspiracy against the work of the great genius Casimir-Bar? She, Marie Léonie, could understand that He, in his difficult situation would not wish to give permission to instal in the Salon works at which *Elle* took umbrage because her possessions did not include objects of art which all the world acknow-ledged to be of classic rank, not to mention the string of pearls which she, Marie Léonie, Riotor by birth, owed to the generosity of him, Mark, and her own economies. And other objects of value and taste. That was reasonable. If your woman is poorly *dot*-ed . . . let us call it *dot*-ed . . . because, certainly she, Marie Léonie, was not one to animadvert upon those in situations of difficulty . . . It would ill become her so to do! Nevertheless a great period of years of honesty, frugality, regularity of life and cleanliness . . . And she asked Mark if he had ever seen in *her* parlour

16

traces of mud such as on wet days she had certainly observed in the salon of a certain person . . . And certain revelations she could make as to what had used to be the condition of a cupboard under the stairs and the state to be observed behind certain presses in the kitchen! But if you have not had experience in the control of domestics, what would you? . . . Nevertheless a stretch of years passed in the state of housewifeliness such as she had already adumbrated upon gave one the right to comment — of course — with delicacy, upon the *ménage* of a young person even though her delicate situation might avert from her comment of an un-Christian nature as to certain other facts. It did however seem to her, Marie Léonie, that to appear before a clergyman in a skirt decorated with no less than three visible *tâches* of petrol, wearing gloves encrusted with mud as you encrust a truffle with paste before baking it under the cinders — and holding, of all implements, a common gardening-trowel . . . And to laugh and joke with him! . . . Surely the situation called for a certain — let them call it, retirement of demeanour. She was far from according to the Priest the extravagant privileges to which priests laid claim. The late Monsieur Casimir-Bar was accustomed to say that if we accorded to our *soi-disant* spiritual

17

advisers all that they would take we should lie upon a bed that had neither sheets, *eidredons*, pillows, bolsters, nor settle. And she, Marie-Léonie, was inclined to agree with Monsieur Casimir-Bar, though, as one of the heroes of the barricades in 1848, he was apt to be a little extreme in his tenets. Still a vicar is in England a functionary of the State and as such should be received with a certain modesty and reserve. On the other hand — she, Marie Léonie — formerly Riotor, her mother having been born Lavigne-Bourdreau and having in consequence a suspicion of Huguenot blood so that she, Marie Léonie, might be expected to know how the Protestant clergy should be received — she, then, Marie Léonie, from the little window on the side of the stairs, had distinctly seen *Elle* lay one hand on the shoulder of that clergyman and point — point, mind you, with the *trowel* — to the open front door and say — she had distinctly heard the words: 'Poor man, if you have hunger you will find Mr. Tietjens in the dining-room. He is just eating a sandwich. It's hungry weather!' ... That was six months ago, but Marie Léonie's ears still tingled at the words and the gesture. A trowel! To point with a *trowel; pensez y!* If a trowel why not a *main de fer,* a dustpan? Or a vessel even more homely! ... And Marie Léonie chuckled.

Her grandmother Bourdreau remembered a crockery-merchant of the ambulating sort who had once filled one of those implements — a *vase de nuit* — but of course new, with milk and had offered the whole gratuitously to any passer-by who would drink the milk. A young woman called Laborde accepted his challenge there in the market-place of Noisy-Lebrun. She has lost her fiancé who found the gesture exaggerated. But he was a farceur, that crockery-dealer!

She drew from the pocket of her pinafore several folded pages of a newspaper and from under the bed a double picture-frame — two frames hinged together so that they would close. She inserted a sheet of the paper between the two frames and then hung the whole on a piece of picture wire that depended from the roof-tree beneath the thatch. Two braces of picture-wire too came from the supporting posts, to right and left. They held the picture-frames motionless and a little inclined towards Mark's face. She was agreeable to look at, stretching up her arms. She lifted his torso with great strength and infinite solicitude, propped it a little with the pillows and looked to see that his eyes fell on

19

the printed sheet. She said:

'You can see well, like that?'

His eyes took in the fact that he was to read of the Newbury Summer Meeting and the one at Newcastle. He closed them twice to signify Yes! The tears came into hers. She murmured:

'Mon pauvre homme! Mon pauvre homme! What they have done to you!' She drew from another pocket in her pinafore a flask of eau de cologne and a wad of cotton-wool. With that, moistened, she wiped even more solicitously his face and then his thin, mahogany hands which she uncovered. She had the air of women in France when they change the white satin clothes and wash the faces of favourite Virgins at the church doors in August.

Then she stood back and apostrophised him. He took in that the King's filly had won the Berkshire Foal plate and the horse of a friend the Seaton Delaval Handicap, at Newcastle. Both might have been expected. He had meant to go to the Newcastle meeting this year and give Newbury a by. During the last year when he had gone racing he had done rather well at Newbury so he had then thought he would try Newcastle for a change and, whilst he was there, take a look at Groby and see what that bitch Sylvia was doing with the house. Well, that was done with. They would presumably bury him at Groby.

She said, in deep, rehearsed, tones:

'My Man!' She might almost have well said: 'My Deity!' 'What sort of life is this we lead here? Was there ever anything so singular and unreasonable? If we sit to drink a cup of tea, the cup may at any moment be snatched from our mouths; if we recline upon a divan — at any moment the divan may go. I do not comment on this that you lie by night as by day for ever here in the open air, for I understand that it is by your desire and consent that you lie here and I will never exhibit aversion from that which you desire and that to which you consent. But cannot you bring it about that we should inhabit a house of some reason, one more suited to human beings of this age, and one that is less of a procession of goods and chattels? You can bring that about. You are all-powerful here. I do not know what are your resources. It was never your habit to tell me. You kept me in comfort. Never did I express a desire that you did not satisfy, though it is true that my desires were always reasonable. So I know nothing though I read once in a paper that you were a man of extravagant riches and that can hardly all have vanished for there can have been fewer men of as great a frugality

21

and you were always fortunate and moderate in your wagers. So I know nothing and I would scorn to ask of these others, for that would imply doubt of your trust in me. I do not doubt that you have made arrangements for my future comfort and I am in no uncertainty of the continuance of those arrangements. It is not material fears that I have. But all this appears to be a madness. Why are we here? What is the meaning of all this? Why do you inhabit this singular erection? It may be that the open air is of necessity for your malady. I do not believe that you lived in perpetual currents of air in your chambers, though I never saw them. But on the days you gave to me you had everything of the most comfortable and you seemed contented with my arrangements. And your brother and his woman appear so mad in all the other affairs of life that they may well be mad in this also. Why then will you not end it? You have the power. You are all-powerful here. Your brother will spring from one corner to the other of this lugubrious place in order to anticipate your slightest wish. *Elle,* too!'

Stretching out her hands she had the air of a Greek woman who invoked a deity, she was so large and fair and her hair was so luxuriantly blonde. And indeed, to her, in his mystery and silence he had the air of a deity who could discharge unthinkable darts and vouchsafe unimaginable favours. Though all their circumstances had changed, that had not changed, so that even his immobility enhanced his mystery. In all their life together, not merely here, he had been silent whilst she had talked. On the two regular days of the week on which he had been used to visit her, from the moment when she would open her door exactly at seven in the evening and see him in his bowler hat with his carefully rolled umbrella, his racing glasses slung diagonally across him, to the moment when, next morning at half-past ten she would brush his bowler and hand him that and his umbrella, he would hardly speak a word — he would speak such few words as to give the idea of an absolute taciturnity whilst she entertained him with an unceasing flow of talk and of comments on the news of the Quartier — of the French colonists of that part of London, or on the news in the French papers. He would remain seated on a hard chair, bending slightly forward, with, round the corners of his mouth little creases that suggested an endless, indulgent smile. Occasionally he would suggest that she should put half a sovereign upon a horse; occasionally he would bring her an opulent present, heavy gold bangles floridly chased and set with large emeralds, sumptuous furs, expensive travelling trunks for when she had visited Paris or went to the seaside in the autumn. That sort of thing. Once he had bought her a complete set of the works of Victor Hugo bound in purple morocco and all the works that had been illustrated by Gustave Doré, in green calf, once a hoof of a racehorse, trained in France, set in silver in the form of an inkstand. On her forty-first birthday — though she had no idea how he had ascertained that it was her forty-first birthday — he had given her a string of pearls and had taken her to a hotel at Brighton kept by an ex-prize-fighter. He had told her to wear the pearls at dinner, but to be careful of them because they had cost five hundred pounds. He asked her once about her investment of her savings and when she had told him that she was investing in French *rentes viagères* he had told her that he could do better than that for her and afterwards; from time to time he had told her of odd but very profitable ways of investing small sums.

In this way, because his gifts filled her with rapture on account of their opulence and weightiness, he had assumed for her the aspect by degrees of a godhead who could bless — and possibly blast — inscrutably. For many years after he had first picked her up in the Edgeware Road outside the old Apollo she had regarded him with suspicion since he was a man and it is the nature of men to treat women with treachery, lust, and meanness. Now she regarded herself as the companion of a godhead, secure and immune from the evil workings of Fortune — as if she had been seated on the shoulder of one of Jove's eagles, beside his throne. The Immortals had been known to choose human companions; when they had so done, fortunate indeed had been the lot of the chosen. Of them she felt herself to be one.

Even his seizure had not deprived her of her sense of his wide-spreading and inscrutable powers and she could not rid herself of the conviction that if he would, he could talk, walk, and perform the feats of strength of a Hercules. It was impossible not to think so; the vigour of his glance was undiminished and it was the dark glance of a man, proud, alert, and commanding. And the mysterious nature and occurrence of the seizure itself only confirmed her subconscious conviction. The fit had come so undramatically that although the several pompous and, for her nearly imbecile, English physicians who had been called in to attend on him, agreed that some sort of fit must have visited him as he lay in his bed, that had done nothing to change her mind. Indeed, even when her own Doctor, Drouant-Rouault, asserted with certitude and knowledge that this was a case of fulminant hemiplegia of a characteristic sort, though her reason accepted his conclusion, her subconscious intuition remained the same. Doctor Drouant-Rouault was a sensible man; that he had proved by pointing out the anatomical excellence of the works of sculpture by Monsieur Casimir-Bar and agreeing that only a conspiracy of rivals could have prevented his arriving at the post of President of the École des Beaux Arts. He was then, a man of sense and his reputation amongst the French tradesmen of the Quarter stood very high. She had never herself needed the attentions of a doctor. But if you needed a doctor, obviously you went to a Frenchman and acquiesced in what he said.

But although she acquiesced in words to others, and indeed to herself, she could not convince herself in her *for intérieur*, nor indeed had she arrived at that amount of exterior conviction without some argument at least. She had pointed out, not only to Doctor Drouant-Rouault, but she had even conceived it to be her duty to point out to the English practitioners to whom she would not otherwise have spoken, that the man lying there in her bed was a North-Countryman, from Yorkshire where men were of an inconceivable obstinacy. She had asked them to consider that it was not unusual for Yorkshire brothers and sisters or other relatives to live for decades together in the same house and never address a word to each other and she had pointed out that she knew Mark Tietjens to be of an unspeakable determination. She knew it from their lifelong intimacy. She had never, for instance, been able to make him change his diet by an ounce in weight or the shaking of a pepper-pot as to flavour — not once in twenty years during which she had cooked for him. She pleaded with these gentlemen to consider as a possibility that the terms of the armistice were of such a nature as to make a person of Mark's determination and idiosyncrasies resolve to withdraw himself for ever from all human contacts and, that if he did so determine, nothing would cause him to change his determination. The last word he had spoken had been whilst one of his colleagues at the Ministry had been telephoning to tell her, for Mark's information, what the terms of the Armistice were. At the news, which she had had to give him over her shoulder, he had made from the bed some remark. He

27

had been recovering from double pneumonia at the time. What the remark had been she could not exactly repeat; she was almost certain that it had been to the effect — in English — that he would never speak again. But she was aware that her own predilection was sufficient to bias her hearing. She had felt herself at the news that the Allies did not intend to pursue the Germans into their own country — she had felt herself as if she could say to the High Official at the other end of the telephone that she would never speak word to him and his race again. It was the first thing that had come into her mind and no doubt it had been the first thing to come into Mark's.

So she had pleaded with the doctors. They had paid practically no attention to her and she was aware that that was very likely due to her ambiguous position as the companion, until lately without any legal security, of a man whom they considered as in no position to continue his protection of her. That she in no way resented; it was in the nature of English male humanity. The Frenchman had naturally listened with deference, bowing even a little. But he had remarked with a sort of deaf obstinacy: Madame must consider that the occasion of the stroke only made more certain that it *was* a stroke. And that argument to her, as Frenchwoman, must seem almost controvertible. For the betrayal of France by her Allies at the supreme moment of triumph had been a crime the news of which might well cause the end of the world to seem desirable.

# 2

She continued to stand beside him and to apostrophise him until it should be time to turn round the framed newspaper so that he could read the other side of the sheet. What he read first contained the remarks of various writers on racing. That he took in rapidly, as if it were a mere *hors d'œuvre*. She knew that he regarded with contempt the opinions of all writers on racing, but the two who wrote in this particular sheet with less contempt than the others. But the serious reading began when she turned the page. Here were endless, serried columns of the names of race-horses, their jockeys, and entrants at various race-meetings, their ages, ancestries, former achievements. That he would peruse with minuteness and attention. It would cost him just under an hour. She would have liked to stay with him whilst he read it, for the intensive study of matters connected with race-horses had always been their single topic of communion. She had spent almost sentimental hours leaning over the back of his arm-chair reading news of the turf simultaneously with himself, and the compliments he had been used to pay her over her predictions of Form, if they were the only compliments he ever paid her, had filled her with the warm pleasure and confusion that she might have felt had he addressed the same compliments to her on the subject of her person. She did not indeed need compliments from him as to her person; his complete contentment with her sufficed — but she had rejoiced in, and now missed, these long, quiet times of communing. She remarked to him indeed that Seattle had won her race as she had several days ago predicted because there had been no other competitors in any way of the same class as the filly, but there had been no answering, half contemptuous grunt of acquiescence such as in the old days had been hers.

An aeroplane had droned overhead and she had stepped out to look up at the bright toy that, shone upon by the sun, progressed slowly across the pellucid sky. When she went in, in answer to the double closing of his lids that meant that he acquiesced in the turning of his news-sheet, she unhitched one brace from the oaken post to his right and, walking round his bed attached the brace on the post to his left, doing the reverse with the brace that had gone to the left. In that way the picture-frames turned completely round and exhibited the other side of the newspaper.

It was a contrivance that daily excited her annoyance and, as usual, she expressed herself. This was another instance of the madness of They — of her brother-in-law and his woman. Why had they not obtained one of those ingenious machines, like an arm of bright brass supporting a reading-shelf of agreeably varnished mahogany, that you clamped to a bedstead and could adjust at any angle? Why indeed had They not procured one of those huts for the tuberculous that she had seen depicted in a catalogue? Such huts could be painted in agreeable stripes of green and vermilion, thus presenting a gay appearance, and they could be turned upon a pivot so as to meet the rays of the sun or avoid the currents of air caused by the wind? What could be the explanation of this mad and gross structure? A thatched roof supported on posts without walls! Did they desire him to be blown out of his bed by the draughts? Did they merely desire to enrage her? Or could it be that their resources were of such exiguity that they could not afford the conveniences of modern civilisation?

She might well have thought that to be the case. But how could it be, in face of the singular behaviour of Monsieur her *beau-frère* in the matter of the statuary of Casimir-Bar the great sculptor? She had offered to contribute to the expenses of the establishment even at the cost of the sacrifice of what she held most dear and how singular had been Monsieur Christophère's behaviour. During their absence on the occasion of the great sale at Wingham Priory she had ordered the amiable if gross Gunning and the semi-imbecile carpenter to descend from her room to the salon that admirable *Niobe* and the admittedly incomparable *Thetis informing Neptune of the death of a Son-in-law*, not to mention her newly re-gilt Second-Empire fauteuil. And in that gloomy wilderness how had they not shone in their respective whiteness and auriference! The pose of the *Niobe* how passionate, the action of the *Thetis* how spirited and how at the same time pathetic! And she had seized the opportunity to varnish with a special preparation imported from the City of the Arts the only chair in the salon that was not too rough to be susceptible of varnish even though it came from Paris herself. A clumsy affair at that — of the epoch of Louis the Thirteenth of France, though heaven knew whose epoch that was here. Without doubt that of Cromwell the regicide!

And Monsieur must needs seize the moment of his entry on this thus enlivened scene to exhibit the only display of emotion that she had ever known him vouchsafe. For otherwise Monsieur had the pose of being at least as self-contained if not as absolutely taciturn as Mark himself. She asked Mark: was that the moment for what was after all, if you analysed it, a manifestation of attachment for his young woman? What else could it be? *Il* — Monsieur their relative, passed for a man of unbounded knowledge. He knew all knowledge. He could not but be aware of the supreme value of the work of Casimir-Bar who, but for the machinations of his rival Monsieur Rodin and his confrères, must have attained to the highest honours in France. But not only had Monsieur with hisses and tut-tuts of anger ordered Gunning and the carpenter at once to remove the statuary and the fauteuil from the salon where she had exhibited them — with heaven knew how much reluctance — with a view to their attracting the attention of a chance customer — for chance customers did come in their absence without rendezvous . . . Not only that, but Monsieur to gratify the perhaps not unnatural envy of *Elle* had cast meretricious doubts on the pecuniary value of the works of Casimir-Bar themselves. Everyone knew how the Americans to-day were stripping the unfortunate land of France of her choicest art treasures; the enormous prices they paid; the avidity they showed. Yet that man had tried to persuade her that her statues were worth no more than a few shillings a-piece. It was incomprehensible. He was in want of money to the extent of turning their house into a mere depot for dilapidated objects in rough wood and battered brass. He had contrived to obtain singular prices for these forlorn objects from insane Yankees who came great distances to purchase these debris from him. Yet when he was offered pieces of the utmost beauty in the most perfect condition he just simply turned the objects down with scoffing.

For herself, she respected passion — though she could have imagined an object of passion more calculated to excite that feeling than *Elle*, whom for convenience she would call her *belle-sœur*. She at least was broad-minded and moreover she understood the workings of the human heart. It was creditable for a man to ruin himself for the object of his affections. But this at least she found exaggerated.

And what, then, was this determination to ignore the developments of modern genius? Why would they not purchase for Mark a reading-desk with a brass arm that should indicate to the neighbours and dependants that at least he was a person of condition? Why no revolving hut? There were certain symptoms of that age that were disquieting. She would be the first to acknowledge that. They had only to read in the papers of the deeds of assassins, highway robbers, of the subversive and the ignorant who everywhere seized the reins of power. But what was to be said against such innocent things as the reading-desk, the revolving hut, and the aeroplane? Yes, the aeroplane!

Why did they ignore the aeroplane? They had told her that the reason why they had been unable to provide her with *navets de Paris* was that the season was becoming too advanced for the sowing of the seeds of those admirable and amusing vegetables which, seen advancing through the pale electric lights of the early hours of the morning, piled symmetrically as high as the first floors of the hotels, on the marketcarts, provided one of the gayest spectacles of the night-life of la Ville Lumière. They had said that to procure the seeds from Paris would demand at least a month. But supposing they had sent a letter by aeroplane, requesting the despatch of the seeds equally by aeroplane, to procure them, as all the world knew, would be a matter merely of a few hours. And, having thus brought the matter back to turnips again she concluded:

'Yes, mon pauvre homme, they have singular natures, our relatives — for I will include the young woman in that category. I at least am broad-minded enough for that. But they have singular natures. It is a strange affair!'

She departed up the path towards the stable, speculating on the nature of her man's relatives. They were the relatives of a godhead — but godheads had relatives of a singular nature. Let Mark figure as Jupiter; well, Jupiter had a son called Apollo who could not be regarded as exactly *fils de famille*. His adventures had been of the most irregular. Was it not known that he had spent a long space of time with the shepherds of King Admetus, singing and carousing? Well, Monsieur Tietjens might for convenience be regarded as a sort of Apollo, now amongst the shepherds of Admetus and complete with female companion. If he did not often sing he also concealed the tendencies that had brought about his downfall. He was quiet enough about the house, extraordinary as the house might be. *Elle* also. If their relationship was irregular it presented no aspects of reprehensible festivity. It was a sufficiently serious *collage*. That at least ran in the family.

She came round the rough balks of the side of the stable upon Gunning, seated on the stone-sill of the door, cutting with a broad-bladed clasp-knife considerable chunks out of a large meat pasty. She surveyed his extended leggings, his immense be-mired boots and his unshaven countenance and remarked in French that the shepherds of Admetus were probably differently dressed. They certainly were in all the performances of the *Alceste* that she had seen. But perhaps he served his turn.

Gunning said that he supposed he had to go on duty again. She, he supposed, was going to bottle off the cider or she would not have had him bring down that 'ere cask. She was to be careful to tie the carks tight; it would get itself a 'ed, proper.

She said that if she, a Norman of a hundred generations did not know how to handle cider it would be a strange thing and he said that it would be a pity if that cider went wrong after all the trouble they 'ad 'ad.

He brushed the crumbs of his demolished pie off the cords of his breeches, carefully picking up the larger fragments of crust and inserting them into his mouth between his broad, red lips. He asked if 'er Ladyship knew whether the Cahptn wanted the mare that afternoon. If not 'e might's well turn 'er on the Common. She said that she did not know; the Captain had said nothing to her about it. He said he supposed 'e might's well. Cramp said 'e would not have the settee ready to go to the station 'fore mornin'. If she would wait there he would go git some tepid water and they would moisten the eggs. She did not ask better.

He scrambled to his feet and lumbered down the stone path towards the house. She stood in the bright day regarding the long grass of the orchard, the gnarled, whitened trunks of the fruit trees, the little lettuces like aligned rosettes in the beds, and the slope of the land towards the old stones of the house that the boughs of the apple trees mostly hid. And she acknowledged that, in effect, she did not ask better. A Norman, if Mark had died in the ordinary course, she would no doubt have gone back to the neighbourhood either of Falaise or Bayeux from which place came the families of her grandmother and grandfather respectively. She would probably have married a rich farmer or a rich grazier and, by choice, she would have pursued a life of bottling off cider and moistening the eggs of sitting hens. She had had her training as a *coryphée* at the Paris Opera and no doubt if she had not made her visit to London with the Paris Opera troupe and if Mark had not

39

picked her up in the Edgeware road where her lodgings had been, she would have lived with some man in Clichy or Auteuil until with her economies she would have been able, equally, to retire to one or other of the *pays* of her families, and marry a farmer, a butcher, or a grazier. She acknowledged, for the matter of that, that she would probably not have raised more succulent *poulets au grain* or more full-bodied cider than came from the nest-boxes and the presses here and that she was leading no other life than that which she had always contemplated. Nor indeed would she have wanted any other henchman than Gunning who if you had given him a blue-blouse with stitchery and a *casquette* with a black leather peak would have passed for any peasant in Caen market.

He swung up the path, carrying gingerly a large blue bowl, just as if his blouse bellied out round him; he had the same expression of the mouth, the same intonation. It was nothing that she obstinately spoke French to him. On his subjects he could tell by intuition what her answers to his questions were and by now she understood him well enough.

He said that he had better take the 'ens off the nesteses fer fear they peck 'er 'ands and giving her the bowl, brought out from the shadows a protesting, ruffled and crooning

40

hen before which he dropped a handful of bran paste and a lettuce leaf. He came out with another and another. Many more! Then he said she could go in and sprinkle the eggs. He said that it always bothered him to turn the eggs; his clumsy ol' 'ands bruk 'em 's often as not. He said:

'Wait whilst I brings out ol' mare. Bit o' grass wunt do 'er much mischief.'

The hens swollen to an enormous size paraded hostilely against one another about her feet; they clucked, crooned, pecked at lumps of paste, drank water eagerly from an iron dog-trough. With an exaggerated clatter of hoofs old mare emerged from the stable. She was aged nineteen, obstinate, bitter, very dark bay, extremely raw-boned. You might fill her with oats and mash five times a day, but she would not put on flesh. She emerged into the light from the door with the trot of a prima donna, for she knew she had once been a famous creature. The hens fled; she bit into the air showing immense teeth. Gunning opened the orchard gate, just at hand; she went out at a canter, checked, crumpled her knees together, fell on her side and rolled and rolled; her immense lean legs were incongruous, up in the air.

'Yes,' Marie Léonie said, 'pour moi-même je ne demanderais pas mieux!'

Gunning remarked:

'Don't show 'er age, do she? Gambolling like a five-day lamb!' His voice was full of pride, his grey face joyful. ''Is Lordship once sed thet ol' mare had orter be put in the 'Orse Show up to Lunnon. Some yeers ago that was!'

She went into the dark, warm, odorous depths of the hen-house-stable shed; the horse-box being divided off from the hen half by wire netting, nest-boxes, blankets extended on use-poles. She had to bend down to get into the hen-half. The cracks of light between the uprights of the walls blinked at her. She carried the bowl of tepid water gingerly, and thrust her hand into the warm hay hollows. The eggs were fever-heat or thereabouts; she turned them and sprinkled in the tepid water; thirteen, fourteen, fourteen, eleven — that hen was a breaker! — and fifteen. She emptied out the tepid water and from other nests took out egg after egg. The acquisition gratified her.

In an upper box a hen brooded low. It crooned menacingly, then screamed with the voice of poultry disaster as her hand approached it. The sympathetic voices of other hens outside came to her, screaming with poultry disaster — and other hens on the Common. A rooster crowed.

She repeated to herself that she did not demand a better life than this. But was it not the self-indulgence to be so contented? Ought she not to be, still, taking steps for her future — near Falaise or Bayeux? Did one not owe that to oneself? How long would this life last here? And, still more, when it broke up, *how* would it break up? What would *Ils* — the strange people — do to her, her savings, her furs, trunks, pearls, turquoises, statuary, and newly gilt Second Empire chairs and clocks? When the Sovereign died what did the Heir, his concubines, courtiers, and sycophants do to the Maintenon of the day? What precautions ought she not to be taking against that wrath to come? There must be French lawyers in London . . .

Was it to be thought that *Il* — Christopher Tietjens, clumsy, apparently slow-witted, but actually gifted with the insight of the supernatural . . . Gunning would say: The Captain, he never says anything, but who knows what he thinks? He perceives everything . . . Was it to be thought then that, once Mark was dead and he actual owner of the place called Groby and the vast stretch of coal-bearing land that the newspaper had spoken of, Christopher Tietjens would maintain his benevolent and frugal dispositions of today? It was truly thinkable. But, just as he appeared slow-witted and was actually gifted with the insight of the supernatural, so he might well now maintain this aspect of despising wealth and yet develop into a true Harpagon as soon as he held the reins of power. The rich are noted for hardness of heart, and brother will prey upon brother's widow sooner than on another.

So that, certainly, she ought to put herself under the protection of the Authorities. But then, what Authorities? The long arm of France would no doubt protect one of her nationals even in this remote and uncivilised land. But would it be possible to put that machinery in motion without the knowledge of Mark — and what dreadful steps might Mark not take in his wrath if he thought that she had set machinery in motion?

There appeared nothing for it but to wait, and that side of her nature being indolent, perhaps being alone indolent, she was aware that she was contented to wait. But was such a course right? Was it doing justice to herself or to France? For it is the duty of the French citizen, by industry, frugality, and vigilance to accumulate goods; and it was above all the duty of the French citizen to carry back accumulated hoards to that distressed country, stripped bare as she was by the perfidious Allies. She might herself rejoice in these

circumstances, these grasses, orchards, poultry, cider-presses, vegetable-gardens — even if
the turnips were not of the Paris *navet*
variety! She might not ask for better. But
there might be a little *pays*, near Falaise, or in
the alternative, near Bayeux, a little spot that
she might enrich with these spoils from the
barbarians. If every inhabitant of a *pays* in
France did the same would not France again
be prosperous, with all its *clochers* tolling out
contentment across smiling acres? Well, then!

Standing gazing at the poultry whilst
Gunning with a hone smoothed out some
notches from his bagging hook, previous to
going on duty again, she began to reflect on
the nature of Christopher Tietjens, for she
desired to estimate what were her chances of
retaining her furs, pearls and gilt articles of
vertu . . . By the orders of the doctor who
attended daily on Mark — a dry, sandy, no
doubt perfectly ignorant person — Mark was
never to be left out of sight. He was of
opinion, this doctor, that one day Mark might
move — physically. And there might be great
danger if ever he did move. The lesions, if
there were in his brain, might then be
re-started with fatal effects — some such talk.
So they must never let him out of their sight.
For the night they had an alarm that was
connected by a wire from his bed to hers.

Hers was in a room that gave onto the orchard. If he so much as stirred in his bed the bell would ring in her ear. But indeed she rose every night, over and over again to look from her window into his hut; a dim lantern illuminated his sheets. These arrangements appeared to her to be barbarous, but they met the views of Mark and she was thus in no position to question them . . . So she had to wait whilst Gunning honed out his sickle-shaped, short-handled blade.

★ ★ ★

It had all then begun — all the calamities of the world began amidst the clamours and intoxications of that dreadful day. Of Christopher Tietjens till then she had known little or nothing. For the matter of that, of Mark himself she had known little or nothing until a very few years ago. She had known neither his name, nor how he occupied himself, nor yet where he lived. It had not been her business to enquire so she had never made enquiries. Then one day — after thirteen years — he had awakened one morning with an attack of bronchitis after a very wet Newmarket Craven Meeting. He had told her to go to his office with a note addressed to his chief clerk, to ask for his letters and to tell them to send a messenger to his chambers to get some clothes and necessaries.

When she had told him that she did not know what his office was nor where were his chambers nor even his surname he had grunted. He had expressed neither surprise nor gratification, but she knew that he had been gratified — probably with himself for having chosen a woman companion who displayed no curiosity rather than with her for having displayed none. After that he had had a telephone installed in her rooms and not infrequently he would stay later of a morning than had been his habit, letting a messenger from the office bring letters or fetch documents that he had signed. When his father had died he had put her into mourning.

By that date, gradually, she had learned that he was Mark Tietjens of Groby, an immense estate somewhere in the North. He employed himself at an office of the Government in Whitehall — apparently with questions of railways. She gathered, chiefly from ejaculations of the messenger, that he treated his Ministry with contempt, but was regarded as so indispensable that he never lost his post. Occasionally the office would ring up and ask her if she knew where he was.

She would gather from the papers afterwards that that was because there had been a great railway accident. On those occasions he would have been absent at a race-meeting. He gave the office, in fact, just as much of his time as he chose, no more and no less. She gathered that, with his overpowering wealth, it was of no account to him except as an occupation of leisure time between meetings and she gathered that he was regarded as an occult power amongst the rulers of the nation. Once, during the war when he had hurt his hand, he dictated to her a note of a confidential nature to one of the Cabinet Ministers. It had concerned itself with Transport and its tone had been that of singular polite contempt.

For her he was in no way astonishing. He was the English Milor with *le Spleen*. She had read of him in the novels of Alexander Dumas, Paul de Kock, Eugene Sue and Ponson du Terrail He represented the England that the Continent applauded — the only England that the Continent applauded. Silent, obstinate, inscrutable, insolent, but immensely wealthy and uncontrollably generous. For herself, *elle ne demandait pas mieux*. For there was about him nothing of the unexpected. He was as regular as the Westminster Chimes; he never exacted the unexpected of her and he was all-powerful and never in the wrong. He was, in short, what her countrywomen called *sérieux*. No Frenchwoman asks better than that of lover or husband. It was the *collage sérieux* par excellence: they were as a *ménage* sober, honest, frugal, industrious, very wealthy, and seriously saving. For his dinner twice a week she cooked him herself two mutton chops with all but an eighth of an inch of the fat pared off, two mealy potatoes, as light and as white as flour, an apple pie with a very flaky crust which he ate with a wedge of Stilton and some pulled bread and butter. This dinner had never varied once in twenty years except during the season of game when on alternate weeks a pheasant, a brace of grouse or of partridges would come from Groby. Nor in the twenty years had they once been separated for a whole week except that every late summer he spent a month at Harrogate. She always had his dress-shirts washed for him by her own laundress in the Quartier. He spent almost every week-end in one country house or another using at most two dress-shirts and that only if he stayed till Tuesday. English people of good class do not dress for dinner on Sundays. That is a politeness to God because theoretically you attend evening service and you do not go to church in the country in evening dress. As a matter of fact you never go to evening service — but it is complimentary to suggest by your dress that you might be visited by the impulse. So, at least Marie Léonie Tietjens understood the affair.

She was looking out on the Common that sloped up to beech trees, at the poultry — bright chestnut birds extremely busy on the intense green of the browsed grass. The great rooster reminded her of the late Monsieur Rodin, the sculptor who had conspired against Casimir-Bar. She had once seen Rodin in his studio, conducting some American ladies round his work and he had precisely resembled a rooster kicking its leg back and drooping its wings in the dust round a new hen. Only round a new one. Naturally! . . . This rooster was a tremendous Frenchman. *Un vrai de la vraie!* You could imagine nothing more unlike Christopher Tietjens! . . . The backward-raking legs on the dancing toes; the gait of a true master of deportment at an academy of young ladies! The vigilant clear eye cocking up every minute . . . Hark! A swift shadow ran over the ground: the sparrow hawk! The loud, piercing croon of that Father of his Country! How the hens all re-echoed it; how the chickens ran to their mothers and all together to the shadow of the hedge! Monsieur the hawk would have no chance amidst that outcry. The hawk flits silent and detests noise. It will bring the poultry-keeper with his gun! . . . All is discovered because of the vigilance of Milord Chantecler . . . There are those who reprove him because his eyes are always on the sky, because he has a proud head. But that is his function — that and gallantry: Perceive him with a grain of corn; how he flies upon it; how he invites with cries! His favourite — the newest — hens run clucking joyously to him! How he bows, droops and prances, holding the grain of corn in his powerful bill, depositing it, pecking to bruise it and then depositing it before his sultana of the moment. Nor will he complain if a little ball of fluff runs quickly and pecks the grain from his bill before Madame Partlet can take it from him. His gallantry has been wasted, but he is a good father! . . . Perhaps there is not even a grain of corn when he issues his invitations: perhaps he merely calls his favourites to him that he may receive their praise or perform the act of Love . . .

He is then the man that a woman desires to have vouchsafed her. When he smites his wing feathers behind his back and utters his clarion cry of victory over the hawk that now glides far away down the hill, his hens come out again from the shadows, the chickens from beneath their mothers' wings. He has given security to his country and in confidence they can return to their avocations. Different indeed from that Monsieur Christopher who even when he was still a soldier more than anything resembled a full, grey, coarse meal-sack short in the wind and with rolling, hard-blue eyes. Not hard eyes, but of a hard blue! And yet, curiously, he too had some of the spirit of Chantecler beneath his rolling shoulders of a farmyard boar. Obviously you could not be your brother's brother and not have some traces of the Milor . . . The spleen too. But no one could say that her Mark was not a proper man. *Chic* in an eccentric manner, but, oh yes, *chic*! And that was his brother.

Naturally he might try to despoil her. That is what brother does to brother's widow and children . . . But, on occasion, he treated her with a pompous courtesy — a parade. On the first time he had seen her — not so long ago that; only during that period of the war that had been without measurable time — he had treated her to heavy but expressive gestures of respect and words of courtesy in an old-fashioned language that he must have learned at the Théatre Français whilst they still played *Ruy Blas*. French was a different thing now, that she must acknowledge. When she went to Paris — which she did every late summer whilst her man went to Harrogate — the language her nephews spoke was a different affair — without grace, courtesy, intelligibility. Certainly without respect! Oh, la, la! When they came to divide up her inheritance that would be a sharper kind of despoilment than ever Christopher Tietjens'! Whilst she lay on her bed of death those young fellows and their wives would be all through her presses and armoires like a pack of wolves . . . *La famille*! Well, that was very proper. It showed the appropriate spirit of acquisition. What was a good mother for if not to despoil her husband's relatives in the interests of their joint children!

So Christopher had been as courteous as a well-trained meal-sack of the *dix-huitième*. Eighteenth-century! Older still, *période Molière*! When he had come into her room that had been dimly lit with a *veilleuse* — a night-light; they are so much more economical than shaded electric lights! — he had precisely suggested to her a lumbering character from Molière as presented at the Comédie Française; elaborate of phrase and character, but protuberant in odd places. She might in that case have supposed that he entertained designs on her person; but with his eyes sticking out in elaborate considerateness he had only come to break to her the news that his brother was about to make an honest woman of her. That had been Mark's phrase. It is of course only God that can do that . . . But the enterprise had had the full concurrence of Monsieur the Heir-Apparent.

He had indeed been active whilst she slumbered in a hooded-chair after four days and three nights on her feet. She would have surrendered the body of Mark to no human being but his brother. Now the brother had come to tell her not to be alarmed — panting with nervousness and shortness of breath . . . Bad lungs both the brothers had! Panting he had come to tell her not to be alarmed at finding in her man's room two priests, an official, a lawyer and a lawyer's clerk . . . These black-robed people attend on death, bringing will-forms and the holy oils. The doctor and a man with oxygen cylinders had been there when she had gone to repose herself. It was a pretty congregation of the vultures that attend on us during life.

She had started at once to cry out. That undoubtedly was what had made him nervous — the anticipation that she would cry out sharply in the black, silent London that brooded between air-raids. In that silence, before sleep had visited her peignoir-enveloped, and therefore clumsyish, form, she had been aware of Christopher's activities on the telephone in the passage. It had struck her that he might have been warning the Pompes Funébres! ... So she had begun to scream: the sound that irresistibly you make when death is about to descend. But he had agitated himself to soothe her — for all the world like Monsieur Sylvain on the boards of Molière's establishment! He spoke that sort of French, in a hoarse whisper, in the shadows of the night-light ... assuring her that the priest was for marriage, with license of the Archevêque de Cantorbéri such as in London you got in those days from Lambeth Palace for thirty pounds sterling. That enabled you to make any woman honest at any hour of the day or night. The lawyer was there to have a will re-signed. Marriage in this singular country invalidates any previous will. So, Tietjens (Christophère) assured her.

But then, if there was that haste there was danger of death! She had often speculated as to whether he would or would not marry her as an act of death-bed contrition. Rather contemptuously as great lords with *le Spleen* make their peace with God. She screamed; in silent, black London. The night-light wavered in its saucer.

He crepitated out that his brother was doubling, in this new will, his posthumous provision for her. With provision for the purchase of a house in France if she would not inhabit the Dower House at Groby. A Louis Treize dower-house. It was his idea of consolation. He affected to be business-like . . . These English. But then, perhaps they do not go through your presses and wardrobes whilst your corpse is still warm!

She screamed out that they might take away their marriage papers and will-forms, but to give her her man again. If they had let her give him her *tisanes* instead of . . .

With her breast heaving she had cried into that man's face:

'I swear that my first act when I am Madame Tietjens and have the legal power will be to turn out all these men and give him infusions of poppy-heads and lime-flowers.' She expected to see him recoil, but he had said:

'In heaven's name do, my dear sister. It might save him and the nation!'

It was silly of him to talk like that. These fellows had too much pride of family. Mark did no more than attend to Transport. Well,

56

perhaps transport in those days had its importance. Still, probably Tietjens, Christopher, over-rated the indispensableness of Tietjens, Mark . . . That would have been three weeks or a month before the Armistice. They were black days . . . A good brother, though . . .

In the other room, whilst papers were signing, after the *curé* in his *calotte* and all, had done reading from his book, Mark had signed to her to bend her head down to him and had kissed her. He whispered:

'Thank God there is one woman-Tietjens who is not a whore and a bitch!' He winced a little; her tears had fallen on his face. For the first time, she had said:

'Mon pauvre homme, ce qu'ils ont fait de toil' She had been hurrying from the room when Christopher had stopped her. Mark had said:

'I regret to put you to further inconvenience . . . ' in French. He had never spoken to her in French before. Marriage makes a difference. They speak to you with ceremony out of respect for themselves and their station in life. You also are at liberty to address them as your *pauvre homme*.

There had to be another ceremony. A man looking like a newly dressed gaol-bird stepped out with his book like an office register. With a blue-black jowl. He married them over again. A civil marriage, this time.

It was then that, for the first time, she had become aware of the existence of another woman-Tietjens, Christopher's wife . . . She had not known that Christopher had a wife. Why was not she there? But Mark with his labouring politeness and chest had told her that he exaggerated the formality of the marriage because if both he and Christopher died she, Marie Léonie Tietjens, might have trouble with a certain Sylvia. The Bitch! . . . Well, she, Marie Léonie, was prepared to face her legitimate sister-in-law.

# 3

The little maid, Beatrice, as well as Gunning, regarded Marie Léonie with paralysed but bewildered obedience. She was 'Er Ladyship, a good mark, a foreign Frenchy. That was bad. She was extraordinarily efficient about the house and garden and poultry-yard, a matter for mixed feelings. She was fair, not black-avised, a good mark; she was buxom, not skinny, like the real Quality. A bad mark because she was, then, not real Quality; but a qualifiedly good mark because if you 'as to 'ave Quality all about you in the 'ouse tis better not to 'ave real Quality . . . But on the whole the general feeling was favourable because like themselves she was floridly blonde. It made 'er 'uman like. Never you trust a dark woman and if you marries a dark man 'e will treat you bad. In the English countryside it is like that.

Cabinet-maker Cramp who was a remnant of the little dark persistent race that once had peopled Sussex regarded her with distrust that mingled with admiration for the quality of the varnish that she imported from Paris. Proper French polish that were. He lived in the cottage just across the path on the Common. 'E couldn' say as 'ow 'e liked the job the Governor give 'im. He had to patch up and polish with beeswax — not varnish — rough stuff such 's 'is granf'er 'ad 'ad. An 'ad got rid of. Rough ol' truck. Moren n 'undred yeers old. N' more!

He had to take bits of old wood out of one sort of old truck and fit it into missing bits of other old truck. Bought old Moley's pig-pound boards that had been Little Kingsworth church stalls, the Cahptn 'ad; n 'ad 'im, Cramp, use'm for all manner of patchin's up. The Captain had bought too ol' Miss' Cooper's rabbit 'utch. Beautifully bevelled the panels was too which cleaned up n beeswaxed. Cramp would acknowledge that. Made him match the bevelling in the timber from Kingsworth Church stalls for one of the missing doors, an' more of the timber fer the patching. Proper job, he, Cramp, had made of it too; he would say that. 'N it looked proper when it was finished — a long, low press, with six bevelled doors; beautiful purfling on the edges. Like some of the stuff 'Is Lordship 'ad in the Tujer Room at Fittleworth House. Moren n 'undred yeers old. Three undred. Four . . . There's no knowin.

'N no accountin' fer tastes. 'E would say 'e

'ad n eye — the Cahptn 'ad. Look at a bit of ol' rough truck the Cahptn would n see it was older than the Monument to Sir Richard Atchinson on Tadworth 'Ill that was set up in the year 1842 to celebrate the glorious victory of Free Trade. So the Monument said. Lug a bit of rough ol' truck out of the back of a cow-house where it had been throwed — the Cahptn would. And his, Cramp's, heart would sink to see the ol' mare come back, some days, the cart full of 'en-coops, n leaden pig-truffs, n pewter plates that 'ad been used to stop up 'oles in cow-byres.

'N off it would all go to Murrikay. Queer place Murrikay must be — full of the leavins of ol' England. Pig-troughs, hen-coops, rabbit-hutches, wash-house coppers that no one now had any use for. He loaded 'em when he'd scrubbed, and silver-sanded and beeswaxed-n-turpentined 'em, onto the ol' cart, n put to ol' mare, n down to station, n on to Southampton n off to New York. Must be a queer place yon! Hadn't they no cabinet-makers or ol' rough truck of ther own?

Well, it took all sorts to make a world n thank God fer that. He, Cramp, had a good job, likely to last 'im 'is lifetime because some folks wus queer in the 'ed. The ol' lumber went out yon and his, Cramp's missus, was gettin' together a proper set of goods. A tidy treat their sittin' room looked with aspidistras in mahogany tripods, 'n a Wilton carpet 'n bamboo cheers 'n mahogany whatnots. A proper woman Missus Cramp was, if sharp in the tongue.

Miss's Cramp she didn't give so much fer 'Er Ladyship. She was agin Foreigners. All German spies they wus. Have no truck with them she wouldn't. 'Oo noo if they wus 's much 's married. Some says they wus, some says they wasn'. But you couldn' take in Miss' Cramp . . . 'N Quality! What was to show that they were real Quality. Livin how they did wasn' Quality manners. Quality was stuck up 'n wore shiny clothes 'n had motor-cars 'n statues 'n palms 'n ball-rooms 'n conservatories. 'N didn' bottle off the cider 'n take the eggs 'n speak queer lingo to th' handy-man. 'N didn' sell the cheers they sat on. The four younger children also didn' like 'Er Ladyship. Never called 'em pretty dears she did nor give 'em sweeties nor rag-dolls nor apples. Smacked 'em if she found 'em in the orchard. Never so much s give 'em red flannel capes in the winter.

But Bill the eldest liked 'Er Ladyship. Called 'er a proper right 'un. Never stopped tarkin' of 'er. 'N *she* 'ad statues in 'er bedroom, 'n fine gilt cheers, 'n clocks, 'n

flowerin plants. Bill e'd made fer 'Er
Ladyship what she called 'n eightyjare. In
three stories, to stand in a corner 'n hold
knick-knacks. Out of fretwork to a pettern
she'd give 'im. Varnished proper, too. A good
piece of work if he shouldn't say so ... But
Miss's Cramp she'd never been allowed in 'er
Ladyship's bedroom. A proper place it was.
Fit fer a Countess! If Miss's Cramp could be
allowed to see it she'd maybe change her
opinions ... But Miss's Cramp she said:
'Never you trust a fair woman,' bein' dark.

The matter of the cider however, did give
him to think. Proper cider it was, when they
was given a bottle or two. But it wasn't
Sussex cider. A little like Devonshire cider,
more like Herefordshire. But not the same as
any. More head it had 'n was sweeter, 'n
browner. 'N not to be drunk s' freely! Fair
scoured you it did if you drunk's much's a
quart!

The little settlement was advancing furtively to the hedge. Cramp put his bald poll
out of his work-shed and then crept out. Mrs.
Cramp, an untidy, dark, very thin woman
emerged over her door-sill, wiping her hands
on her apron. The four Cramp children at
different stages of growth crept out of the
empty pig-pound. Cramp was not going to
buy his winter pigs till next fortnightly fair at

Little Kingsworth. The Elliott children with the milk-can came at a snail's pace down the green path from the farm; Mrs. Elliott, an enormous woman with untidy hair, peered over her own hedge which formed a little enclosure on the Common; Young Hogben, the farmer's son, a man of forty, very thick-set, appeared on the path in the beech-wood, ostensibly driving a great black sow. Even Gunning left his brushing and lumbered to the edge of the stable. From there he could still see Mark in his bed, but also, looking downwards between the apple-trunks he could see Marie Léonie bottle the cider, large, florid and intent, in the open dairying-shed where water ran in a v-shaped wooden trough.

'Runnin't' cider out of cask with a chube!' Mrs. Cramp screamed up the hill to Mrs. Elliott. "Ooever 'eered!' Mrs. Elliott rumbled huskily back at Mrs. Cramp. All these figures closed in furtively; the children peering through tiny interstices in the hedge and muttering one to the other: "Ooever 'eered . . . Foreign ways I call it . . . A glass chube . . . 'Ooever 'eered.' Even Cramp, though, wiping his bald head with his carpenter's apron, he admonished Mrs. Cramp to remember that he had a good job — even Cramp descended from the path to the hedge-side and stood so close — peering over — that the thorns pricked his perspiring chest through his thin shirt. They said to the baker who wearily followed his weary horse up the steep path, coming from the deep woods below: It had ought to be stopped. The police had ought to know. Bottling cider by means of a glass tube. And standing the cider in running water. Where was the excise? Rotting honest folks guts! Poisoning them. No doubt the governor could tell them a tale about that if he could speak or move. The police had ought to know . . . Showing off, with cider in running water — to cool it when first bottled! 'Ooever 'eered! Just because they 'ad a Ladyship to their tail. 'N more money than better folks. Not so much money either. Reckon they'd come to smash 'n be sold up like 'Igginson at Fittleworth. Set 'isself up fer Quality, 'e did too! . . . 'N not so much of a Ladyship, neither. Not so much more of a Ladyship as us if the truth was known. Not an Earl or a Lord, only a baronite-ess at that, supposin' we all 'ad our rights . . . The police had ought to be brought into this affair!

A number of members of the Quality, on shining horses, their leathers creaking beautifully, rode at a walk up the path. They were the real Quality. A fine old gentleman, thin as a lath, clean face, hooky nose, white

65

moustache, lovely cane, lovely leggings. On 'Is Lordship's favourite hack. A bay mare. A fine lady, slim as a boy, riding astride as they do to-day though they did not use to. But times change. On the Countess's own chestnut with white forehead. A bad-tempered horse. She must ride well, that lady. Another lady, grey-haired, but slim too, riding side-saddle in a funny sort of get-up. Long skirt with panniers and three-cornered hat like the ones you see in pictures of highwaymen in the new pub in Queens Norton. Sort of old-fashioned she looked. But no doubt it was the newest pattern. Things is so mixed up nowadays. 'Is Lordship's friends could afford to do as they pleased. A boy, eighteen, maybe. Shiny leggings too: all their clothes is shiny. Rides well, too, the boy. Look how his legs nip into Orlando — the chief whip's horse. Out for an airing. 'Is Lordship's groom of the stud only too glad if the horses can get exercise in hay-cutting time. The real Quality.

They reined in their horses a little further up the road, and sat staring down into the orchard. They had ought to be told what was going on down there. Puts white powder into the cider along o' the sugar. The Quality ought to be told . . . But you do not speak to the Quality. Better if they do not notice you.

You never know. They sticks together. Might be friends of Tietjenses for all you know. You don't *know* Tietjenses ain't Quality. Better git a move on or something might 'appen to you. You hear!

The boy in the shiny leggings and clothes — bareheaded he was, with shiny fair hair and shiny cheeks — exclaimed in a high voice:

'I say, mother, I don't like this spying!' And the horses started and jostled.

You see. They don't like this spying. Get a move on. And all that peasantry got a move on whilst the horses went slowly up hill. Queer things the Gentry can do to you still if they notice you. It is all very well to say this is a land fit for whatever the word is that stands for simple folk. But they have the police and the keepers in their hands, and your cottages and livings.

Gunning went out at the garden gate beside the stable and shouted objurgations at Young Hogben.

'Hey, don't you drive that sow. She's as much right on Common as you.'

The great sow was obstinately preceding the squat figure of Young Hogben who hissed and squeaked behind her. She flapped her great ears and sniffed from side to side, a monument of black imperturbability.

'You keep your 'ogs out of our swedes!' Young Hogben shouted amidst objurgations. 'In our forty acre she is all day 'n all night too!'

'You keep your swedes outen our 'ogs,' Gunning shouted back swinging his gorilla arms like a semaphore. He advanced onto the Common. Young Hogben descended the slope.

'You fence your 'ogs in same's other folks 'as to do,' Young Hogben menaced.

'Folks as abuts on Commons 'as to fence out, not fence in,' Gunning menaced. They stood foot to foot on the soft sward menacing each other with their chins.

'S Lordship sold Tietjens's to the Cahptn without Common rights,' the farmer said. 'Ask Mr. Fuller.'

'S Lordship could no more sell Tietjens's 'thout Common rights 'n you could sell milk without drinking rights. Ast Lawyer Sturgis!' Gunning maintained. Put arsenic in among 'is roots, Young Hogben maintained that he would. Spend seven years up to Lewes Jail if 'e did, Gunning maintained. They continued for long in the endless quarrel that obtains between tenant-farmer who is not Quality but used to brutalising his hinds, and gentleman's henchman who is used to popularity amongst his class and the peasantry. The only thing

68

upon which they agreed was that you wouldn't think there 'adnt been no war. The war ought to have given tenant farmers the complete powers of local tyrants; it should have done the same for gentlemen's bailiffs. The sow grunted round Gunning's boots, looking up for grains of maize that Gunning usually dropped. In that way sows come to heel when you call them however far away they may be on the Common.

Down through the garden by the zig-zag path that dropped right away from the hard road up the hill — Tietjens's went up the slope to the hedge there — descended the elderly lady who was singularly attired in the eyes of the country people. She considered that she was descended, not by blood, but by moral affinity from Madame de Maintenon, therefore she wore a long grey riding skirt with panniers, and a three-cornered, grey felt hat and carried a riding switch of green shagreen. Her thin grey face was tired but authoritative, her hair which she wore in a knot beneath her hat was luminously grey, her pince-nez rimless.

Owing to the steepness of the bank on which the garden rose the path of sea-pebbles zigzagged across most of its width, orange-coloured because it had been lately sanded. She went furtively between quince-trunks,

69

much like the hedge-sparrow, flitting a stretch and then stopping for the boy with the shining leggings stolidly to overtake her.

She said that it was dreadful to think that the sins of one's youth could so find one out. It ought to make her young companion think. To come at the end of one's life to inhabiting so remote a spot! You could not get there with automobiles. Her own Delarue-Schneider had broken down on the hill-road in the attempt to get there yesterday.

The boy, slim in the body, but heavy in the bright red cheeks, with brown hair, truly shiny leggings and a tie of green, scarlet and white stripes, had a temporarily glum expression. He said nevertheless with grumbling determination that he did not think this was playing the game. Moreover hundreds of motors got up that hill; how else would people come to buy the old furniture? He had already told Mrs. de Bray Pape that the carburettors of Delarue-Schneiders were a wash-out.

It was just that, Mrs. Pape maintained, that was so dreadful a thought. She went swiftly down another zigzag of the path and then faltered.

It was that that was dreadful in these old countries, she said. Why could they never learn? Take example! Here were the descendants of a great family, the Tietjenses of Groby, a haunt of ancient peace, the one reduced to a no doubt dreadful state by the sins of his youth, the other to making a living by selling old furniture.

The youth said she was mistaken. She must not believe all that his mother hinted to her. His mother was all right, but her hints went further than facts warranted. If he wanted to let Groby to Mrs. de Bray Pape it was because he hated swank. His uncle also hated swank . . . He mumbled a little and added: 'And . . . my father!' Moreover it was not playing the game. He had soft brown eyes that were now clouded and he was blushing.

He mumbled that mother was splendid but he did not think she ought to have sent him there. Naturally she had her wrongs. For himself he was a Marxist-Communist. All Cambridge was. He therefore, of course, approved of his father's living with whom he wished. But there were ways of doing things. Because you were advanced you did not have to treat women with discourtesy. The reverse, rather. He was painfully agitated by the time he overtook the tired lady at the corner of the next zigzag.

She wanted him not to misunderstand her. No discredit attached in her eyes to the pursuit of selling old furniture. Far from it. Mr. Lemuel of Madison Avenue might be called a dealer in old furniture. It was of course Oriental which made a difference. But Mr. Lemuel was a most cultivated man. His country house at Crugers in the State of New York was kept up in a style that would have done credit to the *grands seigneurs* of pre-Revolutionary France. But from that to this . . . what a downfall!

The house — the cottage — was by now nearly below her feet, the roof extremely high, the windows sunk very deep in grey stone and very small. There was a paved semi-circular court before the door, the space having been cut out of the orchard bank and walled with stones. It was extravagantly green, sunk in greenery and the grass that came nearly to Mrs. Pape's middle was filled with hiding profusions of flowers that were turning to seed. The four counties swept away from under her, hedges like string going away, enclosing fields, to the hills on the very distant horizon; the country near at hand wooded. The boy beside her took a deep breath as he always did when he saw a great view. On the moors above Groby, for instance. Purple they were.

'It *isn't* fit for human habitation!' the lady exclaimed with the triumphant intonation of one who sees great truth confirmed. 'The houses of the poor in these old countries beggar even pity. Do you suppose they so much as have a bath?'

'I should think my father and uncle were personally *clean*!' the boy said. He mumbled that this was supposed to be rather a show-place. He could trust his father indeed to find rather a show-place to live in. Look at the rock plants in the sunk garden! He exclaimed: 'Look here! Let's go back!'

Mrs. Pape's perturbation gave way to obstinacy. She exclaimed.

'Never!' She had a mission from the poor boy's injured mother. She would never look Sylvia Tietjens in the face if she flinched. Sanitation went before anything. She hoped to leave the world a better place before she passed over. She had Authority conferred on her. Metempsychosistically. She believed that the soul of Madame de Maintenon, the companion of Louis the Fourteenth had passed into her. How many convents had not the Maintenon set up and how rigidly had she not looked after the virtue and the sanitation of the inhabitants? That was what she, Mrs. Millicent de Bray Pape, looked to. She had in the South of France — the Riviera — a palace, erected by Mr. Behrens the celebrated architect — after the palace of the

Maintenon at Sans Souci. But sanitated! She asked the young man to believe her. The boudoir appeared to be only a panelled boudoir: very large because of the useless vanity of le Raw Solale. Madame de Maintenon would have been content without such vanity . . . But only touch a spring in the panels and every sort of bathing arrangement presented itself to you hidden in the wall. Sunken baths; baths above ground; douches with sea-water extra-iodised; lateral douches with and without bath-salts dissolved in the water. That was what she called making the world a little better.

The boy mumbled that he was not in principle against the old tree's coming down. He was indeed in principle against his uncle's and his father's adoption of the peasant life. This was an industrial age. The peasant had always spoilt every advance in the ideas of the world. All the men at Cambridge were agreed as to that. He exclaimed:

'Hi! You can't do that . . . Not go through standing *hay*!'

Every fibre of his country-boy landowner's soul was outraged as he saw the long trail of satiny grey that followed Mrs. de Bray Pape's long skirts. How were his father's men to cut hay that had been trampled like that? But, unable to bear any longer the suspense of the spectacular advance towards Mark Tietjens along those orange zigzags, Mrs. de Bray Pape was running straight down the bank towards the unwalled, thatched hut. She could see it through the tops of the apple tree.

The boy, desperately nervous, continued to descend the zigzag paths that would take him into the very purlieus of his father's house — onto the paved court where there were rock plants between the interstices. His mother *ought* not to have forced him to accompany Mrs. de Bray Pape. His mother was splendid. Divinely beautiful; athletic as Atalanta or Betty Nuthall, in spite of her sufferings. But she ought not to have sent Mrs. de Bray Pape. It was *meant* as a sort of revenge. General Campion had not approved. He could see that, though he had said: 'My boy, you ought always to obey your dear mother! She has suffered so much. It is your duty to make it up to her by fulfilling her slightest whim. An Englishman always does his duty to his mother!'

Of course it was the presence of Mrs. de Bray Pape that forced the General to say that. Patriotism. General Campion was deadly afraid of mother. Who wasn't? But he would hardly have enjoined upon a son to go and spy upon his father and his father's

. . . companion if he had not wanted to show Mrs. de Bray Pape how superior English family ties were to those of her country. They ragged each other about that all day long.

And yet he did not know. The dominion of women over those of the opposite sex was a terrible thing. He had seen the old General whimper like a whipped dog and mumble in his poor white moustache . . . Mother was splendid. But wasn't sex a terrible thing . . . His breath came short.

He covered two foot of pebbles with the orange sand rolled into them. A tidy job it must be rolling on that slope! Still the actual gradient was not so steep on the zigzags. One in sixteen perhaps. He covered another two feet of pebbles with orange sand rolled in. How could he? How could he cover another two? His heels were trembling!

Four counties ran out below his feet. To the horizon! *He showed him the kingdoms of the earth.* As great a view as above Groby, but not purple and with no sea. Trust Father to settle where you could see a great view by going up hill. *Vox adhaesit* . . . . 'His feet were rooted to the earth.' . . . No, *vox adhaesit faucibus* meant that his voice stuck to his jaws. Palate rather. His palate was as dry as sawdust! How *could* he do it! . . . A terrible thing! They called it Sex! . . . His mother had coerced him into this dry palate and trembling heels by the force of her sex fever. Dreadful good-nights they had had in her boudoir, she forcing and forcing him with arguments to go. To come here. Beautiful Mother! . . . Cruel! Cruel!

The boudoir all lit up. Warm! Scented! Mother's shoulders! A portrait of Nell Gwynn by Sir Peter Lely. Mrs. de Bray Pape wanted to buy it. Thought she could buy the earth, but Lord Fittleworth only laughed . . . How had they all got forced down there? By Mother . . . To spy on Father. Mother had never taken much stock of Fittleworth — good fellow Fittleworth, good landlord! — till last winter when she had got to know that Father had bought this place. Then it was Fittleworth, Fittleworth, Fittleworth! Lunches, dinner, dances at the Ambassador's. Fittleworth wasn't saying no. Who could say no to Mother, with her figure in the saddle, and her hair?

If he had known when they came down to Fittleworth's last winter what he knew now! He knew now that his mother, come down for the hunting, though she had never taken much stock in hunting . . . Still, she could ride. Jove, she could ride. He had gone queer all over again and again at first in taking those leaps that she took laughing. Diana, that's what she was . . . Well, no, Diana was . . . His mother, come down for the hunting was there to torment Father and his . . . companion. She had told him. Laughing in that way she had . . . It must be sex cruelty! . . . Laughing like those Léonardi-do-da . . . Well, Vinci women. A queer laugh, ending with a crooked smile . . . In corresponding with Father's servants . . . Dressing up as a housemaid and looking over the hedge.

How *could* she do it? *How?* How could she force him to be here? What would Monty, the Prime Minister's son, Dobles, Porter — fat ass because his father was too beastly rich! — what would his set think at Cambridge. They were all Marxist-Communists to a man. But still . . .

What would Mrs. Lowther think if she *really* knew . . . If she could have been in the corridor one night when he came out from his mother's boudoir! He would have had the courage to ask her then. Her hair was like floss silk, her lips like cut pomegranates. When she laughed she threw up her head . . . He was now warm all over, his eyes wet and warm.

When he had asked if he ought to — if *she* wanted him to — do whatever his mother wanted whether or no he approved . . . If his mother asked him to do what he thought was a mean action . . . But that had been on the Peacock Terrace with the famous Fittleworth Seven Sister Roses . . . How she went against the roses! . . . In a yellow . . . No, moth-coloured . . . Not yellow, not yellow. Green's forsaken, but yellow's forsworn. Great pity filled him at the thought that Mrs. Lowther might be forsaken. But she must not be forsworn . . . moth-coloured silk. Shimmering. Against pink roses. Her fine, fine hair, a halo. She had looked up and sideways. She had been going to laugh with her lips like cut pomegranates . . . She had told him that as a rule it was a good thing to do what one's mother wanted when she was like Mrs. Christopher Tietjens. Her soft voice . . . Soft Southern voice . . . Oh, when she laughed at Mrs. de Bray Pape . . . How could she be a friend of Mrs. de Bray Pape's? . . .

If it hadn't been sunlight . . . If he had come on Mrs. Lowther as he came out of his mother's boudoir. He would have had courage. At night. Late. He would have said: 'If you are really interested in my fate tell me if I ought to spy upon my father and his . . . companion!' She would not have laughed, late at night. She would have given him her hand. The loveliest hands and the lightest feet. And her eyes would have dimmed . . . Lovely, lovely pansies!

Pansies are heartsease . . .

Why did he have these thoughts: these wafts of intolerable . . . oh, desire! He was his mother's son . . . His mother was . . . He would kill anyone who said it . . .

Thank God! Oh thank God! He was down on the crazy paving level with the house. *AND there was another path went up to Uncle Mark's shed.* The Blessed Virgin — who was like Helen Lowther! — had watched over him. He had not to walk under those little deep, small-paned windows.

His father's . . . companion might have been looking out. He would have fainted . . .

His father was a good sort of man. But he too must be . . . like Mother. If what they said was true. Ruined by dissolute living. But a good, grey man. The sort of man to be tormented by Mother. Great spatulate fingers. But no one had ever tied flies like Father. Some he had tied years ago were the best he, Mark Tietjens junior of Groby, had yet. And Father loved the wine-coloured moor. *How* could he stifle under these boughs! A house overhung by trees is unsanitary. They all say that . . .

But what a lovely glimpse under the trees. Sweet-williams along the path. Light filtered by boughs. Shadow. Gleams in the little window-panes. Wallstones all lichen. That's

80

England. If he could spend a while here with Father . . .

Father had been matchless with horses. Women too . . . What an inheritance was his, Mark Tietjens, junior's! If he could spend a while here . . . But his Father slept with . . . If she came out of the door . . . She must be beautiful . . . No they said she was not a patch on Mother. He had overheard that at Fittleworth's. Or Helen Lowther . . . But his father had had his pick! . . . If he chose then to sleep with . . .

If she came out of the door he would faint . . . Like the Venus of Botti . . . A crooked smile . . . No, Helen Lowther would protect . . . He might fall in love with his father's . . . What do you know of what will happen to you when you come in contact with the Bad Woman . . . of advanced views . . . They said she was of Advanced Views. And a Latinist . . . He was a Latinist. Loved it!

Or his father might with Hel . . . Hot jealousy filled. His father was the sort of man . . . She might . . . Why did over . . . people like Mother and Father beget children?

He kept his eyes fascinatedly fixed on the stone porch of the cottage whilst he stumbled up the great stone slabs to the path. The path led to Uncle Mark's wall-less thatched hut . . . No form filled the porch. What was to become of him? He had great wealth; terrific temptation would be his. His mother was no guide. His father might have been better . . . Well, there was Marxian-Communism. They all looked to that now, in his set at Cambridge. Monty, the Prime Minister's son with black eyes; Dobles, Campion's nephew, lean as a rat; Porter, with a pig's snout, but witty as hell. Fat ass!

# 4

Mark Tietjens thought that a cow or a hog
must have got into the orchard there was
such a rushing in the grass. He said to himself
that that damn Gunning was always boasting
about his prowess as a hedger; he might see
that his confounded hedges kept out the
beasts from the Common. An unusual voice
— unusual in its intonation — remarked:

'Oh, Sir Mark Tietjens, this is dreadful!'

It appeared to be dreadful. A lady in a long
skirt — an apparently elderly Di Vernon out
of *Waverley* which was one of the few novels
Mark had read — was making dreadful havoc
with the standing grass. The beautiful, proud
heads swayed and went down as she rushed,
knee-deep amongst it; stopped, rushed again
across his view and then stopped apparently
to wring her hands and once more explain
that it was dreadful. A tiny rabbit, scared out
by her approach, scuttered out under his bed
and presumably down into the vegetables.
Marie Léonie's Mistigris would probably get
it and, since it was Friday, Marie Léonie
would be perturbed.

The lady pushed through the remaining tall

grass that stood between them, and had the air of rising up at his bed-foot. She was rather a faint figure — like the hedge-sparrow. In grey, with a grey short coat and a waistcoat with small round buttons and a three-cornered hat. A tired, thin face . . . Well, she must be tired, pushing through that long grass with a long skirt. She had a switch of green shagreen. The hen tomtit that lived in the old shoe they had tucked on purpose under his thatch uttered long warning cries. The hen tomtit did not like the aspect of this apparition.

She was devouring his face with her not disagreeable eyes and muttering:

'Dreadful! Dreadful!' An aeroplane was passing close overhead.

She looked up and remarked almost tearfully:

'Hasn't it struck you that but for the sins of your youth you might be doing stunts round these good-looking hills? Now!'

Mark considered the matter, fixedly returning her glance. For an Englishman the phrase 'the sins of your youth' as applied to a gentleman's physical immobility implies only one thing. It never had occurred to him that that implication might be tacked on to him. But of course it might. It was an implication of a disagreeable, or at least a discrediting, kind because, in his class they had been accustomed to consider that the disease was incurred by consorting with public women of a cheap kind. He had never consorted with any woman in his life but Marie Léonie who was health exaggerated. But if he had had to do with women he would have gone in for the most expensive sort. And taken precautions! A gentleman owes that to his fellows!

The lady was continuing:

'I may as well tell you at once that I am Mrs. Millicent de Bray Pape. And hasn't it struck you that but for *his* depravity — unbridled depravity — your brother might to-day be operating in Capel Court instead of peddling old furniture at the end of the world?'

She added disconcertingly:

'It's nervousness that makes me talk like this. I have always been shy in the presence of notorious libertines. That is my education.'

Her name conveyed to him that this lady was going to occupy Groby. He saw no objection to it. She had indeed written to ask him if he saw any objection to it. It had been a queerly written letter, in hieroglyphs of a straggling and convoluted kind . . . 'I am the lady who is going to rent your mansion Groby from my friend Mrs. Sylvia.'

It had struck him then — whilst Valentine

had been holding the letter up for him to read
. . . pretty piece, Valentine, nowadays; the
country air suited her — that this woman
must be an intimate friend of his brother's
wife Sylvia. Otherwise she would have said
'Mrs. Sylvia Tietjens' at least.

Now he was not so certain. This was not
the sort of person to be an intimate friend of
that bitch's. Then she was a catspaw. Sylvia's
intimates — amongst women — were all
Bibbies and Jimmies and Marjies. If she
spoke to any other woman it was to make use
of her — as a lady's-maid or a tool.

The lady said:

'It must be agony to you to be reduced to
letting your ancestral home. But that does not
seem to be a reason for not speaking to me. I
meant to ask the Earl's housekeeper for some
eggs for you, but I forgot. I am always
forgetting. I am so active. Mr. de Bray Pape
says I am the most active woman from here to
Santa Fé.'

Mark wondered: why Santa Fé? That was
probably because Mr. Pape had olive-tree
plantations in that part of the United States.
Valentine had told him over the letter that
Mr. Pape was the largest olive-oil merchant in
the world. He cornered all the olive-oil and
all the straw-covered flasks in Provence,
Lombardy, California, and informed his

country that you were not really refined if you used in your salads oil that did not come out of a Pape Quality flask. He showed ladies and gentlemen in evening dress starting back from expensively laid dinner tables, holding their noses and exclaiming 'Have you no *Pape's*!' Mark wondered where Christopher got his knowledge, for naturally Valentine had the information from him. Probably Christopher had looked at American papers. But why should one look at American papers? Mark himself never had. Wasn't there the *Field*? . . . He was a queer chap, Christopher.

The lady said:

'It *isn't* a reason for not speaking to me! It isn't!'

Her greyish face flushed slowly. Her eyes glittered behind her rimless pince-nez. She exclaimed:

'You are probably too haughtily aristocratic to speak to me, Sir Mark Tietjens. But I have in me the soul of the Maintenon; you are only the fleshly descendant of a line of chartered libertines. That is what Time and the New World have done to redress the balance of the old. It is we who are keeping up the status of the *grands seigneurs* of old in your so-called ancestral homes.'

He thought she was probably right. Not a bad sort of woman: she would naturally be irritated at his not answering her. It was proper enough.

He never remembered to have spoken to an American or to have thought about America. Except of course during the war. Then he had spoken to Americans in uniform about Transport. He hadn't liked their collars, but they had known their jobs as far as their jobs went — which had been asking to be provided with a disproportionate amount of transport for too few troops. He had had to wring that transport out of the country.

If he had had his way he wouldn't have. But he hadn't had his way because the Governing Classes were no good. Transport is the soul of a war: the spirit of an army had used to be in its feet, Napoleon had said. Something like that. But those fellows had starved the army of transport; then flooded it with so much it couldn't move; then starved it again. Then they had insisted on his finding enormously too much transport for those other fellows who used it for disposing of smuggled typewriters and sewing machines that came over on transports ... It had broken his back, that and solitude. There had not been a fellow he could talk to in the Government towards the end. Not one who knew the difference between the ancestry of Persimmon and the stud form of Sceptre or

Isinglass. Now they were paying for it.

The lady was saying to him that her spiritual affinity was probably a surprise to Sir Mark. There was none the less no mistake about it. In every one of the Maintenon's houses she felt instantly at home; the sight in any Museum of any knick-knack or jewel that had belonged to the respectable companion of Louis Quatorze startled her as if with an electric shock. Mr. Quarternine, the celebrated upholder of the metempsychosistic school had told her that those phenomena proved beyond doubt that the soul of the Maintenon had returned to earth in her body. What, as against that, were the mere fleshly claims of Old Family?

Mark considered that she was probably right. The old families of his country were a pretty inefficient lot that he was thankful to have done with. Racing was mostly carried on by English nobles from Frankfort-on-the-Main. If this lady could be regarded as speaking allegorically she was probably right. And she had had to get a soul from somewhere.

But she talked too much about it. People ought not to be so tremendously fluent. It was tiring; it failed to hold the attention. She was going on.

He lost himself in speculations as to her

89

reason for being there, trampling on his brother's grass. It would give Gunning and the extra hands no end of an unnecessary job to cut. The lady was talking about Marie Antoinette. Marie Antoinette had gone sledging on salt in summer. Trampling down haygrass was really worse. Or no better. If everyone in the country trampled on grass like that it would put up the price of fodder for transport animals to something prohibitive.

Why had she come there? She wanted to take Groby furnished. She might for him. He had never cared about Groby. His father had never had a stud worth talking about. A selling plater or two. He himself had never cared for hunting or shooting. He remembered standing on Groby lawn watching the shooting parties take to the hills on the Twelfth and feeling rather a fool. Christopher, of course, loved Groby. He was younger and hadn't expected to own it.

A pretty muck Sylvia might have made of the place by now — if her mother had let her. Well, they would know pretty soon. Christopher would be back, if the machine did not break his obstinate neck . . . What, then, was this woman doing here? She probably represented a new turn of the screw that that unspeakable woman was administering to Christopher.

His sister-in-law Sylvia represented for him unceasing, unsleeping activities of a fantastic kind. She wanted, he presumed, his brother to go back and sleep with her. So much hatred could have no other motive . . . There could be no other motive for sending this American lady here.

The American lady was telling him that she intended to keep up at Groby a semi-regal state — of course with due domestic modesty. Apparently she saw her way to squaring that circle! . . . Probably there are ways. There must be quite a lot of deucedly rich fellows in that country! How did they reconcile doing themselves well with democracy? Did their valets sit down to meals with them, for instance? That would be bad for discipline. But perhaps they did not care about discipline. There was no knowing.

Mrs. de Bray Pape apparently approved of having footmen in powder and the children of the tenants kneeling down when she drove out in his father's coach and six. Because she intended to use his father's coach and six when she drove over the moors to Redcar or Scarboro'. That, Mrs. de Bray Pape had been told by Sylvia, was what his father had done. And it was true enough. That queer old josser, his father, had always had out that monstrosity when he went justicing or to the

Assizes. That was to keep up his state. He didn't see why Mrs. de Bray Pape shouldn't keep up hers if she wanted to. But he did not see the tenant's children kneeling to the lady! Imagine old Scot's children at it or Long Tom o' th' Clough's; . . . Their grandchildren of course. They had called his father 'Tietjens' — some of them even 'Auld Mark!' to his face. He himself had always been 'Young Mark' to them. Very likely he was still. These things do not change any more than the heather on the moors. He wondered what the tenants would call her. She would have a tough time of it. They weren't her tenants; they were his and they jolly well knew it. These fellows who took houses and castles furnished thought they jolly well hired descent from the family. There had been before the war a fellow from Frankfort-on-the-Main took Lindisfarne or Holy Island or some such place and hired a bagpiper to play round the table while they ate. And closed his eyes whilst the fellow played reels. As if it had been a holy occasion . . . Friend of Sylvia's friends in the Government. To do her credit she would not stop with Jews. The only credit she had to her tail!

Mrs. de Bray Pape was telling him that it was not undemocratic to have your tenants' children kneel down when you passed.

92

A boy's voice said:

'Uncle Mark!' Who the devil could that be? Probably the son of the people he had week-ended with. Bowlby's maybe; or Teddy Hope's. He had always liked children and they liked him.

Mrs. de Bray Pape was saying that, yes, it was good for the tenants' children. The Rev. Dr. Slocombe, the distinguished educationalist, said that these touching old rites should be preserved in the interests of the young. He said that to see the Prince of Wales at the Coronation kneeling before his father and swearing fealty had been most touching. And she had seen pictures of the Maintenon having it done when she walked out. *She* was now the Maintenon, therefore it must be right. But for Marie Antoinette . . .

The boy's voice said:

'I hope you will excuse . . . I *know* it isn't the thing . . . '

He couldn't see the boy without turning his head on the pillow and he was not going to turn his head. He had a sense of someone a yard or so away at his off-shoulder. The boy at least had not come through the standing hay.

He did not imagine that the son of anyone he had ever week-ended with would ever walk through standing hay. The young generation

93

were a pretty useless lot, but he could hardly believe they would have come to that yet. Their sons might . . . He saw visions of tall dining-rooms lit up, with tall pictures, and dresses, and the sunset through high windows over tall grasses in the parks. He was done with that. If any tenants' children ever knelt to him it would be when he took his ride in his wooden coat to the little church over the moors . . . Where his father had shot himself.

That had been a queer go. He remembered getting the news. He had been dining, at Marie Léonie's . . .

The boy's voice was, precisely, apologising for the fact that that lady had walked through the grass. At the same time Mrs. de Bray Pape was saying things to the discredit of Marie Antoinette whom apparently she disliked. He could not imagine why anyone should dislike Marie Antoinette. Yet very likely she was dislikable. The French who were sensible people had cut her head off, so *they* presumably disliked her . . .

He had been dining at Marie Léonie's, she standing, her hands folded before her, hanging down, watching him eat his mutton chops and boiled potatoes when the porter from his Club had phoned through that there was a wire for him. Marie Léonie had answered the telephone. He had told her to tell the porter to open the telegram and read it to her. That was a not unusual proceeding. Telegrams that came to him at the Club usually announced the results of races that he had not attended. He hated to get up from the dinner-table. She had come back slowly and said still more slowly that she had bad news for him; there had been an accident; his father had been found shot dead.

He had sat still for quite a time; Marie Léonie also had said nothing. He remembered that he had finished his chops, but had not eaten his apple-pie. He had finished his claret.

By that time he had come to the conclusion that his father had probably committed suicide and that he — he, Mark Tietjens — was probably responsible for his father's having done that. He had got up, then, told Marie Léonie to get herself some mourning and had taken the night train to Groby. There had been no doubt about it when he got there. His father had committed suicide. His father was not the man, unadvisedly, to crawl through a quicken-hedge with his gun at full-cock behind him, after rabbits . . . It had been proposed.

There was, then, something soft about the Tietjens' stock — for there had been no real and sufficient cause for the suicide. Obviously his father had had griefs. He had never got over the death of his second wife: that was soft for a Yorkshireman. He had lost two sons and an only daughter in the war: other men had done that and got over it. He had heard through him, Mark, that his youngest son — Christopher — was a bad hat. But plenty of men had sons who were bad hats . . . Something soft then about the stock! Christopher certainly was soft. But that came from the mother. Mark's step-mother had been from the south of Yorkshire. Soft people down there; a soft woman. Christopher had been her ewe lamb and she had died of grief when Sylvia had run away from him! . . .

The boy with a voice had got himself into view towards the bottom of the bed, near Mrs. de Bray Pape . . . A tallish slip of a boy, with slightly chawbacony cheeks, high-coloured, lightish hair, brown eyes. Upstanding, but softish. Mark seemed to know him, but could not place him. He asked to be forgiven for the intrusion, saying that he knew it was not the thing.

Mrs. de Bray Pape was talking improbably about Marie Antoinette, whom she very decidedly disliked. She said that Marie Antoinette had behaved with great ingratitude to Madame de Maintenon — which must have been difficult. Apparently, according to Mrs. de Bray Pape, when Marie

Antoinette had been a neglected little girl about the Court of France Madame de Maintenon had befriended her, lending her frocks, jewels, and perfumes. Later Marie Antoinette had persecuted her benefactor. From that had arisen all the woes of France and the Old World in general.

That appeared to Mark to be to mix history. Surely the Maintenon was a hundred years before the other. But he was not very certain. Mrs. de Bray Pape said, however, that she had those little-known facts from Mr. Regibald Weiler, the celebrated professor of social economy at one of the Western universities.

Mark returned to the consideration of the softness of the Tietjens stock whilst the boy gazed at him with eyes that might have been imploring or that might have been merely moonstruck. Mark could not see what the boy could have to be imploring about, so it was probably just stupidity. His breeches, however, were very nicely cut. Very nicely indeed. Mark recognised the tailor — a man in Conduit Street. If that fellow had the sense to get his riding breeches from that man he could not be quite an ass . . .

That Christopher was soft because his mother did not come from the north of Yorkshire or Durham might be true enough

— but that was not enough to account for the race dying out. His, Mark's, father had no descendants by his sons. The two brothers who had been killed had been childless. He himself had none. Christopher . . . Well, that was debatable!

That he, Mark, had practically killed his own father he was ready to acknowledge. One made mistakes: that was one. If one made mistakes one should try to repair them, otherwise one must, as it were, cut one's losses. He could not bring his father back to life; he hadn't, equally, been able to do anything for Christopher . . . Not much, certainly. The fellow had refused his brass . . . He couldn't really blame him.

The boy was asking him if he would not speak to them. He said he was Mark's nephew, Mark Tietjens, junior.

Mark took credit to himself because he did not stir a hair. He had so made up his mind, he found, that Christopher's son was not his son that he had almost forgotten the cub's existence. But he ought not to have made up his mind so quickly: he was astonished to find from the automatic working of his brain that he so had. There were too many factors to be considered that he had never bothered really to consider. Christopher had determined that this boy should have Groby: that had been enough for him, Mark. He did not much care who had Groby.

But the actual sight of this lad whom he had never seen before, presented the problem to him as something that needed solution. It came as a challenge. When he came to think of it, it was a challenge to him to make up his mind finally as to the nature of Woman. He imagined that he had never bothered his head about that branch of the animal kingdom. But he found that, lying there, he must have spent quite a disproportionate amount of his time in thinking about the motives of Sylvia.

He had never spoken much with any but men — and then mostly with men of his own class and type. Naturally you addressed a few polite words to your week-end hostess. If you found yourself in the rose-garden of a Sunday before church with a young or old woman who knew anything about horses, you talked about horses or Goodwood or Ascot to her for long enough to show politeness to your hostess's guests. If she knew nothing about horses you talked about the roses or the irises or the weather last week. But that pretty well exhausted it.

Nevertheless he knew all about women; of that he was confident. That is to say that, when in the course of conversation or gossip he had heard the actions of women narrated

99

or commented on, he had always been able to supply a motive for those actions sufficient to account for them to his satisfaction or to let him predict with accuracy what course the future would take. No doubt twenty years of listening to the almost ceaseless but never disagreeable conversation of Marie Léonie had been a liberal education.

He regarded his association with her with complete satisfaction — as the only subject for complete satisfaction to be found in the contemplation of the Tietjens family. Christopher's Valentine was a pretty piece enough and had her head screwed confoundedly well on. But Christopher's association with her had brought such a peck of troubles down on his head that, except for the girl as an individual, it was a pretty poor choice. It was a man's job to pick a woman who would neither worry him nor be the cause of worries. Well, Christopher had picked two — and look at the results!

He, himself, had been completely unmistaken — from the beginning. He had first seen Marie Léonie on the stage of Covent Garden. He had gone to Covent Garden in attendance on his step-mother, his father's second wife — the soft woman. A florid, gentle, really saintly person. She had passed around Groby for a saint. An Anglican saint, of course. That was what was the matter with Christopher. It was the soft streak. A Tietjens had no business with saintliness in his composition! It was bound to get him looked on as a blackguard!

But he had attended Covent Garden as a politeness to his stepmother who very seldom found herself in Town. And there, in the second row of the ballet he had seen Marie Léonie — slimmer of course in those days. He had at once made up his mind to take up with her and, an obliging commissionaire having obtained her address for him from the stage-door he had, towards twelve-thirty, walked along the Edgeware Road towards her lodgings. He had intended to call on her; he met her, however, in the street. Seeing her there he had liked her walk, her figure, her neat dress.

He had planted himself, his umbrella, his billycock hat and all, squarely in front of her — she had neither flinched nor attempted to bolt round him! — and had said that, if at the end of her engagement in London, she cared to be placed 'dans ses draps,' with two hundred and fifty pounds a year and pin money to be deliberated on, she might hang up her cream-jug at an apartment that he would take for her in St. John's Wood Park which was the place in which in those days most of his friends had establishments. She had preferred the neighbourhood of the Gray's Inn road as reminding her more of France.

But Sylvia was quite another pair of shoes . . .

That young man was flushing all over his face. The young of the tomtit in the old shoe were getting impatient; they were chirruping in spite of the alarm-cries of the mother on the boughs above the thatch. It was certainly insanitary to have boughs above your thatch, but what did it matter in days so degenerate that even the young of tomtits could not restrain their chirpings in face of their appetites.

That young man — Sylvia's by-blow — was addressing embarrassed remarks to Mrs. de Bray Pape. He suggested that perhaps his uncle resented the lady's lectures on history and sociology. He said they had come to talk about the tree. Perhaps that was why his uncle would not speak to them.

The lady said that it was precisely giving lessons in history to the dissolute aristocracy of the Old World that was her mission in life. It was for their good, resent it how they might. As for talking about the tree, the young man had better do it for himself. She now intended to walk around the garden to see how the poor lived.

The boy said that in that case he did not see why Mrs. de Bray Pape had come at all. The lady answered that she had come at the sacred behest of his injured mother. That ought to be answer enough for him. She flitted, disturbedly, from Mark's view.

The boy, swallowing visibly in his throat, fixed his slightly protruding eyes on his uncle's face. He was about to speak, but he remained for a long time, silent and goggling. That was a Christopher Tietjens trick — not a Tietjens family trick. To gaze at you a long time before speaking. Christopher had it, no doubt, from his mother — exaggeratedly. She would gaze at you for a long time. Not unpleasantly of course. But Christopher had always irritated him, even as a small boy ... It is possible that he, Mark, himself, might not be as he was if Christopher hadn't gazed at him for a long time, like a stuck pig. On the morning of that beastly day. Armistice Day ... Beastly.

Cramp's eldest son, a bugler in the second Hampshires, went down the path, his bugle shining behind his khaki figure. Now they would make a beastly row with that instrument. On Armistice Day they had played the Last Post on the steps of the church under Marie Léonie's windows ... The Last Post! ... The Last of England! He remembered thinking that. He had not by then had the full terms of that surrender, but he had had a dose enough of Christopher's stuck-piggedness! . . . A full dose! He didn't say he didn't deserve it. If you make mistakes you must take what you get for it. You shouldn't make mistakes.

The boy at the foot of the bed was making agonised motions with his throat: swallowing at his Adam's apple.

He said:

'I can understand, uncle, that you hate to see us. All the same it seems a little severe to refuse to speak to us!'

Mark wondered a little at the breakdown in communications that there must have been. Sylvia had been spying round that property and round and round and round again. She had had renewed interviews with Mrs. Cramp. It had struck him as curious taste to like to reveal to dependents — to reveal and to dwell upon, the fact that you were distasteful to your husband. If his woman had left him he would have preferred to hold his tongue about it. He certainly would not have gone caterwauling about it to the carpenter of the man she had taken up with. Still, there was no accounting for tastes. Sylvia had, no doubt, been so full of her own griefs that she, very likely had not listened to what Mrs.

Cramp had said about his, Mark's, condition. During the one or two interviews he had had years ago with that bitch she had been like that. She had sailed in with her grievances against Christopher with such vigour that she had gone away with no ideas at all as to the conditions on which she was to be allowed to inhabit Groby. Obviously it taxed her mind to invent what she invented. You could not invent that sort of sex-cruelty stuff without having your mind a little affected. She could not, for instance, have invented the tale that he, Mark, was suffering for the sins of his youth without its taking it out of her. That is the ultimate retribution of Providence on those who invent gossip frequently. They go a little dotty . . . The fellow — he could not call his name to mind, half Scotch, half Jew — who had told him the worst tales against Christopher, had gone a little dotty. He had grown a beard and wore a top-hat at inappropriate functions. Well, in effect, Christopher was a saint and Provvy invents retributions of an ingenious kind against those who libel saints.

At any rate that bitch must have become so engrossed in her tale that it had not come through to her that he, Mark, could not speak. Of course the results of venereal disease are not pleasant to contemplate and

105

no doubt Sylvia having invented the disease for him had not liked to contemplate the resultant symptoms. At any rate that boy did not know — and neither did Mrs. de Bray Pape — that he did not speak; not to them, not to anybody. He was finished with the world. He perceived the trend of its actions, listened to its aspirations and even to its prayers, but he would never again stir lip or finger. It was like being dead — or being a God. This boy was apparently asking for absolution. He was of opinion that it was not a very sporting thing of himself and Mrs. Bray to come there ... It was however sporting enough. He could see that they were both as afraid of him, Mark, as of the very devil. Its taste might, however, be questioned. Still, the situation was unusual — as all situations are.

Obviously it was not in good taste for a boy to come to the house in which his father lived with a mistress, nor for the wife's intimate friend either. Still they apparently wanted, the one to let, the other to take, Groby. They could not do either if he, Mark, did not give permission, or at any rate if he opposed them. It was business, and business may be presumed to cover quite a lot of bad taste.

And in effect the boy was saying that his mother was, of course, a splendid person but that he, Mark junior, found her proceedings in many respects questionable. One could not however expect a woman — and an injured woman . . . The boy with his shining eyes and bright cheeks seemed to beg Mark to concede that his mother was at least an injured woman . . . One could not expect, then, a wronged woman to see things eye to eye with . . . with young Cambridge! For, he hastened to assure Mark, his Set — the son of the Prime Minister, young Doble, and Porter, as well as himself, were unanimously of opinion that a man ought to be allowed to live with whom he liked. He was not therefore questioning his father's actions and, for himself, if the occasion arose, he would be very glad to shake his father's . . . companion . . . by the hand.

His bright eyes became a little humid. He said that he was not in effect questioning anything, but he thought that he, himself, would have been the better for a little more of his father's influence. He considered that he had been too much under his mother's influence. They noticed it, even at Cambridge! That, in effect, was the real snag when it came to be a question of dissolving unions once contracted. Scientifically considered. Questions of . . . of sex-attraction, in spite of all the efforts of scientists, remained fairly mysterious. The best way to look at it . . . the safest way, was that sex attraction occurred as a rule between temperamental and physical opposites because Nature desired to correct extremes. No one in fact could be more different than his father and mother — the one so graceful, athletic and . . . oh, charming. And the other so . . . oh, let us say perfectly honourable but lawless. Because, of course, you can break certain laws and remain the soul of honour.

Mark wondered if this boy was aware that his mother habitually informed everyone whom she met that his father lived on women. On the immoral earnings of women, she would infer when she thought it safe . . .

The soul of honour, then, and masculinely clumsy and damn fine in his way . . . Well, he, Mark Tietjens junior, was not there to judge his father. His Uncle Mark could see that he regarded his father with affection and admiration. But if Nature — he must be pardoned for using anthropomorphic expressions since they were the shortest way — if Nature then, meant unions of opposite characters to redress extremes in the children, the process did not complete itself with . . . in short with the act of physical union. For just as there were obviously inherited physical characteristics and no doubt inherited memory, there yet remained the question of the influence of temperament on temperament by means of personal association. So that for one opposite to leave the fruits of a union exclusively under the personal influence of the other opposite was very possibly to defeat the purposes of Nature . . .

That boy, Mark thought, was a very curious problem. He seemed to be a good, straight boy. A little loquacious: still that was to be excused since he had to do all the talking himself. From time to time he had paused in his speech as if, deferentially, he wished to have Mark's opinion. That was proper. He, Mark, could not stand hobbledehoys — particularly the hobbledehoys of that age who appeared to be opinionative and emotional beyond the normal in hobbledehoys. Anyhow, he could not stand the Young once they were beyond the age of childhood. But he was aware that, if you want to conduct a scientific investigation, if you want to arrive, for yourself, at the truth of an individual's parentage — you must set aside your likes and dislikes.

Heaven knew, he had found Christopher, when he had been only one of the younger ones in his father's — he had found him irritating enough . . . a rather moony, fair brat, interested mostly in mathematics, with a trick of standing with those goggle eyes gazing bluely at you — years ago in and around, at first the nursery, then the stables at Groby. Then, if this lad irritated him it was rather an argument in favour of his being Christopher's son than Sylvia's by-blow by another man . . . What was the fellow's name? A rank bad hat, anyhow.

The probability was that he *was* the other fellow's son. That woman would not have trepanned Christopher into the marriage if she hadn't at least thought that she was with child. There was nothing to be said against any wench's tricking any man into marrying her if she were in that condition. But once having got a man to give a name to your bastard you ought to treat him with some loyalty: it is a biggish service he has done you. That Sylvia had never done . . . They had got this young springald into their — the Tietjenses' — family. There he was, with his fingers on Groby already . . . That was all right. As great families as Tietjens' had had that happen to them.

But what made Sylvia pestilential was that she should afterwards have developed this sex-madness for his unfortunate brother.

There was no other way to look at it. She

110

had undoubtedly lured Christopher on to marry her because she thought rightly or wrongly that she was with child by another man. They would never know — she herself probably did not know! — whether this boy was Christopher's son or the other's. English women are so untidy — shamefaced — about these things. That was excusable. But every other action of hers from that date had been inexcusable — except regarded as actions perpetrated under the impulsion of sex-viciousness.

It is perfectly proper — it is a mother's duty to give an unborn child a name and a father. But afterwards to blast the name of that father is more discreditable than to leave the child nameless. This boy was now Tietjens of Groby — but he was also the legal son of a father who had behaved unspeakably according to the mother ... And the son of a mother who had been unable to attract her man! ... Who advertised the fact to the estate carpenter! If we say that the good of the breed is the supreme law, what sort of virtue was this?

It was all very well to say that every one of Sylvia's eccentricities had in view the sole aim of getting her boy's father to return to her. No doubt they might be. He, Mark, was perfectly ready to concede that even her infidelities, notorious as they had been, might have been merely ways of calling his unfortunate brother's attention back to her — of keeping herself in his mind. After the marriage Christopher, finding out that he had been a mere catspaw, probably treated her pretty coldly or ignored her — maritally . . . And he was a pretty attractive fellow, Christopher. He, Mark, was bound nowadays to acknowledge that. A regular saint and Christian martyr and all that . . . Enough to drive a woman wild if she had to live beside him and be ignored.

It is obvious that women must be allowed what means they can make use of to maintain — to arouse — their sex attraction for their men. That is what the bitches are for in the scale of things. They have to perpetuate the breed. To do that they have to call attention to themselves and to use what devices they see fit to use, each one according to her own temperament. That cruelty was an excitant he was quite ready, too, to concede. He was ready to concede anything to the woman. To be cruel is to draw attention to yourself; you cannot expect to be courted by a man whom you allow to forget you. But there probably ought to be a limit to things. You probably ought in this, as in all other things, to know what you can do and what you can't — and the proof of this particular pudding, as of all others, was in the eating. Sylvia had left no stone unturned in the determination to keep herself in her man's mind and she had certainly irretrievably lost her man: to another girl. Then she was just a nuisance.

A woman intent on getting a man back ought to have some system, some sort of scheme at the very least. But Sylvia — he knew it from the interminable talk that he had had with Christopher on Armistice night — Sylvia delighted most in doing what she called pulling the strings of shower-baths. She did extravagant things, mostly of a cruel kind, for the fun of seeing what would happen. Well, you cannot allow yourself fun when you are on a campaign. Not as to the subject matter of the campaign itself! If then you do what you want rather than what is expedient you damn well have to take what you get for it. *Damn* well!

What would have justified Sylvia, no matter what she did, would have been if she had succeeded in having another child by his brother. She hadn't. The breed of Tietjens was not enriched. Then she was just a nuisance . . .

An infernal nuisance . . . For what was she up to now? It was perfectly obvious that both Mrs. de Bray Pape and this boy were here because she had had another outbreak of . . . practically Sadism. They were here so that Christopher might be hurt some more and she not forgotten. What then was the reason for this visit? What the deuce was it?

The boy had been silent for some time. He was gazing at Mark with the goggle-eyed gasping that had been so irritating in his father — particularly on Armistice Day . . . Well, he, Mark, was apparently now conceding that this boy was probably his brother's son. A real Tietjens after all was to reign over the enormously long, grey house behind the fantastic cedar. The tallest cedar in Yorkshire; in England; in the Empire . . . He didn't care. He who lets a tree overhang his roof calls the doctor in daily . . . The boy's lips began to move. No sound came out. He was presumably in a great state!

He was undoubtedly like his father. Darker . . . Brown hair, brown eyes, high-coloured cheeks all flushed now; straight nose, marked brown eyebrows. A sort of . . . scared, puzzled . . . what was it? . . . expression. Well, Sylvia was fair; Christopher was dark-haired with silver streaks, but fair-complexioned . . . Damn it; this boy was more attractive than Christopher had been at his age and earlier . . . Christopher hanging round the schoolroom door in Groby, puzzled over the

114

mathematical theory of waves. He, Mark, hadn't been able to stand him or indeed any of the other children. There was sister Effie — *born* to be a curate's wife . . . Puzzled! That was it! . . . That bothering woman, his father's second wife — the Saint! — had introduced the puzzlement strain into the Tietjenses . . . This was Christopher's boy, saintly strain and all. Christopher was probably born to be a rural dean in a fat living, writing treatises on the integral calculus all the time except on Saturday afternoons. With a great reputation for saintliness. Well he wasn't the one and hadn't the other. He was an old-furniture dealer who made a stink in virtuous nostrils . . . Provvy works in a mysterious way. The boy was saying now:

'The tree . . . the great tree . . . It darkens the windows . . .'

Mark said: 'Aha!' to himself. Groby Great Tree was the symbol of Tietjens. For thirty miles round Groby they made their marriage vows by Groby Great Tree. In the other Ridings they said that Groby Tree and Groby Well were equal in height and depth one to the other. When they were really imaginatively drunk Cleveland villagers would declare — would knock you down if you denied — that Groby Great

Tree was 365 foot high and Groby Well 365 feet deep. A foot for every day of the year . . . On special occasions — he could not himself be bothered to remember what — they would ask permission to hang rags and things from the boughs. Christopher said that one of the chief indictments against Joan of Arc had been that she and the other village girls of Domrèmy had hung rags and trinkets from the boughs of a cedar. Or maybe a thorn? Offering to fairies . . . Christopher set great store by the tree. He was a romantic ass. Probably he set more store by the tree than by anything else at Groby. He would pull the house down if he thought it incommoded the tree.

Young Mark was bleating, positively bleating:

'The Italians have a proverb . . . He who lets a tree overhang his house invites a daily call from the doctor . . . I agree myself . . . In principle of course . . . '

Well, that was that! Sylvia, then, was proposing to threaten to ask to have Groby Great Tree cut down. Only to threaten to ask. But that would be enough to agonise the miserable Christopher. You couldn't cut down Groby Great Tree. But the thought that the tree was under the guardianship of unsympathetic people would be enough to drive Christopher almost dotty — for years and years.

'Mrs. de Bray Pape,' the boy was stammering, 'is extremely keen on the tree's being . . . I agree in principle . . . My mother wished you to see that — oh, in modern days — a house is practically unlettable if . . . So she got Mrs. de Bray Pape . . . She hasn't had the courage though she swore she had . . . '

He continued to stammer. Then he started and stopped, crimson. A woman's voice had called:

'Mr. Tietjens . . . Mr. Mark . . . Hi . . . hup!'

A small woman, all in white, white breeches, white coat, white wide-awake, was slipping down from a tall bay with a white star on the forehead — a bay with large nostrils and an intelligent head. She waved her hand obviously at the boy and then caressed the horse's nostrils. Obviously at the boy . . . for it was impossible that Mark, Senior, would know a woman who could make a sound like 'Hi, hup!' to attract his attention.

Lord Fittleworth, in a square, hard hat, sat on an immense, coffin-headed dapple-grey. He had bristling, close-cropped moustaches and sat like a limpet. He waved his crop in the direction of Mark — they were such old friends — and went on talking to Gunning, who was at his stirrup. The coffin-headed beast started forward and reared a foot or so; a wild, brazen, yelping sound had disturbed it. The boy was more and more scarlet and as emotion grew on him, more and more like Christopher on that beastly day . . . Christopher with a piece of furniture under his arm, in Marie Léonie's room, his eyes goggling out at the foot of the bed.

Mark swore painfully to himself. He hated to be reminded of that day. Now this lad and that infernal bugle that the younger children of Cramp had got hold of from their bugler-brother, had put it back damnably in his mind. It went on. At intervals. One child had another try, then another. Obviously then Cramp, the eldest, took it. It blared out . . . Ta . . . Ta . . . Ta . . . Ta . . . , ti . . . ta-ta-ti . . . Ta . . . The Last Post. The B—y infernal Last Post . . . Well, Christopher, as that day Mark had predicted, had got himself, with his raw sensibilities, into a pretty bloody infernal mess while some drunken ass had played the Last Post under the window . . . Mark meant that whilst that farewell was being played he had had that foresight. And he hated the bugle for reminding him of it. He hated it more than he had imagined. He could not have imagined himself using profanity even to himself. He must have been profoundly moved. Deucedly and profoundly moved at that beastly noise. It had come over the day like a disaster. He saw every detail of Marie Léonie's room as it was on that day. There was, on the marble mantel-shelf under an immense engraving of the Sistine Madonna a feeding-cup over a night-light in which Marie Léonie had been keeping some sort of pap warm for him. Probably the last food to which he had ever helped himself . . .

# 5

But no . . . that must have been about twelve or earlier or later on that infernal day. In any case he could not remember any subsequent meal he had had then; but he remembered an almost infinitely long period of intense vexation. Of mortification insofar as he could accuse himself of ever having felt mortified. He could still remember the fierce intaking of his breath through his nostrils that had come when Christopher had announced what had seemed to him then his ruinous intentions . . . It had not been till probably four in the morning that Lord Wolstonemark had rung him up to ask him to countermand the transport that was to have gone out from Harwich . . . At four in the morning, the idiotic brutes. His substitute had disappeared in the rejoicings in the sy— and Lord Wolstonemark had wanted to know what code they used for Harwich because transport must at all costs be stopped. There was going to be no advance into Germany . . . He had never spoken after that!

His brother was done for; the country finished; he was as good as down and out, as the phrase was, himself. Already in his deep mortification — yes — mortification! — he had said to Christopher that morning — the 11th November, 1918 — that he would never speak to him again. He hadn't at that moment meant to say that he would never speak to Christopher at all again — merely that he was never going to speak to him about the affairs of Groby! Christopher might take that immense, far-spreading, grey, bothersome house and the tree and the well and the moors and all the John Peel outfit. Or he might leave them. He, Mark, was never going to speak about the matter any more.

He remembered thinking that Christopher might have taken him to mean that he intended to withdraw, for what it was worth, the light of his countenance from the Christopher Tietjens *ménage*. Nothing had been further from his thoughts. He had a soft corner in his heart for Valentine Wannop. He had had it ever since sitting, feeling like a fool, in the ante-room of the War Office, beside her — gnawing at the handle of his umbrella. But, then, he had recommended her to become Christopher's mistress; he had at any rate begged her to look after his mutton chops and his buttons. So that it wasn't likely that when, a year or so later, Christopher announced that he really was at last going to take up with the young woman and to chance what came of it — it wasn't likely that he intended to dissociate himself from the two of them.

The idea had worried him so much that he had written a rough note — the last time that his hand had ever held a pen — to Christopher. He had said that a brother's backing was not of great use to a woman, but in the special circumstances of the case, he being Tietjens of Groby for what it was worth, and Lady Tietjens — Marie Léonie — being perfectly willing to be seen on all occasions with Valentine and her man it might be worth something, at any rate with tenantry and such like.

Well, he hadn't gone back on that!

But once the idea had come into his head it had grown and grown, on top of his mortification and his weariness. Because he could not conceal from himself that he was weary to death — of the office, of the nation, of the world and people . . . People . . . he was tired of them! And of the streets, and the grass, and the sky and the moors! He had done his job. That was before Wolstonemark had telephoned and he still thought that he had done his job of getting things here and there about the world to some purpose.

A man is in the world to do his duty by his

nation and his family . . . By his own
people first. Well, he had to acknowledge
that he had let his own people down pretty
badly — beginning with Christopher.
Chiefly Christopher; but that reacted on the
tenantry.

He had always been tired of the tenantry
and Groby. He had been born tired of them.
That happens. It happens particularly in old
and prominent families. It was odd that
Groby and the whole Groby business should
so tire him; he supposed he had been born
with some kink. All the Tietjenses were born
with some sort of kink. It came from the
solitude maybe, on the moors, the hard
climate, the rough neighbours — possibly
even from the fact that Groby Great Tree
overshadowed the house. You could not look
out of the school-room windows at all for its
great, ragged trunk and all the children's
wing was darkened by its branches. Black
. . . funeral plumes. The Hapsburgs were said
to hate their palaces — that was no doubt
why so many of them, beginning with Juan
Ort, had come muckers. At any rate they had
chucked the royalty business.

And at a very early age he had decided that
he would chuck the country-gentleman
business. He didn't see that he was the one to
bother with those confounded, hardheaded

beggars or with those confounded wind-swept moors and valley bottoms. One owed the blighters a duty, but one did not have to live among them or see that they aired their bedrooms. It had been mostly swank that, always; and since the Corn Laws it had been almost entirely swank. Still, it is obvious that a landlord owes something to the estate from which he and his fathers have drawn their income for generations and generations.

Well, he had never intended to do it because he had been born tired of it. He liked racing and talking about racing to fellows who liked racing. He had intended to do that to the end.

He hadn't been able to.

He had intended to go on living between the office, his chambers, Marie Léonie's and week-ends with race-horse owners of good family until his eyes closed . . . Of course God disposes in the end, even of the Tietjenses of Groby! He had intended to give over Groby, on the death of his father, to whichever of his brothers had heirs and seemed likely to run the estate well. That for a long time had seemed quite satisfactory. Ted, his next brother, had had his head screwed on all right. If he had had children he would have filled the bill. So would the next brother . . . But neither of them had had children and both had managed to get killed in Gallipoli. Even sister Mary who was actually, next to him, a *maitresse femme* if ever there was one, had managed to get killed as a Red Cross matron. *She* would have run Groby well enough — the great, blowsy, grey woman with a bit of a moustache.

Thus God had let him down with a bump on Christopher . . . Well, Christopher would have run Groby well enough. But he wouldn't. Wouldn't own a yard of Groby land; wouldn't touch a penny of Groby money. He was suffering for it now.

They were both, in effect, suffering, for Mark could not see what was to become of either Christopher or the estate.

Until his father's death Mark had bothered precious little about the fellow. He was by fourteen years the younger: there had been ten children altogether, three of his own mother's children having died young and one having been soft. So Christopher had been still a baby when Mark had left Groby for good — for good except for visits when he had brought his umbrella and seen Christopher mooning at the schoolroom door or in his own mother's sitting-room. So he had hardly known the boy.

And at Christopher's wedding he had definitely decided that he would not see him again — a mug who had got trepanned into marrying a whore. He wished his brother no ill, but the thought of him made Mark sickish. And then, for years, he had heard the worst possible rumours about Christopher. In a way they had rather consoled Mark. God knows, he cared little enough about the Tietjens family — particularly for the children by that soft saint. But he would rather have any brother of his be a wrong 'un than a mug.

Then gradually from the gossip that went abroad he had come to think that Christopher was a very bad wrong 'un indeed. He could account for it easily enough. Christopher had a soft streak and what a woman can do to deteriorate a fellow with a soft streak is beyond belief. And the woman Christopher had got hold of — who had got hold of him — passed belief too. Mark did not hold any great opinion of women at all; if they were a little plump, healthy, a little loyal and not noticeable in their dress that was enough for him . . . But Sylvia was as thin as an eel, as full of vice as a mare that's a wrong 'un, completely disloyal, and dressed like any Paris cocotte. Christopher, as he saw it, had had to keep that harlot to the tune of six or seven thousand a year, in a society of Jewish or Liberal cabinet minister's wives, all wrong

'uns too — and on an income of at most two
. . . Plenty for a younger son. But naturally
he had had to go wrong to get the money.

So it had seemed to him . . . and it had
seemed to matter precious little. He gave a
thought to his brother perhaps twice a year.
But then one day — just after the two
brothers had been killed — their father had
come up from Groby to say to Mark at the
Club:

'Has it occurred to you that, since those
two boys are killed that fellow Christopher is
practically heir to Groby? You have no
legitimate children have you?' Mark replied
that he hadn't any bastards either and that he
was certainly not going to marry.

At that date it had seemed to him certain
that he was not going to marry Marie Léonie
Riotor and certainly he was not going to
marry anyone else. So Christopher — or at
any rate Christopher's heir — must surely
come in to Groby. It had not really, hitherto,
occurred to him. But when it was thus put
forcibly into his mind he saw instantly that it
upset the whole scheme of his life. As he saw
Christopher then, the fellow was the last
person in the world to have charge of Groby
— for you had to regard that as to some
extent a cure of souls. And he himself would
not be much better. He was hopelessly out of

127

touch with the estate and, even though his father's land-steward was a quite efficient fellow, he himself at that date was so hopelessly immersed in the affairs of the then war that he would hardly have a moment of time to learn anything about the property.

There was therefore a breakdown in his scheme of life. That was already a pretty shaking sort of affair. Mark was accustomed to regard himself as master of his fate — as being so limited in his ambitions and so entrenched behind his habits and his wealth that, if circumstances need not of necessity bend to his will, fate could hardly touch him.

And it was one thing for a Tietjens younger son to be a bold sort of law-breaker — or at any rate that he should be contemptuous of restraint. It was quite another that the heir to Groby should be a soft sort bad hat whose distasteful bunglings led his reputation to stink in the nostrils of all his own class. If a younger son can be said to have a class! . . . At any rate in the class to which his father and eldest brother belonged. Tietjens was said to have sold his wife to her cousin the Duke at so contemptible a price that he was obviously penniless even after that transaction. He had sold her to other rich men — to bank managers, for instance. Yet even after that he was reduced to giving worthless cheques. If a man sold his soul to the devil he should at least insist on a good price. Similar transactions were said to distinguish the social set in which that bitch moved — but most of the men who, according to Ruggles, sold their wives to members of the government, obtained millions by governmental financial tips — or peerages. Not infrequently they obtained both peerages and millions. But Christopher was such a confounded ass that he had got neither the one nor the other. His cheques were turned down for twopences. And he was such a bungler that he must needs seduce the daughter of their father's oldest friend, must needs get her with child and let the fact be known to the whole world . . .

This information he had from Ruggles — and it killed their father. Well, he, Mark was absolutely to blame: that was that. But — infinitely worse — it had made Christopher fiercely determined not to accept a single penny of the money that had become Mark's and that had been his father's. And Christopher was as obstinate as a hog. For that Mark did not blame him. It was a Tietjens job to be obstinate as a hog.

He couldn't, however, disabuse his mind of the idea that Christopher's refusal of Groby and all that came from Groby was as much a manifestation of the confounded saintliness that he got from his soft mother as of a spirit of resentment. Christopher *wanted* to rid himself of his great possessions. The fact that his father and brother had believed him to be what Marie Léonie would have called *maquereau* and had thus insulted him he had merely grasped at with eagerness as an excuse. He wanted to be out of the world. That was it. He wanted to be out of a disgustingly inefficient and venial world just as he, Mark, also wanted to be out of a world that he found almost more fusionless and dishonest than Christopher found it.

At any rate, at the first word that they had had about the heirship to Groby after their father's death, Christopher had declared that he, Mark, might take his money to the devil and the ownership of Groby with it. He proposed never to forgive either his father or Mark. He had only consented to take Mark by the hand at the urgent solicitation of Valentine Wannop . . .

That had been the most dreadful moment of Mark's life. The country was, even then, going to the devil; his brother proposed to starve himself; Groby, by his brother's wish was to fall into the hands of that bitch . . . And the country went further and further towards the devil and his brother starved

130

worse and worse . . . and as for Groby . . .

The boy who practically owned Groby had, at the first sound of the voice of the woman who wore white riding-kit and called 'Hi-hup!' — at the very first sound of her voice the boy had scampered off through the raspberry canes and was now against the hedge whilst she leaned down over him, laughing, and her horse leaned over behind her. Fittleworth was smiling at them benevolently and at the same time continuing his conversation with Gunning . . .

The woman was too old for the boy who had gone scarlet at the sound of her voice. Sylvia had been too old for Christopher: she had got him on the hop when he had been only a kid . . . The world went on.

He was nevertheless thankful for the respite. He had to acknowledge to himself that he was not as young as he had been. He had a great deal to think of if he was to get the hang of — he was certainly not going to interfere with — the world and having to listen to conversations that were mostly moral apophthegms had tired him. He got too many at too short intervals. If he had spoken he would not have, but, because he did not speak both the lady who was descended from the Maintenon and that boy had peppered him with moral points of view that all

131

required to be considered, without leaving him enough time to get his breath mentally.

The lady had called them a corrupt and effete aristocracy. They were probably not corrupt but certainly, regarded as landowners, they were effete — both he and Christopher. They were simply bored at the contemplation of that terrific nuisance — and refusing to perform the duties of their post they refused the emoluments too. He could not remember that, after childhood, he had ever had a penny out of Groby. They would not accept that post: they had taken others . . . Well, this was his, Mark's, last post . . . He could have smiled at his grim joke.

Of Christopher he was not so sure. That ass was a terrific sentimentalist. Probably he would have liked to be a great landowner, keeping up the gates on the estate — like Fittleworth who was a perfect lunatic about gates. He was probably even now jaw-jawing Gunning about them, smacking his boot-top with his crop-handle. Yes — keeping up the gates and seeing that the tenants' land gave so many bushels of wheat to the acre or supported so many sheep the year round . . . How many sheep would an acre keep all the year round and how many bushels of wheat should it give? He, Mark, had not the least idea. Christopher would know — with the difference to be expected of every acre of all the thousand acres of Groby ... Yes, Christopher had pored over Groby with the intentness of a mother looking at her baby's face!

So that his refusal to take on that stewardship might very well arise from a sort of craving for mortification of the spirit. Old Campion had once said that he believed — he positively believed, with shudders — that Christopher desired to live in the spirit of Christ. That had seemed horrible to the general, but Mark did not see that it was horrible, *per se* .... He doubted, however, whether Christ would have refused to manage Groby had it been his job. Christ was a sort of an Englishman and Englishmen did not as a rule refuse to do their jobs ... They had not used to; now no doubt they did. It was a Russian sort of trick. He had heard that even before the revolution great Russian nobles would disperse their estates, give their serfs their liberty, put on a hair shirt and sit by the roadside begging ... Something like that. Perhaps Christopher was a symptom that the English were changing. He himself was not. He was just lazy and determined — and done with it!

He had not at first been able to believe that Christopher was resolved — with a Yorkshire resolution — to have nothing to do with Groby or his, Mark's, money. He had nevertheless felt a warm admiration for his brother the moment the words had been said. Christopher would take none of his father's money; he would never forgive either his father or his brother. A proper Yorkshire sentiment, uttered coldly and as it were good-humouredly. His eyes, naturally, had goggled, but he had displayed no other emotion.

Nevertheless Mark had imagined that he might be up to some game. He might be merely meaning to bring Mark to his knees . . . But how could Mark be more brought to his knees than by offering to give over Groby to his brother? It is true he had kept that up his sleeve whilst his brother had been out in France. After all there was no sense in offering a fellow who might be going to become food for powder the management of great possessions. He had felt a certain satisfaction in the fact that Christopher *was* going out, though he was confoundedly sorry too. He really admired Christopher for doing it — and he imagined that it might clear some of the smirchiness that must attach to Christopher's reputation in spite of what he now knew to be his brother's complete guiltlessness of the crime that had been attributed to him. He had of course been wrong — he had reckoned without the determined discredit that, after the war was over, the civilian population would contrive to attach to every man who had been to the front as a fighting soldier. After all that was natural enough. The majority of the male population was civilian and once the war was over and there was no more risk they would bitterly regret that they had not gone. They would take it out of the ex-soldiers all right!

So that Christopher had rather been additionally discredited than much helped by his services to the country. Sylvia had been able to put it, very reasonably, that Christopher was by nature that idle and dissolute thing, a soldier. That, in times of peace, had helped her a great deal.

Still, Mark had been pleased with his brother, and, once Christopher had been invalided back and had returned to his old-tin saving depot near Ealing, Mark had at once set wheels in motion to get his brother demobilised so that he might look after Groby. By that time Groby was inhabited by Sylvia, the boy, and Sylvia's mother. The estate just had to be managed by the land-steward who had served his father, neither Sylvia nor her family having any finger in that; though her mother was able to assure him, Mark, that the estate was doing as well as the Agricultural Committee of grocers and stock-jobbers would let it. They insisted on wheat being sown on exposed moors where nothing but heather had a chance, and active moorland sheep being fattened in water-bottoms full of liver fluke. But the land-steward fought them as well as one man could be expected to fight the chosen of a nation of small shop-keepers . . .

And at that date — the date of Christopher's return to Ealing — Mark had still imagined that Christopher had really only been holding out for the possession of Groby. He was therefore disillusioned rather nastily. He had managed to get Christopher demobilised — without telling him anything about it — by just about the time when the Armistice came along . . . And then he found that he really had put the fat in the fire!

He had practically beggared the wretched fellow who, counting on living on his pay for at least a year longer, had mortgaged his blood-money in order to go into a sort of partnership in an old-furniture business with a confounded American. And of course the blood-money was considerably diminished, being an allowance made to demobilised officers computed on the number of their days of service. So he had docked Christopher of two or three hundred pounds. That was the sort of mucky situation into which Christopher might be expected to be got in by his well-wishers . . . There he had been, just before Armistice Day, upon the point of demobilisation and without an available penny! It appeared that he had to sell even the few books that Sylvia had left him when she had stripped his house.

That agreeable truth had forced itself on Mark at just the moment when he had been so rotten bad with pneumonia that he might be expected to cash in at any moment. Marie Léonie had indeed, of her own initiative, telephoned to Christopher that he had better come to see his brother if he wanted to meet him on this side of the grave.

They had at once started arguing — or rather each had started exposing his views. Christopher had stated what he was going to do and Mark had voiced his horror at what Christopher proposed. Mark's horror came from the fact that Christopher proposed to eschew comfort. An Englishman's duty is to secure for himself for ever, reasonable clothing, a clean shirt a day, a couple of mutton chops grilled without condiments, two floury potatoes, an apple pie with a piece of Stilton and pulled bread, a pint of Club medoc, a clean room, in the winter a good fire in the grate, a comfortable armchair, a comfortable woman to see that all these were prepared for you, and to keep you warm in bed and to brush your bowler and fold your umbrella in the morning. When you had that secure for life you could do what you liked provided that what you did never endangered that security. What was to be said against that?

Christopher had nothing to advance except that he was not going to live in that way. He was not going to live in that way unless he could secure that or something like it, by his own talents. His only available and at the same time marketable talent was his gift for knowing genuine old furniture. So he was going to make a living out of old furniture. He had had his scheme perfectly matured; he had even secured an American partner, a fellow who had as great a gift for the cajolement of American purchasers of old stuff as he, Christopher, had for its discovery. It was still the war then, but Christopher and his partner between them had predicted the American mopping up of the world's gold supply and the consequent stripping of European houses of old stuff . . . At that you could make a living.

Other careers, he said, were barred to him.

The Department of Statistics in which he had formerly had a post had absolutely cold-shouldered him. They were not only adamant, they were also vindictive against civil servants who had become serving soldiers. They took the view that those members of their staffs who had preferred serving were idle and dissolute fellows who had merely taken up arms in order to satisfy their lusts for women. Women had naturally preferred soldiers to civilians; the civilians were now getting back on them. That was natural.

Mark agreed indeed that it was natural. Before he had been interested in his brother as a serving soldier he had been inclined to consider most soldiers as incompetent about Transport and, in general, nuisances. He agreed too that Christopher could not go back to the Department. There he was certainly a marked man. He could possibly have insisted on his rights to be taken back even though his lungs, being by now pretty damaged by exposure, might afford them a pretext for legally refusing him. H.M. Civil Service and Departments have the right to refuse employment to persons likely to become unfit for good. A man who has lost an eye may be refused by any Department because he may lose the other and so become liable for a pension. But even if Christopher forced himself on the Department they would have their bad mark against him. He had been too rude to them during the war when they had tried to force him to employ himself in the faking of statistics that the Ministry had coerced the Department into supplying in order to dish the French who demanded more troops.

With that point of view Mark found himself entirely in sympathy. His long association with Marie Léonie, his respect for the way in which she had her head screwed on, the constant intimacy with the life and point of view of French individuals of the *petite bourgeoisie* which her gossip had given him — all these things together with his despair for the future of his own country had given him a very considerable belief in the destinies and indeed in the virtues of the country across the Channel. It would therefore have been very distasteful to him that his brother should take pay from an organisation that had been employed to deal treacherously with our Allies. It had indeed become extremely distasteful to him to take pay himself from a Government that had forced such a course upon the nation and he would thankfully have resigned from his office if he had not considered that his services were indispensable to the successful prosecution of the war which was then still proceeding. He wanted to be done with it, but at the moment he saw no chance. The war was by then obviously proceeding towards a successful issue. Owing to the military genius of the French who by then had the supreme command, the enemy nations were daily being forced to abandon great stretches of territory. But that only made the calls on Transport the greater whilst, if we were successfully and unwastefully to occupy the enemy capital as at that date he imagined that we obviously must, the demand for the provision of Transport must become almost unmeasurable.

Still, that was no argument for the re-entry of his brother into the service of the country. As he saw things, public life had become — and must remain for a long period — so demoralized by the members of the then Government with their devious foreign policies and their intimacies with a class of shady financiers such as had never hitherto had any finger in the English political pie — public life had become so discreditable an affair that the only remedy was for the real governing classes to retire altogether from public pursuits. Things in short must become worse before they could grow better. With the dreadful condition of ruin at home and foreign discredit to which the country must almost immediately emerge under the conduct of the Scotch grocers, Frankfort financiers, Welsh pettifoggers, Midland armament manufacturers and South Country incompetents who during the later years of the war had intrigued themselves into office — with that dreadful condition staring it in the face, the country must return to something like its old standards of North Country common sense and English probity. The old governing class to which he and his belonged might never return to power but, whatever revolutions took place — and he did not care! — the country must return to exacting of whoever might be its governing class some semblance of personal probity and public honouring of pledges. He obviously was out of it or he would be out of it with the end of the war, for even from his bed he had taken no small part in the directing of affairs at his office . . . A state of war obviously favouring the coming to the top of all kinds of devious storm petrels; that was inevitable and could not be helped. But in normal times a country — every country — was true to itself.

Nevertheless he was very content that his brother should in the interim have no share in affairs. Let him secure his mutton chop, his

142

pint of claret, his woman, and his umbrella and it mattered not into what obscurity he retired. But how was that to be secured? There were several ways.

He was aware, for instance, that Christopher was both a mathematician of no mean order and a churchman. He might perfectly well take orders, assume the charge of one of the three family livings that Mark had in his gift and, whilst competently discharging the duties of his cure, pursue whatever are the occupations of a well-cared-for mathematician.

Christopher, however, whilst avowing his predilection for such a life — which as Mark saw it was exactly fitted to his asceticism, his softness in general, and his private tastes — Christopher admitted that there was an obstacle to his assuming such a cure of souls — an obstacle of an insuperable nature. Mark at once asked him if he were in fact living with Miss Wannop. But Christopher answered that he had not seen Miss Wannop since the day of his second proceeding to the front. They had then agreed that they were not the sort of persons to begin a hidden intrigue and the affair had proceeded no further.

Mark was, however, aware that a person of Christopher's way of thinking might well feel inhibited from taking on a cure of souls if, in spite of the fact that he had abstained from seducing a young woman, he nevertheless privately desired to enter into illicit relations with her, and that that was sufficient to justify him in saying that an insuperable obstacle existed. He did not know that he himself agreed, but it was not his business to interfere between any man and his conscience in a matter of the Church. He was himself no very good Christian, at any rate as regards the relationships of men and women. Nevertheless the Church of England was the Church of England. No doubt had Christopher been a Papist he could have had the young woman for his housekeeper and no one would have bothered.

But what the devil, then, was his brother to do? He had been offered, as a sop in the pan, and to keep him quiet, no doubt, over the affair of the Department of Statistics, a vice-consulate in some Mediterranean port — Toulon or Leghorn or something of the sort. That might have done well enough. It was absurd to think of a Tietjens, heir to Groby, being under the necessity of making a living. It was fantastic, but if Christopher was in a fantastic mood there was nothing to be done about it. A vice-consulate is a potty sort of job. You attend to ships' manifests, get members of crews out of gaol, give old lady tourists the addresses of boarding houses kept by English or half-castes, or provide the vice-admirals of visiting British squadrons with the names of local residents who should be invited to entertainments given on the flagship. It was a potty job, but innocuous if it could be regarded as a sort of marking time ... And at that moment Mark still thought that Christopher was still holding out for some sort of concession on Mark's part before definitely assuming the charge of Groby, its tenants, and its mineral rights ... But there were insuperable objections to even the vice-consulate. In the first place the job would have been in the public service, a fact to which as has been said Mark strongly objected. Then the job was offered as a sort of a bribe. And, in addition, the consular service exacts from everyone who occupies a consular or vice-consular post the deposit of a sum of four hundred pounds sterling, and Christopher did not possess even so much as four hundred shillings ... And, in addition, as Mark was well aware, Miss Wannop might again afford an obstacle. A British vice-consul might possibly keep a Maltese or Levantine in a back street and no harm done, but he probably could not live with an English

145

young woman of family and position without causing so much scandal as to make him lose his job . . .

It was at this point that Mark again, but for the last time, asked his brother why he did not divorce Sylvia.

By that time Marie Léonie had retired to get some rest. She was pretty worn out. Mark's illness had been long and serious; she had nursed him with such care that during the whole time she had not been out into the streets except once or twice to go across the road to the Catholic church where she would offer a candle or so to his recovery and once or twice to remonstrate with the butcher as to the quality of the meat he supplied for Mark's broths. In addition, on many days, she had worked late, under Mark's directions on papers that the office had sent him. She either could not or would not put her man into the charge of any kind of night nurse. She alleged that the war had mopped up every kind of available attendant on the sick, but Mark shrewdly suspected that she had made no kind of effort to secure an assistant. There was her national dread of draughts to account for that. She accepted with discipline, if with despair, the English doctor's dictum that fresh air must be admitted to the sick room, but she sat up night after night in a hooded-chair, watching for any change in the wind and moving in accordance a complicated arrangement of screens that she maintained between her patient and the open window. She had, however, surrendered Mark to his brother without a murmur and had quietly gone to her own room to sleep, and Mark, though he carried on almost every kind of conversation with his brother and though he would not have asked her to leave them in order that he might engage on topics that his brother might like to regard as private — Mark seized the opportunity to lay before Christopher what he thought of Sylvia and the relationships of that singular couple.

It amounted in the end to the fact that Mark wanted Christopher to divorce his wife and to the fact that Christopher had not altered in his views that a man cannot divorce a woman. Mark put it that if Christopher intended to take up with Valentine it mattered practically very little whether he married her after a divorce or not. What a man has to do if he means to take up with a woman and as far as possible to honour her is to make some sort of fight of it — as a symbol. Marriage, if you do not regard it as a sacrament — as no doubt it ought to be regarded — was nothing more than a token that a couple intended to stick to each other. Nowadays people — the right people — bothered precious little about anything but that. A constant change of partners was a social nuisance; you could not tell whether you could or couldn't invite a couple together to a tea-fight. And society existed for social functions. That was why promiscuity was no good. For social functions you had to have an equal number of men and women or someone got left out of conversations and so you had to know who, officially in the social sense, went with whom. Everyone knew that all the children of Lupus at the War Office were really the children of a late Prime Minister so that presumably the Countess and the Prime Minister slept together most of the time but that did not mean that you invited the Prime Minister and the woman to social-official functions because they hadn't any ostensible token of union. On the contrary, you invited Lord and Lady Lupus together to all functions that would get into the papers, but you took care to have the Lady at any private, week-endish parties or intimate dinners to which the Chief was coming.

And Christopher had to consider that, if it came to marriage, ninety per cent of the inhabitants of the world regarded the marriage of almost everybody else as invalid. A Papist obviously could not regard a marriage before a registrar or a French *maire* as having any spiritual validity. At best it was no more than a demonstration of aspirations after constancy. You went before a functionary publicly to assert that you and a woman intended to stick to each other. Equally for extreme Protestants a marriage by a Papist priest, or a minister of any other sect, or a Buddhist Lama, had not the blessing of their own brand of Deity. So that really, to all practical intents, it was sufficient if a couple really assured their friends that they intended to stick together, if possible, for ever. If not, at least for years enough to show that they had made a good shot at it. Mark invited Christopher to consult whom he liked in his, Mark's, particular set and he would find that they agreed with his views.

So he was anxious that if Christopher intended to take up with the Wannop young woman he should take at least a shot at a divorce. He might not succeed in getting one. He obviously had grounds enough, but Sylvia might make counter-allegations, he, Mark, couldn't say with what chance of success. He was prepared himself to accept his brother's assertions of complete innocence, but Sylvia was a clever devil and there was no knowing what view a judge might take. Where there had been such a hell of a lot of smoke he might consider that there must be enough flame to justify refusing a divorce. There would no doubt be, thus — a beastly stink. But a beastly stink would be better than the sort of veiled ill-fame that Sylvia had contrived to get attached to Christopher. And the fact that Christopher had faced the stink and made the attempt would be at least that amount of tribute to Miss Wannop. Society was at least good-natured and was inclined to take the view that if a fellow had faced his punishment and taken it he was pretty well absolved. There might be people who would hold out against them, but Mark supposed that what Christopher wanted for himself and his girl was reasonable material comfort with a society of sufficient people of the right sort to give them a dinner or so a week and a week-end or so a month in the week-ending season.

Christopher had listened to his views with so much amiability that Mark began to hope that he would get his way in the larger matter of Groby. He was prepared to go further and to stake as much as his assurance that if Christopher would settle down at Groby, accept a decent income and look after the estate, he, Mark, would assure his brother and Valentine of bearable social circumstances.

Christopher, however, had made no answer at all beyond saying that if he tried to divorce Sylvia it would apparently ruin his old-furniture business. For his American partner assured him that in the United States if a man divorced his wife instead of letting her divorce him no one would do any business with him. He had mentioned the case of a man called Blum, a pretty warm stock-exchange man, who insisted on divorcing his wife against the advice of his friends; he found when he returned to the stockmarket that all his clients cold-shouldered him, so that he was ruined. And as these fellows were shortly going to mop up everything in the world, including the old-furniture trade, Christopher supposed that he would have to study their prejudices. He had come across his partner rather curiously. The fellow, whose father had been a German Jew but a naturalized American citizen, had been in Berlin mopping up German old furniture for sale in the American interior where he had a flourishing business. So, when America had come in on the side that was not German, the Germans had just simply dropped on Mr. Schatzweiler in their pleasant way, incorporated him in their forces and had sent him to the front as a miserable little Tommy before the Americans had been a month in the show.

And there, amongst the prisoners he had had to look after, Christopher had found the little, large-eyed, sensitive creature, unable to speak a word of German, but just crazy about the furniture and tapestries in the French chateaux that the prisoners passed on their marches. Christopher had befriended him; kept him as far as possible separated from the other prisoners, who naturally did not like him, and had a good many conversations with him.

It had appeared that Mr. Schatzweiler had had a good deal to do, in the way of buying, with Sir John Robertson the old old-furniture buying millionaire who was a close friend of Sylvia's and had been so considerable an admirer of Christopher's furniture-buying gifts that he had, years ago, proposed to take Christopher into partnership with himself. At that time Christopher had regarded Sir John's proposals as outside the range of his future; he had then been employed in the Department of Statistics. But the proposal had always amused and rather impressed him. If, that is to say, that hardheaded old Scotsman who had made a vast fortune at his trade made to Christopher a quite serious business proposition on the strength of Christopher's *flair* in the matter of old woods and curves, Christopher himself might take his own gifts with a certain seriousness.

And by the time he came to be in command of the escort over those miserable creatures he had pretty well realised that, after the necessity for escorts was over he would jolly well have to consider how he was going to make a living for himself. That was certain. He was not going to re-insert himself amongst the miserable collection of squits who occupied themselves in his old Department; he was too old to continue in the Army; he was certainly not going to accept a penny from Groby sources. He did not care what became of him — but his not caring did not take any tragico-romantic form. He would be quite prepared to live in a hut on a hillside and cook his meals over three bricks outside the door — but that was not a method of life that was very practicable, and even that needed money. Everyone who served in the Army at the front knew how little it took to keep life going — and satisfactory. But he did not see the world, when it settled down again turning itself into a place fit for old soldiers who had learned to appreciate frugality. On the contrary, the old soldier would be chivvied to hell by a civilian population who abhorred him. So that merely to keep clean and out of debt was going to be a tough job.

In his long vigils in tents, beneath the moon with the sentries walking, challenging from time to time round the barbed wire stockades, the idea of Sir John's proposition had occurred to him with some force. It had gathered strength from his meeting with Mr. Schatzweiler. The little fellow was a shivering artist and Christopher had enough of superstition in him to be impressed by the coincidence of their having come together in such unlikely circumstances. After all Providence must let up on him after a time so why should not this unfortunate and impressively Oriental member of the Chosen people be a sign of a covenant? In a way he reminded Christopher of his former protégé, Macmaster — he had the same dark eyes, the same shape, the same shivering eagerness.

That he was a Jew and an American did not worry Christopher; he had not objected to the fact that Macmaster had been the son of a Scotch grocer. If he had to go into partnership and be thrown into close contact with anyone at all he did not care much who it was as long as it was not either a bounder or a man of his own class and race. To be in close mental communion with either an English bounder or an Englishman of good family would, he was aware, be intolerable to him. But, for a little, shivering artistic Jew, as

154

of old for Macmaster he was quite capable of feeling a real fondness — as you might for an animal. Their manners were not your manners and could not be expected to be and whatever their intelligence they would have a certain little alertness, a certain exactness of thought . . . Besides, if they did you in, as every business partner or protégé must be expected to do, you did not feel the same humiliation as you did if you were swindled by a man of your own race and station. In the one case it was only what was to be expected, in the other you were faced with the fact that your own tradition had broken down. And under the long strain of the war he had outgrown alike the mentality and the traditions of his own family and his own race. The one and the other were not fitted to endure long strains.

So he welcomed the imploring glances and the eventual Oriental gratitude of that little man in his unhappy tent. For, naturally, by communicating in his weighty manner with the United States Headquarters when he happened to find himself in its vicinity, he secured the release of the little fellow who was by now safely back somewhere in the interior of the North American Continent.

But before that happened he had exchanged a certain amount of Correspondence with Sir

John and had discovered from him and from one or two chance members of the American Expeditionary Force that the little man was quite a good old-furniture dealer. Sir John had by that time gone out of business and his letters were not particularly cordial to Tietjens — which was only what was to be expected if Sylvia had been shedding her charms over him. But it had appeared that Mr. Schatzweiler had had a great deal of business with Sir John who had indeed supplied him with a great part of his material and so, if Sir John had gone out of business, Mr. Schatzweiler would need to find in England someone to take Sir John's place. And that was not going to be extraordinarily easy for what with the amount of his money that the Germans had mopped up — they had sold him immense quantities of old furniture and got paid for it and had then enlisted him in the ranks of their Brandenburgers where naturally he could do nothing with carved oak chests that had elaborate steel hinges and locks . . . What, then, with that and his prolonged absence from the neighbourhood of Detroit where he had mostly found his buyers, Mr. Schatzweiler found himself extremely hampered in his activities. It therefore fell to Christopher, if he was to go into partnership with the now sanguine and charming Oriental, to supply an immediate sum of money. That had not been easy, but by means of mortgaging his pay and his blood-money and selling the books that Sylvia had left him he had at least been able to provide Mr. Schatzweiler with enough to make at least a start somewhere across the water . . . And Mr. Schatzweiler and Christopher had between them evolved an ingenious scheme along lines that the American had long contemplated, taking into account the tastes of his countrymen and the nature of the times.

Mark had listened to his brother during all this with indulgence and even with pleasure. If a Tietjens contemplated going into trade he might at least contemplate an amusing trade carried on in a spirited manner. And what Christopher humorously projected was at least more dignified than stock-broking or bill-discounting. And he was pretty well convinced by this time that his brother was completely reconciled to him and to Groby.

It was about then and when he had again begun to introduce the topic of Groby that Christopher got up from the chair at the bedside and having taken his brother's wrist in his cool fingers remarked:

'Your temperature's pretty well down. Don't you think it is about time that you set about marrying Charlotte? I suppose you mean to marry her before this bout is finished and you might have a relapse.'

Mark remembered that speech perfectly well with the addition that if he, Christopher, hurried about it they might get the job done that night. It must therefore then have been about one o'clock of a day about three weeks before the 11th November, 1918.

Mark replied that he would be much obliged to Christopher, and Christopher, having aroused Marie Léonie and told her that he would be back in time to let her have a good night's rest, disappeared saying that he was going straight to Lambeth. In those days, supposing you could command thirty pounds or so there was no difficulty in getting married at the shortest possible notice and Christopher had promoted too many last minute marriages amongst his men not to know the ropes.

Mark viewed the transaction with a good deal of contentment. It had needed no arguing: if the proceeding had the approval of the heir-presumptive to Groby there was nothing more to be said against it. And Mark took the view that if he agreed to a proceeding that Christopher could only have counselled as heir-presumptive that was an additional reason for Mark's expecting that Christopher would eventually consent to administer Groby himself.

# 6

That would have been three weeks before the 11th of November. His head boggled a little at computing what the actual date in October must have been. With his then pneumonia his mind had not much registered dates; days had gone by in fever and boredom. Still, a man ought to remember the date of his wedding. Say it had been the 20th of October, 1918. The 20th of October had been his father's birthday. When he came to think of it he could remember hazily that it was queer that he should be going out of life on the date his father had entered it. It made a sort of full stop. And it made a full stop that, practically on that day Papists entered into their own in Groby. He had, that is to say, made up his mind to the fact that Christopher's son would have Groby as a home even if Christopher didn't. And the boy was by now a full-fledged Papist, pickled and oiled and wafered and all. Sylvia had rubbed the fact in about a week ago by sending him a card for his nephew's provisional baptism and first communion about a week before. It had astonished him that he had not felt more bitter.

He had not any doubt that the fact had reconciled him to his marriage with Marie Léonie. He had told his brother a year or so ago that he would never marry her because she was a Papist, but he was aware that then he was only chipping at Spelden, the fellow that wrote *Spelden on Sacrilege*, a book that predicted all sorts of disaster for families who owned former Papist Church lands or who had displaced Papists. When he had told Christopher that he would never marry Charlotte — he had called her Charlotte for reasons of camouflage before the marriage — he had been quite aware that he was chipping at Spelden's ghost — for Spelden must have been dead a hundred years or so. As it were, he had been saying grimly if pleasantly to that bogey:

'Eh, old 'un. You see. You may prophesy disaster to Groby because a Tietjens was given it over the head of one of your fellows in Dutch William's time. But you can't frighten me into making an honest woman — let alone a Lady of Groby — out of a Papist.'

And he hadn't. He would swear that no idea of disaster to Groby had entered his head at the date of the marriage. Now, he would not say; but of what he felt then he was certain. He remembered thinking whilst the ceremony was going on of the words of Fraser of Lovat before they executed him in the 'Forty Five. They had told him on the scaffold that if he would make some sort of submission to George II they would spare his body from being exhibited in quarters on the spikes of the buildings in Edinburgh. And Fraser had answered: 'An the King will have my heid I care not what he may do with my — ' naming a part of a gentleman that is not now mentioned in drawing-rooms. So, if a Papist was to inhabit Groby House it mattered precious little if the first Lady Tietjens of Groby were Papist or Heathen.

A man as a rule does not marry his mistress whilst he has any kick in him. If he still aims at a career it might hinder him supposing she were known to have been his mistress, or of course a fellow who wants to make a career might want to help himself on by making a good marriage. Even if a man does not want to make a career he may think that a woman who has been his mistress as like as not may cuckold him after marriage, for, if she has gone wrong with him she would be more apt to go wrong elsewhere as well. But if a fellow is practically finished, those considerations disappear and he remembers that you go to hell if you seduce virgins. It is as well at one time or another to make your peace with your Creator. Forever is a long word and God is said to disapprove of unconsecrated unions.

Besides it would very likely please Marie Léonie, though she had never said a word about it and it would certainly dish Sylvia who was no doubt counting on being the first Lady Tietjens of Groby. And then, too, it would undoubtedly make Marie Léonie safer. In one way and another he had given his mistress quite a number of things that might well be desirable to that bitch, and neither his nor Christopher's lives were worth much, whilst Chancery can be a very expensive affair if you get into it.

And he was aware that he had always had a soft spot in his heart for Marie Léonie, otherwise he would not have provided her with the name of Charlotte for public consumption. A man gives his mistress another name if there is any chance of his marrying her so that it may look as if he were marrying someone else when he does it. *Marie Léonie Riotor* looks different from a casual Charlotte. It gives her a better chance in the world outside.

So it had been well enough. The world was changing and there was no particular reason why he should not change with it . . . And he had not been able to conceal from himself that he was getting on the way. Time lengthened out. When he had come in drenched from one of the potty local meetings that they had to fall back on during the war he had known that something was coming to him because after Marie Léonie had tucked him up in bed he could not remember the strain of the winner of some handicap of no importance. Marie Léonie had given him a goodish tot of rum with butter in it and that might have made him hazy — but all the same that had never happened to him in his life before, rum or no rum. And by now he had forgotten even the name of the winner and the meeting . . .

He could not conceal from himself that his memory was failing though otherwise he considered himself to be as sound a man as he had ever been. But when it came to memory, ever since that day his brain had checked at times as a tired horse will at a fence . . . A tired horse!

He could not bring himself to the computation of what three weeks back from the 11th of November came to; his brain would not go at it. For the matter of that he could remember precious little of the events of that three weeks in their due order.

Christopher had certainly been about, relieving Marie Léonie at night and attending to him with a soft, goggle-eyed attentiveness that only a man with a saint for a mother could have put up. For hours and hours he would read aloud in Boswell's *Life of Johnson* for which Mark had had a fancy.

And Mark could remember drowsing off with satisfaction to the sound of the voice and drowsing with satisfaction awake again, still to the sound of the voice. For Christopher had the idea that if his voice went droning on it would make Mark's slumbers more satisfactory.

Satisfaction . . . Perhaps the last satisfaction that Mark was ever to know. For at that time — during those three weeks — he had not been able to believe that Christopher really meant to stick out about the matter of Groby. How could you believe that a fellow who waited on you with the softness of a girl built of mealsacks was determined to . . . call it, break your heart. That was what it came to . . . A fellow too who agreed in the most astounding manner with your views of things in general; a fellow for the matter of that who knew ten times as much as you did. A damned learned fellow . . .

Mark had no contempt for learning — particularly for younger sons. The country

164

was going to the dogs because of the want of education of the younger sons whose business it was to do the work of the nation. It was a very old North Country rhyme that, that when land is gone and money spent then learning is most excellent. No, he had no contempt for learning. He had never acquired any because he was too lazy: a little Sallust, a little Cornelius Nepos, a touch of Horace, enough French to read a novel and follow what Marie Léonie said ... Even to himself he called her Marie Léonie once he was married to her. It had made her jump at first!

But Christopher was a damned learned fellow. Their father, a younger son at the beginning, had been damned learned too. They said that even at his death he had been one of the best Latinists in England — the intimate friend of that fellow Wannop, the Professor ... A great age at which to die by his own hand, his father's! Why, if that marriage had been on the 29th October, 1918, his father, then dead, must have been born on the 29th October what ... 1834 ... No, that was not possible ... No, '44. His father, Mark knew, had been born in 1812 — before Waterloo!

Great stretches of time. Great changes! Yet Father had not been an incult sort of a man. On the contrary, if he was burly and determined, he was quiet. And sensitive. He had certainly loved Christopher very dearly — and Christopher's mother.

Father was very tall; stooping like a toppling poplar towards the end. His head seemed very distant, as if he hardly heard you. Iron-grey; short-whiskered. Absent-minded towards the end. Forgetting where he had put his handkerchief and where his spectacles were when he had pushed them up onto his forehead . . . He had been a younger son who had never spoken to his father for forty years. Grandfather had never forgiven him for marrying Miss Selby of Biggen . . . not because it was marrying below him but because Grandfather had wanted their mother for his eldest son . . . And they had been poor in their early childhood, wandering over the continent to settle at last in Dijon where they had kept some sort of state . . . a large house in the middle of the town with several servants. He never could imagine how their mother had done it on four hundred a year. But she had. A hard woman. But Father had kept in with French people and corresponded with Professor Wannop and Learned Societies. He had always regarded him, Mark, as a dunce . . . Father would sit reading in elegantly bound books, by the hour. His study had been one of the show rooms of the house in Dijon.

*Did* he commit suicide? If so then Valentine Wannop was his daughter. There could not be much getting away from that, not that it mattered much. In that case Christopher would be living with his half-sister . . . Not that it mattered much. It did not matter much, to him, Mark . . . but his father was the sort of man that it might drive to suicide.

A luckless sort of beggar, Christopher! If you took the whole conglobulation at its worst — the father suiciding, the son living with his sister in open sin, the son's son not his son and Groby going over to Papist hands . . . That was the sort of thing that would happen to a Tietjens of the Christopher variety: to any Tietjens who would not get out or get under as he, Mark, had done. Tietjenses took what they damn well got for doing what they damn well wanted to. Well, it landed them in that sort of post . . . A last post, for, if that boy was not Christopher's, Groby went out of Tietjens' hands. There would be no more Tietjenses. Spelden might well be justified.

The Grandfather of Father scalped by Indians in Canada in the war of 1810; the father dying in a place where he should not have been — taking what he got for it and causing quite a scandal for the Court of

167

Victoria; the elder brother of Father killed drunk whilst fox-hunting; Father suicided; Christopher a pauper by his own act with a by-blow in his shoes. If then there were to be any more Tietjenses by both name and blood . . . Poor little devils! They would be their own cousins. Something like that . . .

And possibly none the worse off for that . . . Either Spelden or Groby Great Tree had perhaps done for the others. Groby Great Tree had been planted to commemorate the birth of Great-grandfather who had died in a whoreshop — and it had always been whispered in Groby, amongst the children and servants that Groby Great Tree did not like the house. Its roots tore chunks out of the foundations and two or three times the trunk had had to be bricked into the front wall of the house. They always quoted too the Italian saying about trees over the house. Obviously Christopher had told it to his son and the young man had told it to Mrs. de Bray Pape. That was why the saying had been referred to three times that day . . . Anyway it was an Italian tree! It had been brought as a sapling from Sardinia at a time when gentlemen still thought about landscape gardening. A gentleman in those days consulted his heirs about tree planting. Should you plant a group of copper beeches against a group of white maples over against the haha a quarter of a mile from the house so that the contrast seen from the ball-room windows should be agreeable — in thirty years' time. In those days thought, in families, went in periods of thirty years, owner gravely consulting the heirs who should see that development of light and shade that the owner never would.

Nowadays the heir apparently consulted the owner as to whether the tenant who was taking the ancestral home furnished might not cut down trees in order to suit the sanitary ideas of the day . . . An American day! Well, why not. Those people could not be expected to know how picturesque a contrast the tree would make against the roofs of Groby Great House when seen from Peel's Moorside. They would never hear of Peel's Moorside, or John Peel, or the coat so grey . . .

Apparently that was the meaning of the visit of that young colt and Mrs. de Bray Pape. They had come to ask his, Mark's sanction as owner, to cut down Groby Great Tree. And then they had funked it and bolted. At any rate the boy was still talking earnestly to the woman in white over the hedge. As to where Mrs. de Bray Pape had got to he had no means of knowing; she might be among the potato rows studying the potatoes of the poor for all he knew. He hoped she would not come upon Marie Léonie because Marie Léonie would make short work of Mrs. de Bray Pape and be annoyed on top of it.

But they were wrong to funk talking to *him* about cutting down Groby Great Tree. He cared nothing about it. Mrs. de Bray Pape might just as well have come and said cheerfully: 'Hullo old cock, we're going to cut down your bally old tree and let some light into the house . . . ' if that was the way Americans talked when they were cheerful; he had no means of knowing. He never remembered to have talked to an American . . . Oh, yes, to Cammie Fittleworth. She had certainly been a dreadfully slangy young woman before her husband came into the title. But then Fittleworth was confoundedly slangy too. They said he had to give up in the middle of a speech he tried to make in the House of Lords because he could not do without the word 'toppin' which upset the Lord Chancellor . . . So there was no knowing what Mrs. de Bray Pape might not have said if she had not thought she was addressing a syphilitic member of an effete aristocracy mad about an old cedar tree. But she might just as well have cheerfully announced it. He did not care. Groby Great

Tree had never seemed to like him. It never seemed to like anybody. They say it never forgave the Tietjenses for transplanting it from nice warm Sardinia to that lugubrious climate . . . That was what the servants said to the children and the children whispered to each other in the dark corridors.

But poor old Christopher! He was going to go mad if the suggestion were made to him. The barest hint! Poor old Christopher who was now probably at that very minute in one of those beastly machines overhead, coming back from Groby . . . If Christopher *had* to buy a beastly South Country show-cottage Mark wished he would not have bought it so near a confounded air-station. However, he had expected probably, that beastly Americans would come flying in the beastly machines to buy the beastly old junk. They did indeed do so — sent by Mr. Schatzweiler who was certainly efficient enough in the sending of cheques.

Christopher had nearly jumped out of his skin — that is to say he had sat as still as a lump of white marble — when he had gathered that Sylvia and, still more his own heir, wanted to let Groby furnished. He had said to Mark, over Sylvia's first letter: 'You won't let 'em?' and Mark knew the agony that was behind his tallowy mask and goggle eyes

. . . Perfectly white around the nostrils he went — that was the sign!

And it had been as near an appeal as he had ever come — unless the request for a loan on Armistice Day could be regarded as an appeal. But Mark did not think that that could be regarded as a score. In their game neither of them had yet made a real score. Probably neither of them ever would: they were a stout pair of North Countrymen whatever else could be said against them.

No, it hadn't been a score when Christopher had said: 'You won't let 'em let Groby,' the day before yesterday: Christopher had been in an agony, but he was not *asking* Mark not to let Groby be let; he was only seeking information as to how far Mark would let the degradation of the old place go. Mark had let him pretty well know that Groby might be pulled down and replaced by a terra-cotta hotel before he would stir a finger. On the other hand Christopher had only to stir a finger and not a blade of grass between the cobbles in the Stillroom Yard could be grubbed up . . . But by the rules of the game neither of them could give an order. Neither. Mark said to Christopher: 'Groby's yours!' Christopher said to Mark: 'Groby's yours!' With perfect goodhumour and coldness. So probably the place would fall to pieces or

Sylvia would turn it into a bawdy house . . . It was a good joke! A good, grim Yorkshire joke!

It was impossible to know which of them suffered more. Christopher, it is true, was having his heart broken because the house suffered — but, damn it, wasn't Mark himself pretty well heart-broken because Christopher refused to accept the house from him? . . . It was impossible to know which!

Yes, his confounded heart had been broken on Armistice Day in the morning — between the morning and the morning after . . . Yes: after Christopher had been reading Boswell aloud, night after night for three weeks . . . Was that playing the game? Was it playing the game to get no sleep if you had not forgiven your brother? . . . Oh, no doubt it was playing the game. You don't forgive your brother if he lets you down in a damn beastly way . . . And of course it *is* letting a fellow down in a beastly — a beastly! — way to let him know that you believe he lives on the immoral earnings of his wife . . . Mark had done that to Christopher. It was unforgivable all right. And equally, of course, you do not hurt your brother back except on the lines circum-scribed by the nature of the offence: you are the best friend he has — except on the lines circumscribed by the offence; and you will nurse him like a blasted soft worm — except in so far as the lines circumscribed by the offence do not preclude your ministrations.

For, obviously the best thing Christopher could have done for his brother's health would have been to have accepted the stewardship of Groby — but his brother could die and he himself could die before he would do that. It was nevertheless a pretty cruel affair . . . Over Boswell the two brothers had got as thick as thieves with an astonishing intimacy — and with an astonishing similarity. If one of them made a comment on Bennet Langton it would be precisely the comment that the other had on his lips. It was what asses call telepathy, nowadays . . . a warm, comfortable feeling, late at night with the light shaded from your eyes, the voice going on through the deep silence of London that awaited the crash of falling bombs . . . Well, Mark accepted Christopher's dictum that he himself was an eighteenth-century bloke and was only forestalled when he had wanted to tell Christopher that he was more old-fashioned still — a sort of seventeenth-century Anglican who ought to be strolling in a grove with Greek Testament beneath the arm and all . . .

And, hang it all, there was room for him! The land had not changed . . . There were still the deep beech-woods making groves beside the ploughlands and the rooks rising lazily as the plough came towards them. The land had not changed . . . Well, the breed had not changed . . . There was Christopher . . . Only, the times . . . they had changed. The rooks and the ploughlands and the beeches and Christopher were there still . . . But not the frame of mind in the day . . . The sun might rise and go above the plough till it set behind the hedge and the ploughman went off to the inn settle; and the moon could do the same. But they would — neither sun nor moon — look on the spit of Christopher in all their journeys. Never. They might as well expect to see a mastodon . . . And he, Mark, himself was an old-fashioned buffer. That was all right. Judas Iscariot himself was an old-fashioned ass, once upon a time!

But it was almost on the edge of not playing the game for Christopher to let that intimacy establish itself and all the time to cherish that unforgivingness . . . Not quite not playing the game, but almost. For hadn't Mark held out feelers? Hadn't he made concessions? Hadn't his very marrying of Marie Léonie been by way of a concession to Christopher? Didn't Christopher, if the truth was to be known, want Mark to marry Marie Léonie because he, Christopher, wanted to marry Valentine Wannop and hadn't a hope? If the truth were known ... Well, he had made that concession to Christopher, who was a sort of a person anyhow. But ought Christopher to have exacted — to have telepathically willed — that concession if he wasn't himself going to concede something? Ought he to have forced him, Mark, to accept his mooning, womanly services when the poor devil was already worn out with his military duties of seeing old tins cleaned out day after day, and when he meant to become a beastly old-furniture dealer and refuse Groby? For, upon his soul, till the morning of Armistice Day Mark had accepted Christopher's story of Mr. Schatzweiler as merely a good-humoured, grim threat ... A sort of a feint at a threat ...

Well, probably it was playing the game all right: if Christopher thought it was jonnock, jonnock it was!

But ... a damn beastly shock ... Why he had been practically convalescent, he had been out of bed in a dressing gown and had told Lord Wolstonemark that he could pile in as many papers as he liked from the office ... And then Christopher, without a hat and in a beastly civilian suit of light mulberry coloured Harris tweed, had burst into the room with a beastly piece of old furniture under his arm . . . A sort of inlaid toy writing-desk. A model. For cabinet-makers! A fine thing to bring into a convalescent bedroom, to a man quietly reading Form T. O. LOUWR 1962. E 17 of the 10/11/18 in front of a clean fire . . . And chalk-white about the gills the fellow was — with an awful lot of silver in his hair . . . What age was he? Forty? Forty-three? God knew!

Forty . . . He wanted to borrow forty quid on that beastly piece of furniture. To have an Armistice Day Beanfeast and set up house with his gal! Forty quid! My God! Mark felt his bowels turning over within him with disgust . . . The gal — that fellow's half-sister as like as not — was waiting in an empty house for him to go and seduce her. In order to celebrate the salvation of the world by seven million deaths!

If you seduce a girl you don't do it on forty pounds: you accept Groby and three, seven, ten thousand a year. So he had told Christopher.

And then he had got it. Full in the face. Christopher was not going to accept a penny from him. Never. Not ever! . . . No doubt about that, either. That fact had gone into Mark as a knife goes into a stag's throat. It had hurt as much, but it hadn't killed! Damn it, it might as well have! It might as well have

. . . Does a fellow do that to his own brother just because his own brother has called him . . . what is the word? *Maquereau!* . . . Probably a maquereau is worse than a pimp . . . The difference between a flea and a louse, as Dr. Johnson said.

Eh, but Christopher was bitter! . . . Apparently he had gone round first to Sir John Robertson's with that jigamaree. Sir John had promised to buy it for a hundred pounds. It was a special sort of model signed by some duke of a Bath cabinet-maker in 1762 . . . Wasn't that the year of the American Rebellion? Well, Christopher had bought it in a junk-shop of sorts for a fiver and Sir John had promised him a hundred quid. He collected cabinet-maker's models; extraordinarily valuable they were. Christopher had spat out that this was worth a thousand dollars, . . . Thinking of his old-furniture customers!

When Christopher had used that word — with the blue pebbles sticking out of his white lard head — Mark had felt the sweat break out all over him. He had known it was all up . . . Christopher had gone on: you expected him to spit electric sparks, but his voice was wooden. Sir John had said to him:

'Eh, no mon. You're a fine soldier now, raping half the girls in Flanders an Ealing and

178

asking us to regard you as heroes. Fine heroes. And now you're safe . . . A hundred pounds is a price to a Christian that is faithful to his lovely wife. Five pounds is as much as I'll give you for the model and be thankful it is five, not one, for old sake's sake!'

That was what Sir John Robertson had said to Christopher; that was what the world was like to serving soldiers in that day. You don't have to wonder that Christopher was bitter — even to his own brother with the sweat making his underlinen icy. He had said:

'My good chap. I won't lend you a penny on that idiotic jigamaree. But I'll write you a cheque for a thousand pounds this minute. Give me my cheque book from the table . . . '

Marie Léonie had come into the room on hearing Christopher's voice. She liked to hear the news from Christopher. And she liked Christopher and Mark to have heated discussions. She had observed that they did Mark good: on the day when Christopher had first come there, three weeks before, when they certainly had heatedly discussed, she had observed that Mark's temperature had fallen from ninety-nine point six to ninety-eight point two. In two hours . . . After all, if a Yorkshire man can quarrel he can live. They were like that, those others, she said.

Christopher had turned on her and said:

'Ma belle amie m'attend à ma maison; nous voulons célébrer avec mes camarades de régiment. Je n'ai pas le soue. Prêtez moi quarante livres, je vous en prie, madame!' He had added that he would leave his cabinet as a pledge. He was as stiff as a sentry outside Buckingham Palace. She had looked at Mark with some astonishment. After all, she might well be astonished. He himself had made no sign and suddenly Christopher had exclaimed:

'Prêtez les moi, prêtez les moi, pour l'amour de Dieu!'

Marie Léonie had gone a little white, but she had turned up her skirt and turned down her stocking and took out the notes.

'Pour le dieu d'amour, monsieur, je veux bien,' she had said . . . You never knew what a Frenchwoman would not say. That was out of an old song.

But the sweat burst out all over his face at the recollection: great drops of sweat.

# 7

Marie Léonie, a strong taste of apples in her mouth, strong odours of apples on the air, wasps around her and as if a snow-drift of down descending about her feet, was frowning seriously over Burgundy bottles into which ran cider from a glass tube that she held to their necks. She frowned because the task was serious and engrossing, because the wasps annoyed her and because she was resisting an impulse inside herself. It told her that something ailed Mark and urged her to go and look at him.

It annoyed her because as a rule she felt presages of something ailing Mark only at night. Only at night. During the day usually she felt in her for *intérieur* that Mark was like what he was only because he wanted so to be. His glance was too virile and dominant to let you think otherwise — the dark, liquid, direct glance! But at nightfall — or at any rate shortly after supper when she had retired to her room terrible premonitions of disaster to Mark visited her. He was dying where he lay; he was beset by the spectral being of the countryside; robbers, even, had crept upon him, though that was unreasonable. For all the countryside knew that Mark was paralysed and unable to store wealth in his mattress . . . Still, nefarious strangers might see him and imagine that he kept his gold repeater watch beneath his pillow . . . So she would rise a hundred times in a night and, going to the low, diamond-casement window, would lean out and listen. But there would be no sound: the wind in the leaves; the cry of water-birds overhead. The dim light would be in the hut, seen unmoving through the apple boughs.

Now, however, in broad daylight, towards the hour of tea, with the little maid on a stool beside her plucking the boiling-hens that were to go to market next day, with the boxes of eggs on their shelves, each egg wired to the bottom of its box waiting till she had time to date-stamp it — in the open potting-shed in the quiet, broad light of a summer day she was visited by a presage of something ailing Mark. She resented it, but she was not the woman to resist it.

There was, however, nothing to warrant it. From the corners of the house, to which she proceeded, she could see quite well the greater part of Mark's solitary figure. Gunning, being talked to by the English lord, held a spare horse by the bridle and was looking at Mark over the hedge, too. He exhibited no emotions. A young man was walking along the inside of the hedge between it and the raspberries. That was no affair of hers: Gunning was not protesting. The head and shoulders of a young woman — or it might be another young man — were proceeding along the outside of the hedge nearly level with the first one. That was equally no affair of hers. Probably they were looking at the bird's nest. There was some sort of bird's nest she had heard, in that thick hedge. There was no end to the folly of the English in the country as in the town: they would waste time over everything. This bird was a bottle ... bottle something and Christopher and Valentine and the parson and the doctor and the artist who lived down the hill were crazy about it. They walked on tip-toe when they were within twenty yards. Gunning was allowed to trim the hedge, but apparently the birds knew Gunning ... For Marie Léonie all birds were *moineaux*, as who should say 'sparrers' as in London they called them — just as all flowers were *giroflées* — as you might say wall-flowers ... No wonder this nation was going to rack and ruin when it wasted its time over preserving the nests of sparrers and naming innumerable wall-flowers! The country was well enough

— a sort of suburb of Caen: but the people!
... No wonder William, of Falaise, in
Normandy subjugated them with such ease.

Now she had wasted five minutes, for the
glass tubes, hinged on rubber, that formed
her siphon from barrel to bottle had had
perforce, to be taken out of the spile-hole, the
air had entered into it, and she would have to
put it back and suck once more at the tube
until the first trickle of cider entered her
mouth. She disliked having to do that; it
wasted the cider and she disliked the flavour
in the afternoon when one had lunched. The
little maid also would say: 'A — oh,
meladyship, Ah *du* call thet queer!' . . . Nothing would cure that child of saying that
though she was otherwise *sage et docile*. Even
Gunning scratched his head at the sight of
those tubes.

Could these savages never understand that
if you want to have *cidre mousseux*
— foaming — you must have as little
sediment as possible? And that in the bottom
of casks, even if they had not been moved for
a long time there will always be sediment
— particularly if you set up a flow in the
liquids by running it from a tap near the
bottom. So you siphon off the top of the great
casks for bottling *mousseux* and bottle the
rest of the cask and run the thickest into little

184

thin-wood kegs with many hopes for freezing in the winter ... To make *calvados*, where you cannot have alembics because of the excise ... In this unhappy country you may not have alembics for the distilling of apple-jack, plum-brandy or other *fines* — because of the excise! *Quel pays! Quels gens!*

They lacked industry, frugality — and above all, spirit! Look at that poor Valentine, hiding in her room upstairs because there were people about whom she suspected of being people from the English lord's house ... By rights that poor Valentine should be helping her with the bottling and ready to sell that lugubrious old furniture to visitors whilst her lord was away buying more old rubbish ... And she was distracted because she could not find some prints. They represented — Marie Léonie was well aware because she had heard the facts several times — street criers of ambulant wares in London years ago. There were only eight of these to be found. Where were the other four? The customer, a lady of title, was anxious for them. For presents for an immediate wedding! Monsieur my brother-in-law had come upon the four that were to make up the set at a sale two days before. He had recounted with satisfaction how he had found them on the grass . . . It was supposed that he had brought them home; but they were not in the warehouse at Cramp the carpenter's, they were not to be found, left in the cart. They were in no drawer or press . . . What was to prove that *mon beau-frère* had brought them home from the sale. He was not there: he was gone for a day and a half. Naturally he would be gone for a day and a half when he was most needed . . . And where was he gone, leaving his young wife in that nervous condition? For a day and a half! He had never before been gone for a day and a half . . . There was then something brewing; it was in the air; it was in her bones . . . It was like that dreadful day of the Armistice when this miserable land betrayed the beautiful *pays de France!* . . . When monsieur had borrowed forty pounds off her . . . In the name of heaven why did not he borrow another forty — or eighty — or a hundred, rather than be distracted and distract Mark and his unhappy girl? . . .

She was not unsympathetic, that girl. She had civilisation. She could talk of Philémon and Baucis. She had made her *bachot*, she was what you would call *fille de famille* . . . . But without *chic* . . . Without . . . Without . . . Well, she neither displayed enough erudition to be a *bas bleu* — though she had enough erudition! — not enough *chic* to be a *femme légère* — a *poule* who would *faire la noce* with her gallant. Monsieur the brother-in-law was no gay spark. But you never know with a man . . . The cut of a skirt; a twist of the hair . . . Though to-day there was no hair to twist; but there is the equivalent.

And it was a fact that you never knew a man. Look at the case of Eleanor Dupont who lived for ten years with Duchamp of the Sorbonne . . . Eleanor would never attend scrupulously to her attire because her man wore blue spectacles and was a *savant* . . . . But what happened . . . There came along a little piece with a hat as large as a cartwheel covered with greenstuff and sleeves up above her ears — as the mode was then . . .

That had been a lesson to her, Marie Léonie, who had been a girl at the time. She had determined that if she achieved a *collage sérieux* with a monsieur of eighty and as blind as a bat she would study the modes of the day right down to the latest perfume. These messieurs did not know it, but they moved among *femmes du monde* and the fashionable cocottes and however much she at home might be the little brown bird of the domestic hearth, the lines of her dresses, her hair, her personal odour, must conform. Mark did not imagine; she did not suppose he had ever seen a fashionable journal in her apartments that were open to him or had ever suspected that she walked in the Row on a Sunday when he was away . . . But she had studied these things like another. And more. For it is difficult to keep with the fashion and at the same time appear as if you were a serious *petite bourgeoise*. But she had done it: and observe the results . . .

But that poor Valentine . . . Her man was attached enough, and well he should be considering the affair in which he had landed her. But always there comes the *pic des tempêtes*, the Cape Horn, round which you must go. It is the day when your man looks at you and says: 'H'm, h'm,' and considers if the candle is not more valuable than the game! Ah then . . . There are wise folk who put that at the seventh year; other wise ones, at the second; others again at the eleventh . . . But in fact you may put it at any day on any year — to the hundredth . . . And that poor Valentine with four spots of oil on her only skirt but two. And that so badly hung, though the stuff no doubt was once good. One must concede that! They make admirable tweeds in this country: better certainly than in Roubaix. But is that enough to save a country — or a woman dependant on a man who has introduced her into a bad affair?

A voice behind her said:

'I see you have plenty of eggs!' — an unusual voice of a sort of breathless nervousness. Marie Léonie continued to hold the mouth of her tube into the neck of a burgundy bottle; into this she had already introduced a small screw of sifted sugar and an extremely minute portion of a powder that she got from a pharmacist of Rouen. This, she understood, made the cider of a rich brownness. She did not see why cider should be brown but it was considered to be less fortifying if it were light golden. She continued also to think about Valentine who would be twittering with nerves at the window whose iron-leaded casement was open above their heads. She would have put down her Latin book and have crept to the window to listen.

The little girl beside Marie Léonie had risen from the three-legged stool and held a dead, white fowl with a nearly naked breast by its neck. She said hoarsely:

'These 'ere be 'er Ladyship's settins of prize Reds.' She was blonde, red-faced and wore on her dull fair hair a rather large cap, on her thin body a check blue cotton gown. ''Arf a crownd a piece the heggs be or twenty-four shillings a dozen if you take a gross.'

Marie Léonie heard the hoarse voice with some satisfaction. This girl whom they had only had for a fortnight seemed to be satisfactory mentally; it was not her business to sell the eggs but Gunning's; nevertheless she knew the details. Marie Léonie did not turn round: it was not *her* business to talk to anyone who wanted to buy eggs and she had no curiosity as to customers. She had too much else to think about. The voice said:

'Half a crown seems a great deal for an egg. What is that in dollars? This must be that tyranny over edibles by the producer of which one has heard so much.'

'Tiddn nothin' in dollars,' the girl said. ''Arf a dollar is two bob. 'Arf a crown is two 'n six.'

The conversation continued, but it grew dim in Marie Léonie's thoughts. The child and the voice disputed as to what a dollar was — or so it appeared, for Marie Léonie was not familiar with either of the accents of the disputants. The child was a combative child. She drove both Gunning and the cabinet-maker Camp with an organ of brass. Of tin perhaps, like a penny whistle. When she was not grubbily working, she read books with avidity — books about Blood if she could get them. She had an exaggerated respect for the

Family but none for any other soul in the world . . .

Marie Léonie considered that, by now, she might have got down to the depth of the cask where you find sediment. She ran some cider into a clear glass, stopping the tube with her thumb. The cider was clear enough to let her bottle another dozen, she judged; then she would send for Gunning to take the spile-bung out of the next cask. Four sixty-gallon casks she had to attend to; two of them were done. She began to tire: she was not unfatigable if she was indefatigable. She began at any rate to feel drowsy. She wished Valentine could have helped her. But that girl had not much backbone and she, Marie Léonie, acknowledged that for the sake of the future it was good that she should rest and read books in Latin or Greek. And avoid nervous encounters.

She had tucked her up under an eiderdown on their four-post bed because They would have all the windows open and currents of air must above all be avoided by women . . . *Elle* had smiled and said that it had once been her dream to read the works of Æschylus beside the blue Mediterranean. They had kissed each other . . .

The maid beside her was saying that orfen 'n orfen she'd 'eared 'er farver 'oo was a

191

dealer wen a lot of ol' 'ens, say, 'ad gone to three an nine say: 'Make it two arf dollars!' They didn' 'ave dollars in thet country but they did 'ave 'arf dollars. N Capt'n Kidd th' pirate: 'e 'ad dollars, n' pieces of eight 'n' moi-dors too!

A wasp annoyed Marie Léonie; it buzzed almost on her nose, retired, returned, made a wide circuit. There were already several wasps struggling in the glass of cider she had just drawn; there were others in circles round spots of cider on the slats of wood on which the barrels were arranged. They drew in their tails and then expanded, ecstatically. Yet only two nights before she and Valentine had gone with Gunning all over the orchard with a lantern, a trowel and a bottle of prussic acid, stopping up holes along the paths and in banks. She had liked the experience; the darkness, the ring of light from the lantern on the rough grass; the feeling that she was out, near Mark and that yet Gunning and his lantern kept spiritual visitors away . . . What she suffered between the desire to visit her man in the deep nights and the possibility of coming up against *revenants* . . . Was it reasonable? . . . What women had to suffer for their men! Even if they were faithful . . .

What the unfortunate *Elle* had not suffered! . . .

Even on what you might call her *nuit de noces* . . . . At the time it had seemed incomprehensible. She had had no details. It had merely seemed fantastic: possibly even tragic because Mark had taken it so hardly. Truly she believed he had become insane. At two in the morning, beside Mark's bed. They had — the two brothers — exchanged words of considerable violence whilst the girl shivered; and was determined. That girl had been determined. She would not go back to her mother. At two in the morning . . . Well, if you refuse to go back to your mother at two in the morning you kick indeed your slipper over the mill!

The details of that night came back to her, amongst wasps and beneath the conversation of the unseen woman, in the shed where the water ran in the trough. She had set the bottles in the trough because it is a good thing to cool cider before the process of fermentation in the bottles begins. The bottles with their shining necks of green glass were an agreeable spectacle. The lady behind her back was talking of Oklahoma . . . The cowboy with the large nose that she had seen on the film at the Piccadilly Cinema had come from Oklahoma. It was no doubt somewhere in America. She had been used to go to the Piccadilly Cinema on a Friday. You do not go to the theatre on a Friday if you are *bien pensant*, but you may regard the cinema as being to the theatre what a *repas maigre* is as against a meal with meat . . . The lady speaking behind her came apparently from Oklahoma: she had eaten prairie chickens in her time. On a farm. Now, however, she was very rich. Or so she told the little maid. Her husband could buy half Lord Fittleworth's estate and not miss the money. She said that if only people here would take example . . .

On that evening they had come thumping on her door. The bell had failed to wake her after all the noise in the street that day . . . She had sprung into the middle of the floor and flown to save Mark . . . from an air-raid. She had forgotten that it was the Armistice . . . But the knocking had gone on on the door.

Before it had stood monsieur the brother-in-law and that girl in a dark blue girl-guides' sort of uniform. Both chalk-white and weary to death. As if they leaned one against another . . . She had been for bidding them go away, but Mark had come out of the bedroom; in his nightshirt with his legs bare. And hairy! He had bidden them come in, roughly, and had got back into bed . . . That had been the last time he had been on his legs! Now, he having been in bed so long, his legs were no longer hairy, but polished. Like thin glazed bones!

She had recalled his last gesture. He had positively used a gesture, like a man raving . . . And indeed he was raving. At Christopher. And dripping with sweat. Twice she had wiped his face whilst they shouted at each other.

It had been difficult to understand what they said because they had spoken a sort of *patois*. Naturally they returned to the language they spoke in their childhoods — when they were excited, these unexcitable people! It resembled the *patois* of the Bretons. Harsh . . .

And, for herself she had been all concerned for the girl. Naturally she had been concerned for the girl. One is a woman . . . At first she had taken her for a little piece from the streets . . . But even for a little piece from the streets . . . Then she had noticed that there had been no rouge; no imitation pearl necklace . . .

Of course when she had gathered that Mark was pressing money on them she had felt different. Different in two ways. It could not be a little piece. And then her heart contracted at the idea of money being given away. They might be ruined. It might be these people instead of her Paris nephews who would pillage her corpse. But the brother-in-law pushed the thought of money away from him with both hands. If she — *Elle* — wanted to go with him she must share his fortune . . . What a country! What people!

There had seemed to be no understanding them then . . . It had appeared that Mark insisted that the girl should stop there with her lover; the lover on the contrary insisted that she should go home to her mother. The girl kept saying that on no account would she leave Christopher. He could not be left. He would die if he was left . . . And indeed that brother-in-law had seemed sick enough. He panted worse than Mark.

She had eventually taken the girl to her own room. A little, agonised, fair creature. She had felt inclined to enfold her in her arms but she had not done so. Because of the money . . . She might as well have. It was impossible to get these people to touch money. She would now give no little to lend that girl twenty pounds for a frock and some undergarments.

The girl had sat there without speaking. It had seemed for hours. Then some drunken man on the church steps opposite had begun to play the bugle. Long calls . . . Tee . . . Teee . . . TEEEE . . . Ta-heee . . . To-hee . . . Continuing for ever . . .

The girl had begun to cry. She had said that it was dreadful. But you could not object. It was the Last Post they were playing. For the Dead. You could not object to their playing the Last Post for the Dead that night. Even if it was a drunken man who played and even if it drove you mad. The Dead ought to have all they could get.

If she had not made the necessary allowance that would have seemed to Marie Léonie an exaggerated sentiment. The English bugle notes could do no good to the French dead and the English losses were so negligible in quantity that it hardly seemed worth while to become *emotionnée* when their funeral call was played by a drunken man. The French papers estimated the English losses at a few hundreds; what was that as against the millions of her own people? . . . But she gathered that this girl had gone through something terrible that night with the wife, and being too proud to show emotion over her personal vicissitudes she pretended to find an outlet because of the sounds of that bugle . . . Well, it was mournful enough. She had understood it when Christopher, putting his face in at the crack of the door had whispered to her that he was going to stop the bugle because its sound was intolerable to Mark.

The girl apparently had been in a reverie

for she had not heard him. She, Marie Léonie, had gone to look at Mark and the girl sat there, on the bed. Mark was by then quite quiescent. The bugle had stopped. To cheer him she had made a few remarks about the inappropriateness of playing, for a negligible number of dead, a funeral call at three in the morning. If it had been for the French dead — or if her country had not been betrayed. It was betraying her country to have given those assassins an armistice when they were far from their borders. Merely that was treachery on the part of these sham Allies. They should have gone right through those monsters slaying them by the million, defenceless, and then they should have laid waste their country with fire and sword. Let them too know what it was to suffer as France had suffered. It was treachery enough not to have done that and the child unborn would suffer for it.

But there they waited, then, even after that treachery had been done, to know what were the terms of even that treachery. They might even now not intend to be going to Berlin . . . What then was Life for?

Mark had groaned. In effect he was a good Frenchman. She had seen to that. The girl had come into the room. She could not bear to be alone . . . What a night of movement

198

and cross movement. She had begun to argue with Mark. Hadn't there, she had asked, been enough of suffering? He agreed that there had been enough of suffering. But there must be more . . . Even out of justice to the poor bloody Germans . . . He had called them the poor bloody Germans. He had said that it was the worst dis-service you could do to your foes not to let them know that remorseless consequences follow determined actions. To interfere in order to show fellows that if they did what they wanted they need not of necessity take what they got for it was in effect to commit a sin against God. If the Germans did not experience that in the sight of the world there was an end of Europe and the world. What was to hinder endless recurrences of what had happened near a place called Gemmenich on the 4th of August, 1914, at six o'clock in the morning? There was nothing to hinder it. Any other state from the smallest to the largest might . . .

The girl had interrupted to say that the world had changed and Mark, lying back exhausted on his pillows had said with a sort of grim sharpness:

'It is you who say it . . . Then you must run the world . . . I know nothing about it . . . ' He appeared exhausted.

It was singular the way those two discussed — discussed 'the situation' at three-thirty in the morning. Well, nobody wanted to be asleep that night, it seemed. Even in that obscene street mobs went by, shouting and playing concertinas. She had never heard Mark discuss before — and she was never to hear him discuss again. He appeared to regard that girl with a sort of aloof indulgence; as if he were fond of her but regarded her as over-learned, too young, and devoid of all experience. Marie Léonie had watched them and listened with intentness. In twenty years, these three weeks had for the first time showed her her man in contact with his people. The contemplation had engrossed her.

She could nevertheless see that her man was exhausted in his inner being and obviously that girl was tried beyond endurance. Whilst she talked she appeared to listen for distant sounds . . . She kept on recurring to the idea that punishment was abhorrent to the modern mind. Mark stuck to his point that to occupy Berlin was not punishment, but that not to occupy Berlin was to commit an intellectual sin. The consequences of invasion is counter-invasion and symbolical occupation, as the consequence of over-pride, is humiliation. For the rest of the world, he knew nothing of it; for his own country that was logic — the logic by which she had lived. To abandon that logic was to abandon clearness of mind: it was mental cowardice. To show the world Berlin occupied, with stands of arms and colours on her public places was to show that England respected logic. Not to show the world that was to show that England was mentally cowardly. We dare not put the enemy nations to pain because we shrank from the contemplation.

Valentine had said: 'There has been too much suffering!'

He had said:

'Yes, you are afraid of suffering . . . But England is necessary to the world . . . To my world . . . Well, make it your world and it may go to rack and ruin how it will. I am done with it. But then . . . do you accept the responsibility!'

A world with England presenting the spectacles of moral cowardice will be a world on a lower plane . . . If you lower the record for the mile you lower the standard of blood-stock. Try to think of that. If Persimmon had not achieved what it did the French Grand Prix would be less of an event and the trainers at Maisons Laffite would be less efficient; and the jockeys, and the stable lads, and the sporting writers . . . A world profits by the example of a steadfast nation . . .

Suddenly Valentine said:

'Where is Christopher?' with such intentness that it was like a blow.

Christopher had gone out. She exclaimed:

'But you must not let him go out . . . He is not fit to go out alone . . . He has gone out to go back . . . '

Mark said:

'Don't go . . . ' For she had got to the door. 'He went out to stop the Last Post. But you may play the Last Post, for me. Perhaps he has gone back to the Square. He had presumably better see what has happened to his wife. I should not myself.'

Valentine had said with extraordinary bitterness:

'He shall not. He shall not.' She had gone.

It had come through to Marie Léonie partly then and partly subsequently that Christopher's wife had turned up at Christopher's empty house that was in the Square only a few yards away. They had gone back late at night probably for purposes of love and had found her there. She had come for the purpose of telling them that she was going to be operated on for cancer so that with their sensitive natures they could hardly contemplate going to bed together at that moment.

202

It had been a good lie. That Mrs. Tietjens was a *maîtresse femme*. There was no denying that. She herself was engaged for those others both by her own inclinations and the strong injunctions of her husband, but Mme Tietjens was certainly ingenious. She had managed to incommode and discredit that pair almost as much as any pair could be incommoded and discredited, although they were the most harmless couple in the world.

They had certainly not had an agreeable festival on that Armistice Day. Apparently one of the officers present at their dinner of celebration had gone raving mad; the wife of another of Christopher's comrades of the regiment had been rude to Valentine; the colonel of the regiment had taken the opportunity to die with every circumstance of melodrama. Naturally all the other officers had run away and had left Christopher and Valentine with the madman and the dying colonel on their hands.

An agreeable *voyage de noces* . . . . It appeared that they had secured a four-wheel cab in which with the madman and the other they had driven to Balham — an obscure suburb, with sixteen celebrants hanging all over the outside of the cab and two on the horse's back — at any rate for a couple of miles from Trafalgar Square; they were not of course interested in the interior of the cab; they were merely gay because there was to be no more suffering. Valentine and Christopher had got rid of the madman somewhere in Chelsea at an asylum for shell-shock cases. There he had remained ever since. But the authorities would not take the colonel so they had driven on to Balham, the colonel making dying speeches about the late war, his achievements, the money he owed Christopher . . . Valentine had appeared to find that extremely trying. The man died in the cab.

They had had to walk back into Town because the driver of the four-wheeler was so upset by the death in his cab that he could not drive. Moreover the horse was foundered. It had been twelve, midnight, before they reached Trafalgar Square. They had had to struggle through packed crowds nearly all the way. Apparently they were happy at the accomplishment of their duty — or their benevolence. They stood on the top step of St. Martin's Church, dominating the square that was all illuminated and packed and roaring, with bonfires made of the paving wood and omnibuses and the Nelson Column going up and the fountain-basins full of drunkards, and orators and bands . . . They stood on the top step, drew deep breaths and fell into each other's arms . . .

For the first time — though apparently they had loved each other for a lustrum or more . . . What people!

Then, at the top of the stairs in the house in the Inn they had perceived Sylvia, all in white! . . .

Apparently she had been informed that Christopher and that girl were in communication — by a lady who did not like Christopher because she owed him money. A Lady Macmaster. Apparently there was no one in the world who did not dislike Christopher because they owed him money. The colonel and the lunatic and the husband of the lady who had been rude to Valentine . . . all, all! Right down to Mr. Schatzweiler who had only paid Christopher one cheque for a few dollars out of a great sum and had then contracted a nervous break-down on account of the sufferings he had gone through as a prisoner of war.

But what sort of a man was that Christopher to have in his hands the fortunes of a woman . . . Any woman!

Those were practically the last words her Mark had ever spoken to her, Marie Léonie. She had been supporting him whilst he drank a *tisane* she had made in order that he might sleep, and he had said gravely:

'It is not necessary that I should ask you to

be kind to Mademoiselle Wannop. Christopher is incapable of looking after her . . . ' His last words, for immediately afterwards the telephone bell had rung. He had just before seemed to have a good deal of temperature and it had been whilst his eyes were goggling at her, the thermometer that she had stuck in his mouth gleaming on his dark lips, and whilst she was regretting letting him be tormented by his family that the sharp drilling of the telephone had sounded from the hall. Immediately the strong German accent of Lord Wolstonemark had, with its accustomed disagreeableness, burred in her ear. He had said that the Cabinet was still sitting and they desired to know at once the code that Mark used in his communications with various ports. His second-in-command appeared to be lost amongst the celebrations of that night. Mark had said with a sort of grim irony from the bedroom that if they wanted to stop his transport going out they might just as well not use cypher. If they wanted to use a twopenny halfpenny economy as window dressing for the elections they'd have to have, they might as well give it as much publicity as they could. Besides, he did not believe they would get into Germany with the transport they had. A good deal had been smashed lately.

The Minister had said with a sort of heavy joy that they were not going into Germany, and that had been the most dreadful moment of Marie Léonie's life; but with her discipline she had just simply repeated the words to Mark. He had then said something she did not quite catch, and he would not repeat what he had said. She said as much to Lord Wolstonemark and the chuckling accent said that he supposed that that was the sort of news that would rattle the old boy. But one must adapt oneself to one's day; the times were changed.

She had gone from the instrument to look at Mark. She spoke to him; she spoke to him again. And again — rapid words of panic. His face was dark purple and congested; he gazed straight before him. She raised him; he sank back inertly.

She remembered going to the telephone and speaking in French to the man at the other end. She had said that the man at the other end was a German and a traitor; her husband should never speak to him or his fellows again. The man had said: 'Eh, what's that? Eh? . . . Who are you?'

With appalling shadows chasing up and down in her mind she had said:

'I am Lady Mark Tietjens. You have murdered my husband. Clear yourself from off my line, murderer!'

It had been the first time she had ever given herself that name; it was indeed the first time she had ever spoken in French to that Ministry. But Mark had finished with the Ministry, with the Government, with the nation ... With the world.

As soon as she could get that man off the wire she had rung up Christopher. He had come round with Valentine in tow. It had certainly not been much of a *nuit de noces* for that young couple.

# Part Two

# 1

Sylvia Tietjens, using merely the persuasion of her left knee edged her chestnut bay nearer to the bay mare of the shining General. She said:

'If I divorce Christopher, will you marry me?'

He exclaimed with the vehemence of a shocked hen:

'Good God, no!'

He shone everywhere except in such parts of his grey tweed suit as would have shown by shining that they had been put on more than once. But his little white moustache, his cheeks, the bridge but not the tip of his nose, his reins, his Guards' tie, his boots, martingale, snaffle, curb, fingers, fingernails — all these gave evidence of interminable rubbings ... By himself, by his man, by Lord Fittleworth's stable-hands, grooms ... Interminable rubbings and supervisions at the end of extended arms. Merely to look at him you would know that he was something like Lord Edward Campion, Lieutenant General retired, K.C.M.G. (military) M.P.V.C., M.C., D.S.O ... So he exclaimed: 'Good

God, no!' and using a little-finger touch on his snaffle-rein made his mare recoil from Sylvia Tietjens' chestnut. Annoyed at its mate's motion, the bad-tempered chestnut with the white forehead showed its teeth at the mare, danced a little and threw out some flakes of foam. Sylvia swayed a little backwards and forwards in her saddle, and smiled downwards into her husband's garden.

'You can't, you know,' she said, 'expect to put an idea out of my head just by flurrying the horses . . .'

'A man,' the General said between 'Comeups' to his mare, 'does not marry his . . .'

His mare went backwards a pace or two into the bank and then a pace forwards.

'His what?' Sylvia asked with amiability. 'You can't be going to call me your cast mistress. No doubt most men would have a shot at it. But I never have been even your mistress . . . I have to think of Michael!'

'I wish,' the General said vindictively, 'that you would settle what that boy is to be called . . . Michael or Mark!' He added: 'I was going to say: 'his godson's wife.' . . . A man may not marry his godson's wife.'

Sylvia bent over to stroke the neck of the chestnut.

'A man,' she said, 'cannot marry any man's

wife . . . But if you think that I am going to be the second Lady Tietjens after that . . . French hairdresser's widow . . . '

'You would prefer,' the General said, 'to go to India . . . '

Visions of India went through their hostile minds. They looked down from their horses over Tietjens's in West Sussex, over a house with a high-pitched, tiled roof with deep windows in the grey local stone. He nevertheless saw names like Akhbar Khan, Alexander of Macedon, the son of Philip, Delhi, the Massacre at Cawnpore . . . His mind, given over from boyhood to the contemplation of the largest jewel in the British Crown, spewed up those romances. He was member for the West Cleveland Division and a thorn in the side of the Government. They *must* give him India. They knew that if they did not he could publish revelations as to the closing days of the late war . . . He would naturally never do that. One does not blackmail even a Government.

Still, to all intents he *was* India.

Sylvia also was aware that he was to all intents and purposes India. She saw receptions in Government Houses in which, habited with a tiara, she too would be INDIA . . . As someone said in Shakespeare:

213

I am dying, Egypt, dying! Only
I will importune Death a while until
Of many thousand kisses this poor last
Is laid upon thy lips . . .

She imagined it would be agreeable, supposing her to betray this old Pantaloon India to
have a lover, gasping at her feet, exclaiming: 'I
am dying, India, dying . . . ' And she with her
tiara, very tall. In white, probably. Probably
satin!

The General said:

'You know you cannot possibly divorce my
godson. You are a Roman Catholic.'

She said, always with her smile:

'Oh, *can't* I? . . . Besides it would be of the
greatest advantage to Michael to have for a
step-father the Field Marshal . . . '

He said with impotent irritation:

'I wish you would settle whether that boy's
name is Michael or Mark!'

She said:

'He calls himself Mark . . . I call him
Michael because I hate the name of
Mark . . . '

She regarded Campion with real hatred.
She said that upon occasion she would be
exemplarily revenged upon him. 'Michael'
was a Satterthwaite name, 'Mark,' the name
for a Tietjens eldest son. The boy had

originally been baptised and registered as Michael Tietjens. At his reception into the Roman Church he had been baptised 'Michael Mark.' Then had followed the only real deep humiliation of her life. After his Papist baptism the boy had asked to be called Mark. She had asked him if he really meant that. After a long pause — the dreadful long pauses of children before they render a verdict! — he had said that he intended to call himself Mark from then on . . . By the name of his father's brother, of his father's father, grandfather, great-grandfather . . . By the name of the irascible apostle of the lion and the sword . . . The Satterthwaites, his mother's family, might go by the board.

For herself, she hated the name of Mark. If there was one man in the world whom she hated because he was insensible of her attraction it was Mark Tietjens who lay beneath the thatched roof beneath her eyes . . . Her boy, however, intended, with a child's cruelty to call himself Mark Tietjens . . .

The General grumbled:

'There is no keeping track with you . . . You say now you would be humiliated to be Lady Tietjens after that Frenchwoman . . . But you have always said that that Frenchwoman is only the concubine of Sir Mark . . . You say one thing, then you say another . . .

What is one to believe?'

She regarded him with sunny condescension. He grumbled on:

'One thing, then another . . . You say you cannot divorce my godson because you are a Roman Catholic. Nevertheless you begin divorce proceedings and throw all the mud you can over the miserable fellow. Then you remember your creed and don't go on . . . What sort of game is this?' She regarded him still ironically but with good humour across the neck of her horse.

He said:

'There's *really* no fathoming you . . . A little time ago — for months on end — you were dying of . . . of internal cancer in short . . . '

She commented with the utmost good temper:

'I didn't want that girl to be Christopher's mistress . . . You would think that no man with any imagination at all *could* . . . I mean with his wife in that condition . . . But of course when she insisted . . . Well, I wasn't going to stop in bed, in retreat, all my life . . . '

She laughed good-humouredly at her companion.

'I don't believe you know anything about women,' she said. 'Why should you? Naturally

216

Mark Tietjens married his concubine. Men always do as a sort of deathbed offering. You will eventually marry Mrs. Partridge if I do not choose to go to India. You think you will not, but you will ... As for me I think it would be better for Michael if his mother were Lady Edward Campion — of India! — than if she were merely Lady Tietjens the second of Groby with a dowager who was once a cross-Channel fly-by-night ... ' She laughed and added: 'Anyhow, the sisters at the Blessed Child said that they never saw so many lilies — symbols of purity — as there were at my tea-parties when I was dying ... You'll admit yourself you never saw anything so ravishing as me amongst the lilies and the tea-cups with the great crucifix above my head ... You were singularly moved! You swore you would cut Christopher's throat yourself on the day the detective told us that he was really living here with that girl ... '

The General exclaimed:

'About the Dower House at Groby ... It's really damned awkward ... You swore to me that when you let Groby to that damned American madwoman I could have the Dower House and keep my horses in Groby stables. But now it appears I can't ... It appears ... '

'It appears,' Sylvia said, 'that Mark Tietjens

217

means to leave the Dower House at the disposal of his French concubine . . . Anyhow you can afford a house of your own. You're rich enough!'

The General groaned:

'Rich enough! My God!'

She said:

'You have still — trust you! — your younger son's settlement. You have still your Field Marshal's pay. You have the interest on the grant the nation made you at the end of the war. You have four hundred a year as a member of Parliament. You have cadged on me for your keep and your man's keep and your horses' and grooms' at Groby for years and years . . . '

Immense dejection covered the face of her companion. He said:

'Sylvia . . . Consider the expenses of my constituency . . . One would almost say you hated me!'

Her eyes continued to devour the orchard and garden that were spread out below her. A furrow of raw, newly turned earth ran from almost beneath their horses' hoofs nearly vertically to the house below. She said:

'I suppose that is where they get their water supply. From the spring above here. Cramp the carpenter says they are always having trouble with the pipes!'

The General exclaimed:

'Oh, Sylvia. And you told Mrs. de Bray Pape that they had no water-supply so they could not take a bath!'

Sylvia said:

'If I hadn't she would never have dared to cut down Groby Great Tree . . . Don't you see that for Mrs. de Bray Pape people who do not take baths are outside the law? So, though she's not really courageous, she will risk cutting down their old trees . . . ' She added: 'Yes, I almost believe I do hate misers, and you are more next door to a miser than anyone else I ever honoured with my acquaintance . . . ' She added further: 'But I should advise you to calm yourself. If I let you marry me you will have Satterthwaite pickings. Not to mention the Groby pickings till Michael comes of age and the — what is it — ten thousand a year you will get from India. If out of all that you cannot skimp enough to make up for house-room at my expense at Groby you are not half the miser I took you for!'

A number of horses with Lord Fittleworth and Gunning came up from the soft track outside the side of the garden and onto the hard road that bordered the garden's top. Gunning sat one horse without his feet in the stirrups and had the bridles of two others over his elbows. They were the horses of Mrs. de Bray Pape, Mrs. Lowther and Mark Tietjens. The garden with its quince trees, the old house with its immensely high-pitched roof such as is seen in countries where wood was plentiful, the thatch of Mark Tietjens' shelter and the famous four counties ran from the other side of the hedge out to infinity. An aeroplane droned down towards them, miles away. Up from the road ran a slope covered with bracken to many great beech trees, along a wire hedge. That was the summit of Cooper's Common. In the stillness the hoofs of all those horses made a noise like that of desultorily approaching cavalry. Gunning halted his horses at a little distance; the beast Sylvia rode was too ill-tempered to be approached.

Lord Fittleworth rode up to the General and said:

'God damn it, Campion, Helen Lowther ought not to be down there. Her ladyship will give me no rest for a fortnight!' He shouted at Gunning: 'Here you, blast you, you old scoundrel, where's the gate Speeding complains you have been interfering with.' He added to the general: 'This old scoundrel was in my service for thirty years yet he's always counterswinging the gates in your godson's beastly fields. Of course a man has to look after his master's interests, but we shall have to come to some arrangement. We can't go on like this.' He added to Sylvia:

'It isn't the sort of place Helen ought to go to, is it? All sorts of people living with all sorts. If what you say is true . . . '

The Earl of Fittleworth gave in all places the impression that he wore a scarlet tail coat, a white stock with a fox-hunting pin, white buckskin breeches, a rather painful eyeglass and a silk tophat attached to his person by a silken cord. Actually he was wearing a square, black felt hat, pepper and salt tweeds and no eyeglass. Still he screwed up one eye to look at you and his lucid dark pupils, his contracted swarthy face with grey whiskers and bristling black-grey moustache gave him, perched on his immense horse, the air of a querulous but very masterful monkey.

He considered that he was out of earshot of Gunning and so continued to the other two: 'Oughtn't to give away masters before their servants . . . But it *isn't* any place for the niece of the President of a Show that Cammie has most of her money in. Anyhow she will comb my whiskers!' Before marrying the Earl Lady Fittleworth had been Miss Camden Grimm. 'Regular Aga . . . Agapemone if what you say is true. A queer go for old Mark at his age.'

221

The General said to Fittleworth:

'Here, I say, she says I am a regular miser . . . You don't have any complaints, say, from your keepers that I don't tip enough? That's the real sign of a miser!'

Fittleworth said to Sylvia:

'You don't mind my talking like that of your husband's establishment, do you?' He added that in the old days they would not have talked like that before a lady about her husband. Or perhaps, by Jove, they would have! His grandfather had kept a . . .

Sylvia was of opinion that Helen Lowther could look after herself. Her husband was said not to pay her the attentions that a lady has a right to expect of a husband. So if Christopher . . .

She took an appraising sideways glance at Fittleworth. That peer was going slightly purple under his brown skin. He gazed out over the landscape and swallowed in his throat. She felt that her time for making a decision had come. Times changed, the world changed; she felt heavier in the mornings than she had ever used to. She had had a long, ingenious talk with Fittleworth the night before, on a long terrace. She had been ingenious even for her, but she was aware that afterwards Fittleworth had had a longer bedroom talk with his Cammie. Over even the greatest houses a certain sense of suspense broods when the Master is talking to the Mistress. The Master and the Mistress — upon a word, usually from the Master — take themselves off and the house-guests, at any rate in a small party, straggle, are uncertain as to who gives the signal to retire, suppress yawns even. Finally the butler approaches the most intimate guest and says that the Countess will not be coming down again.

That night Sylvia had shot her bolt. On the terrace she had drawn for the Earl a picture of the *ménage* whose garden she now looked down on. It stretched out below her, that little domain as if she were a goddess dominating its destinies. But she was not so certain of that. The dusky purple under Fittleworth's skin showed no diminution. He continued to gaze away over his territory, reading it as if it were a book — a clump of trees gone here, the red roof of a new villa grown up there in among the trees, a hop-oast with its characteristic cowl gone from a knoll. He was getting ready to say something. She had asked him the night before to root that family out of that slope.

Naturally not in so many words. But she had drawn such a picture of Christopher and Mark as made it, if the peer believed her, almost a necessity for a conscientious nobleman to do his best to rid his countryside of a plague-spot . . . The point was whether Fittleworth would choose to believe her because she was a beautiful woman with a thrilling voice. He was terribly domestic and attached to his Trans-Atlantic female as only very wicked dark men late in life can contrive to be when they come of very wicked, haughty, and influential houses. They have as it were attended on the caprices of so many opera singers and famous professionals that they get the knack when, later in life they take capricious or influential wives, of very stiffly but minutely showing every sort of elaborate deferences to their life-partners. That is born with them.

So that the fate of that garden and that high-pitched roof was in fact in the hands of Cammie Fittleworth — in so far as great peers to-day have influence over the fates of their neighbours. And it is to be presumed that they have some.

And men are curious creatures. Fittleworth stiffened at queer places. He had done so last night. He had nevertheless stood a good deal in the way of allegations from her. It had to be remembered that Mark Tietjens was an old acquaintance of his — not as intimate as he would have been if the Earl had had children, for Mark preferred houses of married people who had children. But the Earl knew Mark very well . . . Now a man listening to gossip about another man whom he knows very well will go pretty far in the way of believing what a beautiful woman will tell him about that other man. Beauty and truth have a way of appearing to be akin; and it is true that no man knows what another man is doing when he is out of sight.

So that in inventing or hinting at a ruinous, concealed harem, with consequent disease to account for Mark's physical condition and apparent ruin she thought she was not going altogether too far. She had at any rate been ready to chance it. It is the sort of thing a man will believe about his best friend even. He will say: 'Only think . . . all the while old X . . . was appearing such a quiet codger he was really . . . ' And the words rivet conviction.

So that appeared to get through.

Her revelations as to Christopher's financial habits had not appeared to do so well. The Earl had listened with his head on one side whilst she had let him gather that Christopher lived on women — on the former Mrs. Duchemin, now Lady Macmaster, for instance. Yes, to that the Earl had listened with deference, and it had seemed a fairly safe allegation to make. Old Duchemin was known to have left a pot of money to his widow. She had a very nice little place not six or seven miles away from where they stood.

And it had come rather naturally to bring in Edith Ethel, for not so long ago Lady Macmaster had actually paid Sylvia a visit. It was about the late Macmaster's debt to Christopher. That was a point about which Lady Macmaster was and always had seemed to be a little cracky. She had actually visited Sylvia in order to see if Sylvia would not use her influence with Christopher. To get him to remit the debt!

Apparently Christopher had not carried his idiocy as far as might be expected. He had dragged that wretched girl down to those penurious surroundings, but he was not going to let her and the child she appeared to be going to have suffer actual starvation or even to suffer from too great worry. And apparently, to satisfy a rather uneasy vanity, years before Macmaster had given Christopher a charge on his life insurance. Macmaster, as she well knew, had sponged unmercifully on her husband and Christopher had certainly formerly regarded the money he had advanced as a gift. She herself had many times upbraided him about it: it had appeared to her one of Christopher's worst unbearablenesses.

But apparently the charge on the life insurance still existed and was now a charge on that miserable fellow's rather extensive estate. At any rate the insurance company refused to pay over any money to the widow until the charge was satisfied ... And the thought that Christopher was doing for that girl what, she was convinced, he never would have done for herself had added a new impulse to Sylvia's bitterness. Indeed her bitterness had by now given way almost entirely to a mere spirit of tormentingness — she wanted to torture that girl out of her mind. That was why she was there now. She imagined Valentine under the high roof suffering tortures because she, Sylvia, was looking down over the hedge.

But the visit of Lady Macmaster had certainly revived her bitterness as it had suggested to her new schemes of making herself a nuisance to the household below her. Lady Macmaster in widow's weeds of the most fantastic crape that gave to her at once the elegance and the portentousness of a funeral horse had really seemed more than a little out of her mind. She had asked Sylvia's opinion of all sorts of expedients for making Christopher loosen his grip and she had continued her supplications even in correspondence. At last she had hit on a singular expedient . . . Some years before, apparently, Edith Ethel had had an affair of the heart with a distinguished Scottish Litterateur, now deceased. Edith Ethel, as was well known, had acted as Egeria to quite a number of Scottish men of letters. That was natural; the Macmasters' establishment was Scottish, Macmaster had been a Critic and had had government funds for the relief of indigent men of letters and Edith Ethel was passionately cultured. You could see that even in the forms her crape took and in how she arranged it around her when she sat or agitatedly rose to wring her hands.

But the letters of this particular Scot had outpassed the language of ordinary Egerianishness. They spoke of Lady Macmaster's eyes, arms, shoulders, feminine aura . . . These letters Lady Macmaster had proposed to entrust to Christopher for sale to Trans-Atlantic collectors. She said they ought to fetch $30,000 at least and with the 10% commission that Christopher might take he might consider himself as amply repaid for the four thousand odd that Macmaster's estate owed him.

And this had appeared to Sylvia to be so eccentric an expedient that she had felt the utmost pleasure in suggesting that Edith Ethel should drive up to Tietjens's with her letters and have an interview — if possible with Valentine Wannop in the absence of Tietjens. This she calculated would worry her rival quite a bit — and even if it did not do that she, Sylvia, would trust herself to obtain subsequently from Edith Ethel a great many grotesque details as to the Wannop's exhausted appearance, shabby clothing, worn hands.

For it is to be remembered that one of the chief torments of the woman who has been abandoned by a man is the sheer thirst of curiosity for material details as to how that man subsequently lives. Sylvia Tietjens for a great number of years had tormented her husband. She would have said herself that she had been a thorn in his flesh, largely because he had seemed to her never inclined to take his own part. If you live with a person who suffers from being put upon a good deal and if that person will not assert his own rights you are apt to believe that your standards as gentleman and Christian are below his, and the experience is lastingly disagreeable. But in any case Sylvia Tietjens had had reason to believe that for many years, for better or for worse — and mostly for worse — she had been the dominating influence over Christopher Tietjens. Now, except for extraneous annoyances, she was aware that she could no longer influence him either for evil or for good. He was a solid, four-square lump of meal-sacks too heavy for her hauling about.

So that the only real pleasure she had was when, at night in a circle of cosy friends she could assert that she was not even yet out of his confidence. Normally she would not — the members of her circle would not have — made confidantes of her ex-husband's domestics. But she had had to chance whether the details of Christopher's *ménage* as revealed by the wife of his carpenter would prove to her friends sufficiently amusing to make them forget the social trespass she committed in consorting with her husband's dependants and she had to chance whether the carpenter's wife would not see that, by proclaiming her wrongs over the fact that her husband had left her, she was proclaiming her own unattractiveness.

She had hitherto chanced both, but the time, she was aware, was at hand when she would have to ask herself whether she would not be better off if she were what the French call *rangée* as was the wife of the Commander in Chief in India than as a free-lance woman owing her popularity entirely to her own exertions. It would be slightly ignominious to owe part of her prestige to a pantaloon like General Lord Edward Campion K.C.B., but how restful might it not be! To keep your place in a society of Marjies and Beatties — and even of Cammies, like the Countess of Fittleworth — meant constant exertion and watchfulness, even if you were comfortably wealthy and well-born — and it meant still more exertion when your staple capital for entertainment was the domestic misfortune of a husband that did not like you.

She might well point out to Marjie, Lady Stern, that her husband's clothes lacked buttons and his companion all imaginable chic; she might well point out to Beattie, Lady Elsbacher, that according to her husband's carpenter's wife, the interior of her husband's home resembled a cave encumbered with packing cases in dark-coloured wood, whereas in her day . . . Or she might even point out to Cammie, Lady Fittleworth, to Mrs. de Bray Pape and Mrs. Luther that, having a defective water supply, her husband's woman probably provided him only with difficulty with baths . . . But every now and then someone — as had been the case once or twice with the three American ladies — would point out, a little tentatively, that her husband was by now Tietjens of Groby to all intents and purposes. And people — and in particular American ladies — would attach particular importance before her to English county gentlemen who had turned down titles and the like. Her husband had not turned down a title; he had not been able to, for much as Mark had desired to refuse a baronetcy at the last moment he had been given to understand that he couldn't. But her husband had practically turned down a whole great estate and the romantic aspect of that feat was beginning to filter through to her friends. For all her assertions that his seeming poverty was due to dissolute living and consequent bankruptcy, her friends would occasionally ask her whether in fact his poverty was not simply a voluntary affair, the result either of a wager or a strain of mysticism. They would point out that she and her son at least had all the symptoms of considerable wealth as a sign rather that Christopher did not desire wealth or was generous, than that he had no longer money to throw away . . .

There were symptoms of that sort of questioning of the mind rising up in the American ladies whom Cammie Fittleworth liked to have staying with her. Hitherto Sylvia had managed to squash them. After all, the

Tietjens household below her feet was a singular affair for those who had not the clue to its mystery. She had the clue herself; she knew both about the silent feud between the two brothers and about their attitude to life. And if it enraged her that Christopher should despise things that she so valued it none the less gratified her to know that, in the end, she was to be regarded as responsible for that silent feud and the renunciation that it had caused. It was her tongue that had set going the discreditable stories that Mark once had believed against his brother.

But if she was to retain her power to blast that household with her tongue she felt she ought to have details. She must have corroborative details. Otherwise she could not so very convincingly put over her picture of abandoned corruption. You might have thought that her coercing Mrs. de Bray Pape and her son into making that rather outrageous visit and in awakening Mrs. Lowther's innocent curiosity as to the contents of the cottage she had been inspired solely by the desire to torment Valentine Wannop. But she was aware that there was more than that to it. She might get details of all sorts of queernesses that, triumphantly, to other groups of listeners she could retail as proof of her intimacy with that household.

If her listeners showed any signs of saying that it was queer that a man like Christopher who appeared to be a kindly group of sacks should actually be a triply crossed being compounded of a Lovelace, Pandarus, and a Satyr she could always answer: 'Ah, but what can you expect of people who have hams drying in their drawing room!' Or if others alleged that it was queer, if Valentine Wannop had Christopher as much under her thumb as she was said to have, even by Sylvia, that she should still allow Christopher to run an Agapemone in what was after all her own house, Sylvia would have liked to be able to reply: 'Ah, but what can you expect of a woman upon whose stairs you will find, side by side, a hairbrush, a frying pan, and a copy of Sappho!'

That was the sort of detail that Sylvia needed. The one item she had: The Tietjenses, she knew from Mrs. Carpenter Cramp, had an immense fireplace in their living-room and, after the time-honoured custom they smoked their hams in that chimney. But to people who did not know that smoking hams in great chimneys was a time-honoured custom the assertion that Christopher was the sort of person who dried hams in his drawing room would bring up images of your finding yourself in a sort of place where hams reclined on the sofa-cushions. Even that to the reflective would not necessarily be proof that the perpetrator was a Sadic lunatic — but few people are reflective and at any rate it was queer, and one queerness might be taken as implying another.

But as to Valentine she could not get details enough. You had to prove that she was a bad housekeeper and a blue stocking in order that it should be apparent that Christopher was miserable — and you had to prove that Christopher was miserable in order to make it apparent that the hold that Valentine Wannop certainly had over him was something unholy. For that, it was necessary to have details of misplaced hairbrushes, frying pans, and copies of Sappho.

It had, however, been difficult to get those details. Mrs. Cramp when appealed to had made it rather plain that, far from being a bad housekeeper Valentine Wannop did no house-keeping at all whereas Marie Léonie — Lady Mark — was a perfect devil of a ménagère. Apparently Mrs. Cramp was allowed no further into the dwelling than the wash house — because of half-pounds of sugar and dusters that Mrs. Cramp in the character of charwoman had believed to be her perquisites. Marie Léonie hadn't.

The local doctor and the parson, both of whom visited the house, had contributed only palely coloured portraits of the young woman. Sylvia had gone to call on them and making use of the Fittleworth ægis — hinting that Lady Cammie wanted details of her humbler neighbours for her own instruction — Sylvia had tried to get behind the professional secrecy that distinguished parsons and doctors. But she had not got much behind. The parson gave her the idea that he thought Valentine rather a jolly girl, very hospitable and with a fine tap of cider at disposal and fond of reading under trees — the classics mostly. Very much interested also in rock-plants as you could see by the bank under Tietjens's windows . . . Their house was always called Tietjens's. Sylvia had never been under those windows and that enraged her.

From the doctor, Sylvia, for a faint flash, gained the impression that Valentine enjoyed rather poor health. But it had only been an impression arising from the fact that the doctor saw her every day — and it was rather discounted by the other fact that the doctor said that his daily visits were for Mark who might be expected to pop off at any moment. So he needed careful watching. A little excitement and he was done for . . .

Otherwise Valentine seemed to have a sharp eye for old furniture as the doctor knew to his cost, for in a small way he collected himself. And he said that at minor cottage-sales and for small objects Valentine could drive a bargain that Tietjens himself never achieved.

Otherwise, from both the doctor and the parson, she had an impression of Tietjens's as a queer household — queer because it was so humdrum and united. She really herself had expected something more exciting! Really. It did not seem possible that Christopher should settle down into tranquil devotion to brother and mistress after the years of emotion she had given him. It was as if a man should have jumped out of a frying pan into — a duckpond.

So, as she looked at the red flush on Fittleworth's face an almost mad moment of impatience had overcome her. This fellow was about the only man who had ever had the guts to stand up to her . . . A fox-hunting squire: an extinct animal!

The trouble was, you could not tell quite how extinct he was. He might be able to bite as hard as a fox. Otherwise she would be running down, right now, running down that zigzag orange path to that forbidden land.

That she had hitherto never dared. From a social point of view it would have been outrageous, but she was prepared to chance that. She was sure enough of her place in Society and if people will excuse a man's leaving his wife they will excuse the wife's making at least one or two demonstrations that are a bit thick. But she had simply not dared to meet Christopher; he might cut her.

Perhaps he would not. He was a gentleman and gentlemen do not usually cut women with whom they have slept . . . But he might . . . She might go down there and in a dark low-ceilinged room be making some sort of stipulation — God knew what, the first that came into her head — to Valentine. You can always make up some sort of reason for approaching the woman who has supplanted you. But he might come mooning in, and suddenly stiffen into a great, clumsy — oh adorable! — face of stone.

That was what you would not dare to face. That would be death. She could imagine him going out of the room, rolling his shoulders. Leaving the whole establishment to her, closing only himself in invisible bonds — closed to her by the angel with the flaming sword . . . That was what he would do. And that before the other woman. He had come once very near it and she had hardly recovered from it. That pretended illness had not been so much pretended as all that! She had smiled angelically, under the great crucifix, in the convent that had been her nursing-home — angelically, amongst lilies, upon the General, the sisters, the many callers that gradually came to her teas. But she had had to think that Christopher was probably in the arms of his girl, and he had let her go when she had, certainly physically, needed his help.

But that had not been a calm occasion, in that dark empty house . . . And he had not, at that date, enjoyed the favours, the domesticity, of that young woman. He hadn't had a chance of comparison, so that the turning-down need not count. He had treated her barbarously — as social counters go it had been helpful to her — but only at the strong urge of a young woman driven to fury. That could be palliated. It hardly indeed affected her now as a reverse. Looked at reasonably, if a man comes home intending to go to bed with a young woman who has bewitched him for a number of years and finds another woman who tells him that she has cancer and does a very creditable faint from the top of the stairs and then — in spite of practice and being as hard as nails — puts her ankle out of joint, he has got to choose between the one and the other. And the other in this case had been vigorous, determined on her man, even vituperative. Obviously Christopher was not the sort of man who would *like* seducing a young woman whilst his wife was dying of internal cancer, let alone a sprained ankle. But the young woman had arrived at a stage when she did not care for any delicacies or their dictates.

No; that Sylvia had been able to bear. But if now the same thing happened, in dim, quiet daylight, in a tranquil old room . . . that she would not be able to face! It is one thing to acknowledge that your man has gone — there is no irrevocability about going. He may come back when the other woman is insignificant, a blue stocking, entirely unnoticeable . . . But if he took the step — the responsibility! — of cutting you, that would be to put between you a barrier that no amount of weariness with your rival could overstep.

Impatience grew upon her. The fellow was away in an aeroplane. Gone North. It was the only time she had ever *known* of him as having gone away. It was her only chance of running down those orange zigzags. And now — it was all Lombard Street to a China apple that Fittleworth intended to disapprove of her running down. And you could not ignore Fittleworth.

# 2

No, you could not ignore Fittleworth. As a fox-hunting squire he might be an extinct monster — though then again he might not: there was no knowing. But as a wicked, dark, adept with bad women, and come of a race that had been adepts with women good and bad for generations, he was about as dangerous a person as you could find. That gross, slow, earthy, obstinate fellow, Gunning, could stand grouchily up to Fittleworth, answer him back and chance what Fittleworth could do to him. So could any cottager. But then they were his people. She wasn't ... she, Sylvia Tietjens, and she did not believe she could afford to outface him. Nor could half England.

Old Campion wanted India — probably she herself wanted Campion to have India. Groby Great Tree was cut down and if you have not the distinction — if you rid yourself of the distinction, of Groby Great Tree just to wound a man to the heart — you may as well take India. Times were changing but there was no knowing how the circumstances of a man like Fittleworth changed. He sat his horse like a monkey and gazed out over his land as his people had done for generations, bastard or legitimate. And it was all very well to regard him as merely a country squire married to a Trans-Atlantic nobody and so out of it. He hopped up to London — he and his Cammie too — and he passed unnoticeably about the best places and could drop a word or so here and there; and for all the countess' foreign and unknown origin she had access to ears that could well be dangerous for aspirants to India. Campion might have his war-services and his constituency. But Cammie Fittleworth was popular in high places and Fittleworth had his hounds and, when it came even to constituencies, the tradesmen of a couple of counties. And he was wicked.

It had been obvious to her for a long time that God would one day step in and intervene for the protection of Christopher. After all Christopher was a good man — a rather sickeningly good man. It is, in the end, she reluctantly admitted, the function of God and the invisible Powers to see that a good man shall eventually be permitted to settle down to a stuffy domestic life . . . even to chaffering over old furniture. It was a comic affair — but it was the sort of affair that you had to admit. God is probably — and very rightly — on the side of the stuffy domesticities. Otherwise the world could not continue — the children would not be healthy. And certainly God desired the production of large crops of healthy children. Mind doctors of to-day said that all cases of nervous breakdown occurred in persons whose parents had not led harmonious lives.

So Fittleworth might well have been selected as the lightning conductor over the house of Tietjens. And the selection was quite a good one on the part of the Unseen Powers. And no doubt predestined! There was no accident about Mark's being under the ægis — if that was what you called it — of the Earl. Mark had for long been one of the powers of the land, so had Fittleworth. They had moved in the same spheres — the rather mysterious spheres of Good People — who ruled the destinies of the nation in so far as the more decorative and more splendid jobs were concerned. They must have met about, here and there, constantly for years. And Mark had indicated that it was in that neighbourhood that he wanted to end his days simply because he wanted to be near the Fittleworths who could be calculated on to look after his Marie Léonie and the rest of them.

For the matter of that, Fittleworth himself,

like God, was on the side of the stuffy domesticities and on the side of women who were in the act of producing healthy children. Early in life he had had a woman to whom he was said to have been hopelessly attached and whom he had acquired in romantic circumstances — a famous dancer whom he had snapped up under the nose of a very Great Person indeed. And the woman had died in childbirth — or had given birth to an infant child and gone mad and committed suicide after that achievement. At any rate for months and months, Fittleworth's friends had had to sit up night after night with him so that he might not kill himself.

Later — after he had married Cammie in the search for a domesticity that, except for his hounds he had made really almost stuffy — he had interested himself — and of course his countess — in the cause of providing tranquil conditions for women before childbirth. They had put up a perfectly lovely lying-in almshouse right under their own windows, down there.

So there it was — and, as she took her sideways glance at Fittleworth high up there in the air beside her, she was perfectly aware that she might be in for such a duel with him as had seldom yet fallen to her lot.

He had begun it by saying: 'God damn it,

Campion, ought Helen Lowther to be down there?' Then he had put it, as upon her, Sylvia's information, that the cottage was in effect a disorderly house. But he had added: 'If what you say is true?'

That of course was distinctly dangerous, for Fittleworth probably knew quite well that it had been at her, Sylvia's instigation that Helen Lowther *was* down there. And he was letting her know that if it *was* at her instigation and if the house was really in her belief a brothel, his countess would be frightfully displeased. Frightfully!

Helen Lowther was of no particular importance, except to the Countess — and, of course, to Michael. She was one of those not unattractive Americans that drift over here and enjoy themselves with frightfully simple things. She liked visiting ruins and chattering about nothing in particular and galloping on the downs and talking to old servants and she liked the adoration of Michael. Probably she would have turned down the adoration of anyone older.

And the Countess liked to preserve the innocence of young American women. The Countess was fiftyish now and of a generation that preserved a certain stiffness along with a certain old-fashioned broadness of mind and outspokenness. She was of a class of

American that had once seemed outrageously wealthy and who, if in the present stage of things they did not seem overwhelming, yet retained an aspect of impressive comfort and social authority and she moved in a set most of whose individuals, American, English, or even French, were of much the same class, at least by marriage, as herself. She tolerated — she even liked — Sylvia, but she might well get mad if from under her roof Helen Lowther, who was in her charge, should come into social contact with an irregular couple. You never knew when that point of view might not crop up in women of that date and class.

Sylvia, however, had chanced it. She had to — and in the end it could only be pulling the string of one more showerbath. It was a showerbath formidably charged — but that was her vocation in life and, if Campion had to lose India, she could always pursue her vocation in other countrysides. She was tired, but not as tired as all that!

So Sylvia had chanced saying that she supposed Helen Lowther could look after herself and had added a salacious quip to keep the speech in character. She knew nothing really of Helen Lowther's husband, who was probably a lean man with some avocation in a rather dim West. But he could not be very *impressionné* or he would not let his attractive young wife roam for ever over Europe, alone.

His Lordship gave no further sign beyond repeating that if that fellow was the sort of fellow Mrs. Tietjens said he was, her Ladyship would properly curl his whiskers. And in face of that Sylvia simply had to make a concession to the extent of saying that she did not see why Helen Lowther could not visit a show cottage that was known, apparently, over half America. And perhaps buy some old sticks.

His Lordship removed his gaze from the distant hills and turned a long, cool, rather impertinent glance on her. He said:

'Ah, if it's only that . . . ' and nothing more. And, at that, she chanced it again:

'If,' she said slowly too, 'you think Helen Lowther is in need of protection I don't mind if I go down and look after her myself!'

The General, who had tried several interjections, now exclaimed:

'Surely you wouldn't meet that fellow!' . . . And that rather spoilt it.

For Fittleworth could take the opportunity to leave her to do what he was at liberty to regard as the directions of her natural protector. Otherwise he must have said something to give away his attitude. So she had to give away more of her own with the words:

'Christopher is not down here. He has taken an aeroplane to York — to save Groby Great Tree. Your man Speeding saw him when he went to get your saddle. Getting into a plane.' She added: 'But he's too late. Mrs. de Bray Pape had a letter yesterday to say the tree had been cut down. At her orders!'

Fittleworth said: 'Good God!' Nothing more!

The General regarded him as one fearing to be struck by lightning. Campion had already told her over and over again that Fittleworth would rage like a town bull at the bare idea that the tenant of a furnished house should interfere with its owner's timber . . . But Fittleworth merely continued to look away, communing with the handle of his crop. That called, Sylvia knew for another concession and she said:

'Now, Mrs. de Bray Pape has got cold feet. Horribly cold feet. That's why she's down there. She's got the idea that Mark may have her put in prison!' She added further:

'She wanted to take my boy, Michael, with her to intercede. As the heir he has some right to a view!'

And from those speeches of hers Sylvia had the measure of her dread of that silent man.

She was more tired than she thought and the idea of India more attractive.

At that point Fittleworth exclaimed:

'Damn it all, I've got to settle the hash of that fellow Gunning!'

He turned his horse's head along the road and beckoned the General towards him with his crop-handle. The General gazed back at her appealingly, but Sylvia knew that she had to stop there and await Fittleworth's verdict from the General's lips. She wasn't even to have any duel of *sous-entendus* with Fittleworth.

She clenched her fingers on her crop and looked towards Gunning . . . If she was going to be asked by the Countess through old Campion to pack up, bag and baggage, and leave the house she would at least get what she could out of that fellow whom she had never yet managed to approach.

&#9733;  &#9733;  &#9733;

The horses of the General and Fittleworth, relieved to be out of the neighbourhood of Sylvia's chestnut, minced friendlily along the road, the mare liking her companion.

'This fellow Gunning,' his Lordship began . . . He continued with great animation:

'About these gates . . . You are aware that

my estate carpenter repairs . . . '

Those were the last words she heard and she imagined Fittleworth continuing for a long time about his bothering gates in order to put the General quite off his guard — and no doubt for the sake of manners. Then he would drop in some shot that would be terrible to the old General. He might even cross-question him as to facts, with sly, side questions, looking away over the country.

For that she cared very little. She did not pretend to be a historian: she entertained rather than instructed. And she had conceded enough to Fittleworth. Or perhaps it was to Cammie. Cammie was a great, fat, good-natured dark thing with pockets under her liquid eyes. But she had a will. And by telling Fittleworth that she had not incited Helen Lowther and the two others to make an incursion into the Tietjens' household Sylvia was aware that she had made an important concession.

She hadn't intended to weaken. It had happened. She had intended to chance conveying the idea that she wanted to worry Christopher and his companion into leaving that country.

The heavy man with the three horses approached slowly, with the air of a small army in the narrow road. He was grubby and unbuttoned, but he regarded her intently with eyes a little bloodshot. He said from a distance something that she did not altogether understand. It was about her chestnut. He was asking her to back that 'ere chestnut's tail into the hedge. She was not used to being spoken to by the lower classes. She kept her horse along the road. In that way the fellow could not pass. She knew what was the matter. Her chestnut would lash out at Gunning's charges if they got near its stern. In the hunting season it wore a large 'K' on its tail.

Nevertheless the fellow must be a good man with horses; otherwise he would not be perched on one with the stirrups crossed over the saddle in front of him and lead two others. She did not know that she would care to do that herself nowadays; there had been a time when she would have. She had intended to slip down from the chestnut and hand it over to Gunning. Once she was down on the road he could not very well refuse. But she felt disinclined to cock her leg over the saddle. He looked like a fellow who could refuse.

He refused. She had asked him to hold her horse whilst she went down and spoke to his master. He had made no motion towards doing so; he had continued to stare fixedly at her. She had said:

251

'You're Captain Tietjens' servant, aren't you? I'm his wife. Staying with Lord Fittleworth!'

He had made no answer and no movement except to draw the back of his right hand across his left nostril — for lack of a handkerchief. He said something incomprehensible — but not conciliatory. Then he began a longer speech. That she understood. It was to the effect that he had been thirty years, boy and man with his Lordship and the rest of his time with the Cahptn. He also pointed out that there was a hitching post and chain by the gate there. But he did not advise her to hitch to it. The chestnut would kick to flinders any cart that came along the road. And the mere idea of the chestnut lashing out and injuring itself caused her to shudder; she was a good horsewoman.

The conversation went with long pauses. She was in no hurry; she would have to wait till Campion or Fittleworth came back — with the verdict, probably. The fellow, when he used short sentences, was incomprehensible because of his dialect. When he spoke longer she got a word or two out of it.

It troubled her a little, now, that Edith Ethel might be coming along the road. Practically she had promised to meet her at that spot and at about that moment, Edith

Ethel proposing to sell her love-letters to Christopher — or through him . . . The night before she had told Fittleworth that Christopher had bought the place below her with money he had from Lady Macmaster because Lady Macmaster had been his mistress. Fittleworth had boggled at that . . . it had been at that moment that he had gone rather stiff to her.

As a matter of fact Christopher had bought that place out of a windfall. Years before — even before she had married him — he had had a legacy from an aunt and in his visionary way had invested it in some Colonial — very likely Canadian — property or invention or tramway concession because he considered that some remote place, owing to its geographical position on some road — was going to grow. Apparently during the war it had grown and the completely forgotten investment had paid nine and sixpence in the pound. Out of the blue. It could not be helped. With a monetary record of visionariness and generosity such as Christopher had behind him, some chickens must now and then come home — some visionary investment turn out sound, some debtor turn honest. She understood even that some colonel who had died on Armistice night and to whom Christopher had lent a good sum in hundreds had turned honest. At any rate his executors had written to ask her for Christopher's address with a view to making payments. She hadn't at the time known Christopher's address, but no doubt they had got it from the War Office or somewhere.

No doubt with windfalls like those he had kept afloat; for she did not believe the old-furniture business as much as paid its way. She had heard through Mrs. Cramp that the American partner had embezzled most of the money that should have gone to Christopher. You should not do business with Americans. Christopher, it is true, had years ago — during the war — predicted an American invasion — as he always predicted everything. He had indeed said that if you wanted to have money you must get it from where money was going to; in other words, if you wanted to sell, you must prepare to sell what was wanted. And they wanted old furniture more than anything else. She didn't mind. She was already beginning a little campaign with Mrs. de Bray Pape to make her re-furnish Groby — to make her export all the clumsy eighteen-forty mahogany that the great house contained, to Sante Fé or wherever it was that Mr. Pape lived alone, and to re-furnish with Louis Quatorze as befitted the spiritual descendant of the Maintenon. The worst of it was that Mr. Pape was stingy.

She was, indeed, in a fine taking that morning — Mrs. de Bray Pape. In hauling out the stump of Groby Great Tree the woodcutters had apparently brought down two-thirds of the ball-room exterior wall and that vast, gloomy room, with its immense lustres was wrecked along with the old school-rooms above it. As far as she could make out from the steward's letter Christopher's boyhood's bedroom had practically disappeared ... Well, if Groby Great Tree did not like Groby House it had finely taken its dying revenge ... A nice shock Christopher would get! Anyhow Mrs. de Bray Pape had pretty well mangled the great dovecote in erecting in it a new power station.

But apparently it was going to mangle the Papes to the tune of a pretty penny and apparently Mr. Pape might be expected to give his wife no end of a time ... Well, you can't expect to be God's Vicegerent of England without barking your shins on old, hard things.

No doubt Mark knew all about it by now. Perhaps it had killed him. She hoped it hadn't because she still hoped to play him some tidy little tricks before she had done with him ...

If he were dead or dying beneath that parallelogram of thatch down among the apple boughs all sorts of things might be going to happen. Quite inconvenient things.

There would be the title. She quite definitely did not want the title and it would become more difficult to decry Christopher. People with titles and great possessions are vastly more difficult to decry than impoverished commoners, because the scale of morality changes. Titles and great possessions expose you to great temptations — you may be excused if you succumb. It is scandalous, on the other hand, that the indigent should have any fun!

So that sitting rather restfully in the sunlight on her horse, Sylvia felt like a general who is losing the fruits of victory. She did not much care. She had got down Groby Great Tree: that was as nasty a blow as the Tietjenses had had in ten generations.

But then a queer, disagreeable thought went through her mind, just as Gunning at last made again a semi-comprehensible remark. Perhaps in letting Groby Great Tree be cut down God was lifting the ban off the Tietjenses. He might well.

Gunning, however, had said something like:

'Shuddn' gaw dahn theer. Ride Boldro up

to farm n' put he in loose box.' She gathered that if she would ride her horse to some farm he could be put in a loose box and she could rest in the farmer's parlour. Gunning was looking at her with a queer, intent look. She could not just think what it meant.

Suddenly it reminded her of her childhood. Her father had had a head gardener just as gnarled and just as apparently autocratic. That was it. She had not been much in the country for thirty years. Apparently country people had not changed much. Times change; probably people do not, much.

For it came back to her with sudden extraordinary clearness. The side of a greenhouse, down there in the west where she had been 'Miss Sylvia, oh, Miss *Sylvia,*' for a whole army of protesting retainers, and that old, brown, gnarled fellow, who was equally 'Mr. Carter' for them all, except her father. Mr. Carter had been potting geranium shoots and she had been teasing a little white kitten. She was thirteen with immense plaits of blonde hair. The kitten had escaped from her and was rubbing itself, its back arched against the leggings of Mr. Carter, who had a special affection for it. She had proposed — merely to torment Mr. Carter — to do something to the kitten, to force its paws into walnut shells perhaps. She had so little meant to hurt the kitten that she had forgotten what it was she had proposed to do. And suddenly the heavy man, his bloodshot eyes fairly blazing, had threatened if she so much as blew on that kitten's fur, to thrash her on a part of her anatomy on which public school-boys rather than young ladies are usually chastised . . . so that she would not be able to sit down for a week, he had said.

Oddly enough it had given a queer pleasure, that returned always with the recollection. She had never otherwise in her life been threatened with physical violence, but she knew that within herself the emotion had often and often existed: If only Christopher had thrashed her within an inch of her life . . . Or yes — there had been Drake . . . He had half killed her on the night before her wedding to Christopher. She had feared for the child within her! That emotion had been unbearable!

She said to Gunning — and she felt for all the world as if she were trying a torment on Mr. Carter of years ago:

'I don't see why I need go to the farm. I can perfectly well ride Boldero down this path. I must certainly speak to your master.'

She had really no immediate notion of doing anything of the sort, but she turned her horse towards the wicket gate that was a little beyond Gunning.

He scrambled off his horse with singular velocity and under the necks of those he led. It was like the running of an elephant and, with all the reins bunched before him, he almost fell with his back on the little wicket back towards whose latch she had been extending the handle of her crop . . . She had not meant to raise it. She swore she had not meant to raise it. The veins stood out in his hairy, open neck and shoulders. He said: No, she didn'!

Her chestnut was reaching its teeth out towards the led horses. She was not certain that he heard her when she asked if he did not know that she was the wife of the Captain, his master; and guest of Lord Fittleworth, his ex-master. Mr. Carter certainly had not heard her years ago when she had reminded him that she was his master's daughter. He had gone on fulminating. Gunning was doing that, too — but more slowly and heavily. He said first that the Cahptn would tan her hide if she so much as disturbed his brother by a look; he would hide her within an inch of her life. As he had done already.

Sylvia said that by God he never had; if he said he had, he lied. Her immediate reaction was to resent the implication that she was not as good a man as Christopher. He seemed to have been boasting that he had physically corrected her.

Gunning continued drily:

'You put it in th' papers yourself. My ol' missus read it me. Powerful set on Sir Mark's comfort, the Cahptn is. Throw you down stairs, the Cahptn did n' give you cancer. It doesn' show!'

That was the worst of attracting chivalrous attentions from professional people. She had begun divorce proceedings against Christopher, in the way of a petition for restitution of conjugal rights, compounding with the shade of Father Consett and her conscience as a Roman Catholic by arguing that a petition for the restoration of your husband from a Strange Woman is not the same as divorce proceedings. In England at that date it was a preliminary measure and caused as much publicity as the real thing to which she had no intention of proceeding. It caused quite a terrific lot of publicity because her counsel, in his enthusiasm for the beauty and wit of his client — in his chambers the dark, Gaelic, youthful K. C. had been impressively sentimental in his enthusiasm — learned counsel had overstepped the rather sober bounds of the preliminary stage of these

260

cases. He knew that Sylvia's aim was not divorce, but the casting of all possible obloquy on Christopher, and in his fervid Erse oratory he had cast as much mud as an enthusiastic terrier with its hind legs out of a fox's hole. It had embarrassed Sylvia herself, sitting brilliantly in Court. And it had roused the judge, who knew something of the case, having, like half London of his class, taken tea with the dying Sylvia beneath the crucifix and amongst the lilies of the nursing-home that was also a convent. The judge had protested against the oratory of Mr. Sylvian Hatt but Mr. Hatt had got in already a lurid picture of Christopher and Valentine in a dark, empty house on Armistice Night, throwing Sylvia downstairs and so occasioning her a fell disease from which, under the Court's eyes, she was now fading. This had distressed Sylvia herself, for, rather with the idea of showing the court and the world in general what a fool Christopher was to have left her for a little brown sparrow, she had chosen to appear in all radiance and health. She had hoped for the appearance of Valentine in Court. It had not occurred.

The judge had asked Mr. Hatt if he really proposed to bring in evidence that Captain Tietjens and Miss Wannop had enticed Mrs. Tietjens into a dark house — and on a shake of the head that Sylvia had not been able to refrain from giving Mr. Hatt, the judge had made some extremely rude remarks to her counsel. Mr. Hatt was at that time standing as parliamentary candidate for a Midland borough and was anxious to attract as much publicity as that or any other case would give him. He had, therefore, gone bald-headed for the judge, even accusing him of being indifferent to the sufferings he was causing to Mr. Hatt's fainting client. Rightly handled impertinence to a judge will gain quite a number of votes on the Radical side of Midland constituencies, judges being supposed to be all Tories.

Anyhow the case had been a fiasco and for the first time in her life Sylvia had felt mortification; in addition she had felt a great deal of religious fear. It had come into her mind in court — and it came with additional vividness there above that house, that, years ago in her mother's sitting-room in a place called Lobscheid, Father Consett had predicted that if Christopher fell in love with another woman, she, Sylvia, would perpetrate acts of vulgarity. And there she had been, not only toying with the temporal courts in a matter of marriage, which is a sacrament, but led undoubtedly into a position that she had to

262

acknowledge was vulgar. She had precipitately left the court when Mr. Hatt had for the second time appealed for pity for her — but she had not been able to stop him ... Pity! She appeal for pity! She had regarded herself as — she had certainly desired to be regarded as — the sword of the Lord smiting the craven and the traitor to Beauty! And was it to be supported that she was to be regarded as such a fool as to be decoyed into an empty house! Or as to let herself be thrown downstairs! ... But *qui facit per alium* is herself responsible and there she had been in a position as mortifying as would have been that of any city clerk's wife. The florid periods of Mr. Hatt had made her shiver all over and she had never spoken to him again.

And her position had been broadcasted all over England — and now, here in the mouth of this gross henchman it had recurred. At the most inconvenient moment. For the thought suddenly recurred, sweeping over with immense force: God had changed sides at the cutting down of Groby Great Tree.

The first intimation she had had that God might change sides had occurred in that hateful court and had, as it were, been prophesied by Father Consett. That dark saint and martyr was in Heaven, having died

263

for the Faith, and undoubtedly he had the ear of God. He had prophesied that she would toy with the temporal courts. Immediately she had felt herself degraded, as if strength had gone out from her.

Strength had undoubtedly gone out from her. Never before in her life had her mind not sprung to an emergency. It was all very well to say that she could not move physically either backwards or forwards for fear of causing a stampede amongst all those horses and that, therefore, her mental uncertainty might be excused. But it was the finger of God — or of Father Consett, who as saint and martyr, was the agent of God . . . Or, perhaps, God, Himself, was here really taking a hand for the protection of His Christopher, who was undoubtedly an Anglican saint . . . The Almighty might well be dissatisfied with the relatively amiable Catholic saint's conduct of the case in which the saint of the other persuasion was involved. For surely Father Consett might be expected to have a soft spot for her whereas you could not expect the Almighty to be unfair even to Anglicans . . . At any rate, up over the landscape, the hills, the sky, she felt the shadow of Father Consett, the arms extended as if in a gigantic cruciform — and then above and behind that an . . . an August Will!

Gunning, his bloodshot eyes fixed on her, moved his lips vindictively. She had, in face of those ghostly manifestations across hills and sky, a moment of real panic. Such as she had felt when they had been shelling near the hotel in France when she had sat amidst palms with Christopher under a glass roof . . . A mad desire to run — or as if your soul ran about inside you like a parcel of rats in a pit awaiting an unseen terrier.

What was she to do? What the devil was she to do? . . . She felt an itch . . . She felt the very devil of a desire to confront at least Mark Tietjens . . . even if it should kill the fellow. Surely God could not be unfair! What was she given beauty — the dangerous remains of beauty! — for if not to impress it on the unimpressible! She ought to be given the chance at least once more to try her irresistible ram against that immovable post . . . She was aware . . .

Gunning was saying something to the effect that if she caused Mrs. Valentine to have a miscarriage or an idiot child 'Is Lordship would flay all the flesh off 'er bones with 'is own ridin' crop. 'Is Lordship 'ad fair done it to 'im. Gunning 'isself, when 'e lef 'is missis then eight and a 'arf munce gone to live with old Mother Cressy! The child was bore dead.

The words conveyed little to her . . . She

was aware . . . She was aware . . . What was she aware of? She was aware that God — or perhaps it was Father Consett that so arranged it, more diplomatically, the dear! — desired that she should apply to Rome for the dissolution of her marriage with Christopher and that she should then apply to the civil courts. She thought that probably God desired that Christopher should be freed as early as possible, Father Consett suggesting to Him the less stringent course.

A fantastic object was descending at a fly-crawl the hill road that went almost vertically up to the farm amongst the beeches. She did not care!

Gunning was saying that that wer why 'Is Lordship giv 'im th' sack. Took away the cottage an ten bob a week that 'Is Lordship allowed to all as had been in his service thritty yeer.

She said: 'What! What's that?' Then it came back to her that Gunning had suggested that she might give Valentine a miscarriage . . .

Her breath made in her throat a little clittering sound like the trituration of barley ears; her gloved hands, reins and all were over her eyes, smelling of morocco leather; she felt as if within her a shelf dropped away — as the platform drops away from beneath the feet of a convict they are hanging. She said:

'Could . . . ' Then her mind stopped, the clittering sound in her throat continuing. Louder. Louder.

Descending the hill at the fly's pace was the impossible. A black basket-work pony phaeton, the pony — you always look at the horse first — four hands too big; as round as a barrel, as shining as a mahogany dining-table, pacing for all the world like a *haute école* circus steed and in a panic bumping its behind into that black vehicle. It eased her to see . . . But, . . . fantastically horrible, behind that grotesque coward of a horse, holding the reins, was a black thing, like a funeral charger; beside it a top hat, a white face, a buff waistcoat, black coat, a thin, Jewish beard. In front of that a bare, blond head, the hair rather long — on the front seat, back to the view. Trust Edith Ethel to be accompanied by a boy-poet cicisbeo! Training Mr. Ruggles for his future condition as consort!

She exclaimed to Gunning:

'By God, if you do not let me pass I will cut your face in half . . . '

It was justified! This in effect was too much — on the part of Gunning and God and Father Consett. All of a heap they had given her perplexity, immobility and a dreadful

thought that was gripping her vitals . . .
Dreadful! Dreadful!

She must get down to the cottage. She must get down to the cottage.

She said to Gunning:

'You damn fool . . . You *damn* fool . . . I want to save . . . '

He moved up — interminably — sweating and hairy from the gate on which he had been leaning, so that he no longer barred her way. She trotted smartly past him and cantered beautifully down the slope. It came to her from the bloodshot glance that his eyes gave her that he would like to outrage her with ferocity. She felt pleasure.

She came off her horse like a circus performer to the sound of 'Mrs. Tietjens! Mrs. Tietjens,' in several voices from above. She let the chestnut go to hell.

It seemed queer that it did not seem queer. A shed of log-parings set upright, the gate banging behind her. Apple branches spreading down; grass up to the middle of her grey breeches. It was Tom Tiddler's Grounds; it was near a place called Gemmenich on the Fourth of August 1914 . . . But just quietude: quietude.

Mark regarded her boy's outline with beady, inquisitive eyes. She bent her switch into a half loop before her. She heard herself say:

'Where are all these fools? I want to get them out of here!'

He continued to regard her, beadily, his head like mahogany against the pillows. An apple bough caught in her hair.

She said:

'Damn it all, *I* had Groby Great Tree torn down: not that tin Maintenon. But, as God is my Saviour I would not tear another woman's child in the womb!'

He said:

'You poor bitch! You poor bitch! The riding has done it!'

★   ★   ★

She swore to herself afterwards that she had heard him say that, for at the time she had had too many emotions to regard his speaking as unusual. She took indeed a prolonged turn in the woods before she felt equal to facing the others. Tietjens's had its woods onto which the garden gave directly.

Her main bitterness was that they had this peace. She was cutting the painter, but they were going on in this peace; her world was waning. It was the fact that her friend Bobbie's husband, Sir Gabriel Blantyre — formerly Bosenheir — was cutting down

269

expenses like a lunatic. In her world there was the writing on the wall. Here they could afford to call her a poor bitch — and be in the right of it, as like as not!

# 3

Valentine was awakened by the shrill overtones of the voice of the little maid coming in through the open window. She had fallen asleep over the words '*Saepe te in somnis vidi*!' to a vision of white limbs in the purple Adriatic. Eventually the child's voice said:

'We only sez 'mem' to friends of the family!' shrilly and self-assertively.

She was at the casement, dizzy and sickish with the change of position and the haste — and violently impatient of her condition. Of humanity she perceived only the top of a three-cornered grey hat and a grey panniered skirt in downward perspective. The sloping tiles of the potting-shed hid the little maid; aligned small lettuce plants like rosettes on the dark earth ran from under the window, closed by a wall of sticked peas, behind them the woods, slender grey ash trunks going to a great height. They were needed for shelter. They would have to change their bedroom; they could not have a night nursery that faced the north. The spring onions needed pricking out; she had meant to put the garden pellitory into the rocks in the half-circle, but the operation had daunted her. Pushing the little roots into crevices with her fingers; removing stones, trowelling in artificial manure, stooping, dirtying her fingers would make her retch . . .

She was suddenly intensely distressed at the thought of those coloured prints. She had searched the whole house — all imaginable drawers, cupboards, presses. It was like their fate that when they had at last got a good — an English — client their first commission from her should go wrong. She thought again of every imaginable, unsearched parallelogram in the house, standing erect, her head up, neglecting to look down on the intruder.

She considered all their customers to be intruders. It was true that Christopher's gifts lay in the way of old-furniture dealing — and farming. But farming was ruinous. Obviously if you sold old furniture straight out of use in your own house it fetched better prices than from a shop. She did not deny Christopher's ingenuity — or that he was right to rely on her hardihood. He had at least the right so to rely. Nor did she mean to let him down. Only . . .

She passionately desired little Chrissie to be born in that bed with the thin fine posts, his blond head with the thin, fine hair on those pillows. She passionately desired that he should lie with blue eyes gazing at those curtains on the low windows . . . *Those!* With those peacocks and globes. Surely a child should lie gazing at what his mother had seen whilst she was awaiting him!

And, where were those lost prints? . . . Four parallelograms of faint, silly colour. Promised for to-morrow morning. The margins needed breadcrumbing . . . She imagined her chin brushing gently, gently back and forward on the floss of his head; she imagined holding him in the air as, in that bed, she lay, her arms extended upwards, her hair spread on those pillows! Flowers perhaps spread on that quilt. Lavender!

But if Christopher reported that one of those dreadful people with querulous voices wanted a bedroom complete . . .

If she begged him to retain it for her! Well, he would. He prized her above money. She thought — ah, she knew — that he prized the child within her above the world.

Nevertheless she imagined that she would go all on to the end with her longings unvoiced . . . Because there was the game . . . His game . . . oh, hang it, *their* game! And you have to think whether it is worse for the unborn child to have a mother with unsatisfied longings or a father beaten at his

. . . No, you must not call it a game. Still, roosters beaten by other roosters lose their masculinity . . .  Like roosters, men . . . Then, for a child to have a father lacking masculinity . . . for the sake of some peacock and globe curtains, spindly bed-posts, old, old glass tumblers with thumb-mark indentations . . .

On the other hand, for the mother, the soft feeling that those things give! . . . The room had a barrel-shaped ceiling, following the lines of the roof almost up to the roof tree; dark oak beams, beeswaxed — ah, that beeswaxing! Tiny, low windows almost down to the oaken floor . . . You would say, too much of the show-place, but you lived into it. You lived yourself into it in spite of the Americans who took, sometimes embarrassed, peeps from the doorway.

Would they have to peek into the nursery? Oh, God, who knew? What would he decree? It was an extraordinary thing to live with Americans all over you, dropping down in aeroplanes, seeming to come up out of the earth . . . There, all of a sudden, you didn't know how . . .

That woman below the window was one, now. How in the world had she got below that window?  . . . But there were so many entrances — from the spinney, from the

274

Common, through the fourteen-acre, down from the road . . . You never knew who was coming. It was eerie; at times she shivered over it. You seemed to be beset — with stealthy people, creeping up all the paths . . .

Apparently the little tweeny was disputing the right of that American woman to call herself a friend of the family and thus to be addressed as: 'Mem!' The American was asserting her descent from Madame de Maintenon . . . It was astonishing the descents they all had! She herself was descended from the surgeon-butler to Henry VII — Henry the Somethingth. And of course from the great Professor Wannop, beloved of lady-educators and by ladies whom he had educated . . . And Christopher was eleventh Tietjens of Groby — with an eventual burgomaster of Scheveningen or somewhere in some century or other: time of Alva. Number one came over with Dutch William, the Protestant Hero! . . . If he had not come and if Professor Wannop had not educated her, Valentine Wannop — or educated her differently — she would not have . . . Ah, but she would! If there had not been any HE, looking like a great Dutch *treckschluyt* or whatever you call it — she would have had to invent one to live with in open sin. But her father might have educated her so as to have

275

— at least presentable underclothes . . .

He could have educated her so as to be able to say — oh, but tactfully:

'Look here, you . . . Examine my . . . my *cache-corsets* . . . . Wouldn't some new ones be better than a new pedigree sow? . . . '

The fellow never had looked at her . . . *cache-corsets*. Marie Léonie had!

Marie Léonie was of opinion that she would lose Christopher if she did not deluge herself with a perfume called Houbigant and wear pink silk next the skin. Elle ne demandait pas mieux — but she could not borrow twenty pounds from Marie Léonie. Nor yet forty . . . Because although Christopher might never notice the condition of her all-wools he jolly well would be struck by the ocean of Houbigant and the surf of pink . . . She would give the world for them . . . But he would notice — and then she might lose his love, because she had borrowed the forty pounds. On the other hand she might lose it because of the all-wools. And heaven knew what condition the other pair would be in when they came back from Mrs. Cramp's newest laundry attentions . . . You could never teach Mrs. Cramp that wool must not be put into boiling water!

Oh God, she ought to lie between

lavendered linen sheets with little Chrissie on soft, pink silk, air-cushionish bosoms! . . . Little Chrissie, descended from surgeon-butler — surgeon-barber, to be correct! — and burgomaster. Not to mention the world-famous Professor Wannop . . . Who was to become . . . who was to become, if it was as she wished it . . .

But she did not know what she wished because she did not know what was to become of England or the world . . . But if he became what Christopher wished he would be a contemplative parson farming his own tythe-fields and with a Greek testament in folio under his arm . . . A sort of White of Selborne . . . Selborne was only thirty miles away, but they had never had the time to go there . . . As who should say: *Je n'ai jamais vu Carcassonne* . . . . For if they had never found time, because of pigs, hens, pea-sticking, sales, sellings, mending all-wool undergarments, sitting with dear Mark — before Chrissie came with the floss silk on his palpitating soft poll and his spinning pebble-blue eyes; if they had never found time now, before, how in the world would there be time when, added on to all the other, there should be the bottles, and the bandagings and the bathing before the fire with the warm, warm water and feeling the slubbing of the soap-saturated flannel on the adorable, adorable limbs? And Christopher looking on ... He would never find time to go to Selborne, nor Arundel, nor Carcassonne nor after the Strange Woman ... Never. Never!

He had been away now for a day and a half. But it was known between them — without speaking! — that he would never be away for a day and a half again. Now, before her pains began he could ... seize the opportunity! Well, he had seized it with a vengeance ... A day and a half! To go to Wilbraham sale! With nothing much that they wanted ... She believed ... she believed that he had gone to Groby in an aeroplane ... He had once mentioned that. Or she knew that he had thought of it. Because the day before yesterday when he had been almost out of his mind about the letting of Groby he had suddenly looked up at an aeroplane and had remained looking at it for long, silent ... Another woman it could not be.

He had forgotten about those prints. That was dreadful. She knew that he had forgotten about them. How could he, when they wanted to get a good, English client, for the sake of little Chrissie? How could he? How could he? It is true that he was almost out of his mind about Groby and Groby Great Tree. He had begun to talk about that in his sleep as for years, at times, he had talked, dreadfully, about the war.

'*Bringt dem Hauptmann eine Kerze* . . . . Bring the Major a candle,' he would shout dreadfully beside her in the blackness. And she would know that he was remembering the sound of picks in the earth beneath the trenches. And he would groan and sweat dreadfully and she would not dare to wake him . . . And there had been the matter of the boy, Aranjuez' eye. It appeared that he had run away over a shifting landscape, screaming and holding his hand to his eye. After Christopher had carried him out of a hole . . . Mrs. Aranjuez had been rude to her at the Armistice night dinner . . . The first time in her life that anyone — except of course Edith Ethel — had ever been rude to her. Of course you did not count Edith Ethel Duchemin, Lady Macmaster! . . . But it's queer. Your man saves the life of a boy at the desperate risk of his own. Without that there would not have been any Mrs. Aranjuez; then Mrs. Aranjuez is the first person that ever in your life is rude to you. Leaving permanent memories that made you shudder in the night! Hideous eyes!

Yet, but for a miracle there might have

been no Christopher! Little Aranjuez — it had been because he had talked to her for so long, praising Christopher, that Mrs. Aranjuez had been rude to her! — little Aranjuez had said that the German bullets had gone over them as thick as the swarm of bees that came out when Gunning cut the leg off the skep with his scythe! . . . Well, there might have been no Christopher. Then there would have been no Valentine Wannop! She could not have lived . . . But Mrs. Aranjuez should not have been rude to her. The woman must have seen with half an eye that Valentine Wannop could not live without Christopher . . . Then, why should she fear for her little, imploring, eyeless soldier boy!

It was queer. You would almost say that there was a Provvy who delighted to torment you with: 'If it hadn't been that . . .' Christopher probably believed that there was a Provvy or he would not dream for his little Chrissie a country parsonage . . . He proposed, if they ever made any money, to buy a living for him — if possible near Salisbury . . . What was the name of the place . . . a pretty name? . . . Buy a living where George Herbert had been parson . . .

She must, bye the bye, remember to tell Marie Léonie that it was the Black Orpington labelled 42, not the Red 16 that she had put the setting of Indian Runners under. She had found that Red 16 was not really broody, though she had come on afterwards. It was queer that Marie Léonie had not the courage to put eggs under broody hens because they pecked her whereas she, Valentine, had no courage to take the chickens when the settings hatched, because of the shells and gumminesses that might be in the nests . . . Yet neither of them wanted courage . . . Hang it all, neither of them wanted courage or they would not be living with Tietjens's. It was like being tied to buffaloes!

And yet . . . How you wanted them to change!

Bremersyde . . . No that was the home of the Haigs . . . Tide what will and tide what tide, there shall be Haigs at Bremersyde . . . . Perhaps it was Bemersyde! . . . Bemerton, then. George Herbert, rector of Bemerton, near Wilton, Salisbury . . . That was what Chrissie was to be like . . . She was to imagine herself sitting with her cheek on Chrissie's floss-silk head, looking into the fire and seeing in the coals, Chrissie, walking under elms beside plough-lands. *Elle ne demandait*, really, *pas mieux*!

If the country would stand it! . . .

Christopher presumably believed in England as he believed in Provvy

— because the land was pleasant and green and comely. It would breed true. In spite of showers of Americans descended from Tiglath Pileser and Queen Elizabeth and the end of the industrial system and the statistics of the shipping trade, England with its pleasant, green comeliness would go on breeding George Herberts with Gunnings to look after them . . . Of course with Gunnings!

The Gunnings of the land were the rocks on which the lighthouse was built — as Christopher saw it. And Christopher was always right. Sometimes a little previous. But always right. Always right. The rocks had been there a million years before the lighthouse was built, the lighthouse made a deuce of a movable flashing — but it was a mere butterfly. The rocks would be there a million years after the light went for the last time out.

Gunnings had been in the course of years, painted blue, a Druid-worshipper, later, a Duke Robert of Normandy, illiterately burning towns and begetting bastards — and eventually — actually at the moment — a man of all works, half-full of fidelity, half blatant, hairy. A retainer you would retain as long as you were prosperous and dispensed hard cider and overlooked his blear-eyed peccadilloes with women. He would go on . . .

The point was whether the time had come for another Herbert of Bemerton. Christopher thought it had; he was always right, always right. But previous. He had predicted the swarms of Americans buying up old things. Offering fabulous prices. He was right. The trouble was they did not pay when they offered the fabulous prices: when they did pay they were as mean as . . . she was going to say Job. But she did not know that Job was particularly mean. That lady down below the window would probably want to buy the signed cabinet of Barker of 1762 for half the price of one bought in a New York department store and manufactured yesterday . . . And she would tell Valentine she was a bloodsucker — even if — to suppose the ridiculous! — Valentine let her have it at her own price. On the other hand Mr. Schatzweiler talked of fantastic prices . . .

Oh, Mr. Schatzweiler, Mr. Schatzweiler, if you would only pay us ten per cent. of what you owe us I could have all the pink fluffies, and three new gowns and keep the little old lace for Chrissie — and have a proper dairy, and not milk goats. And cut the losses over the confounded pigs and put up a range of glass in the sunk garden where it would not be an eye-sore . . . As it was, the age of fairy-tales was not, of course, past. They had had windfalls, lovely windfalls when infinite ease had seemed to stretch out before them . . . A great windfall when they had bought this place; little ones for the pigs and old mare . . . Christopher was that sort of fellow; he had sowed so many golden grains that he could not be always reaping whirlwinds. There must be some halcyon days . . .

Only it was deucedly awkward now — with Chrissie coming and Marie Léonie hinting all day that, as she was losing her figure, if she could not get the grease stains out of her skirt she would lose the affections of Christopher. And they had not got a stiver . . . Christopher had cabled Schatzweiler. But what was the use of that? . . . Schatzweiler would be finely dished if she lost the affections of Christopher — because poor old Chris could not run any old junk shop without her! . . . She imagined cabling Schatzweiler — about the four stains on the skirt and the necessity for elegant lying-in gowns. Or else he would lose Christopher's assistance . . .

The conversation down below raised its tones. She heard the tweeny maid ask why, if the American lady was a friend of the family, she did not know 'Er Ladyship theere? . . . Of

284

course it was easy to understand: these people came, all of them, with letters of introduction from Schatzweiler. Then they insisted that they were friends of the family. It was perhaps nice of them — because most English people would not want to know old-furniture dealers.

The lady below exclaimed in a high voice: 'That Lady Mark Tietjens! That! Mercy me, I thought it was the cook!'

She, Valentine, ought to go down and help Marie Léonie. But she was not going to. She had the sense that hostile presences were creeping up the paths and Marie Léonie had given her the afternoon off . . . For the sake of the future, Marie Léonie had said. And *she* had said that she had once expected her own future to offer the reading of Æschylus beside the Ægean sea. Then Marie Léonie had kissed her and said she knew that she, Valentine would never rob her of her belongings after Mark died!

An unsolicited testimonial, that; but of course Marie Léonie would desire her not to lose the affections of Christopher: Marie Léonie would say to herself that in that case Christopher might take up with a woman who *would* want to rob Marie Léonie of her possessions after Mark died.

The woman down below announced

herself as Mrs. de Bray Pape, descendant of the Maintenon, and wanted to know if Marie Léonie did not think it reasonable to cut down a tree that overhung your house. Valentine desired to spring to the window: she sprang to the old panelled door and furiously turned the key in the lock. She ought not to have turned the key so carelessly; it had a knack of needing five or ten minutes' manipulation before you could unlock the door again . . . She ought to have sprung to the window and cried out to Mrs. de Bray Pape:

'If you so much as touch a leaf of Groby Great Tree we will serve you with injunctions that it will take half your life and money to deal with!'

She ought to have done that to save Christopher's reason. But she could not, she could not! It was one thing living with all the tranquillity of conscience in the world in open sin. It was another, confronting elderly Americans who knew the fact. She was determined to remain shut in there. An Englishman's house may no longer be his castle — but an Englishwoman's castle is certainly her own bedroom. When once, four months or so ago, the existence of little Chrissie being manifest, she had expressed to Christopher the idea that they ought no

286

longer to go stodging along in penury, the case being so grave; they ought to take some of the Groby money — for the sake of future generations . . .

Well, she had been run down . . . At that stage of parturition, call it, a woman is run down and hysterical . . . It had seemed to her overwhelmingly the fact that a breeding woman ought to have pink fluffy things next her quivering skin and sprayings of, say, Houbigant all over her shoulders and hair. For the sake of the child's health.

So she had let out violently at poor wretched old Chris who was faced with the necessity for denying his gods and she had slammed to and furiously locked that door. Her castle had been her bedroom with a vengeance then — for Christopher had been unable to get in or she to get out. He had had to whisper through the keyhole that he gave in; he was dreadfully concerned for her. He had said that he hoped she would try to stick it a little longer, but, if she would not, he would take Mark's money.

Naturally she had not let him — but she *had* arranged with Marie Léonie for Mark to pay a couple of pounds more a week for their board and lodging and as Marie Léonie had perforce taken over the housekeeping they had found things easing off a little. Marie

287

Léonie had run the house for thirty shillings a week less than she, Valentine, had ever been able to do — and run it streets better. Streets and streets! So they had had money at least nearly to complete their equipments of table linen and the layette . . . The long and complicated annals!

It was queer that her heart was nearly as much in Christopher's game as was his own. As house-mother she ought to have grabbed after the last penny — and goodness knew the life was strain enough. Why do women back their men in unreasonable romanticisms? You might say that it was because if their men had their masculinities abated — like defeated roosters! — the women would suffer in intimacies . . . Ah, but it wasn't that! Nor was it merely that they wanted the buffaloes to which they were attached to charge.

It was really that she had followed the convolutions of her man's mind. And ardently approved. She disapproved with him of riches, of the rich, of the frame of mind that riches confers. If the war had done nothing else for them — for those two of them — it had induced them at least to instal Frugality as a deity. They desired to live hard even if it deprived them of the leisure in which to think high! She agreed with him that if a ruling class loses the capacity to rule — or the desire! — it should abdicate from its privileges and get underground.

And having accepted that as a principle, she could follow the rest of his cloudy obsessions and obstinacies.

Perhaps she would not have backed him up in his long struggle with dear Mark if she had not considered that their main necessity was to live high . . . And she was aware that why, really, she had sprung to the door rather than to the window, had been that she had not desired to make an unfair move in that long chess game; on behalf of Christopher. If she had had to see Mrs. de Bray Pape or to speak to her it would have been disagreeable to have that descendant of a king's companion look at her with the accusing eyes of one who thinks: 'You live with a man without being married to him!' Mrs. de Bray Pape's ancestress had been able to force the king to marry her . . . But that she would have chanced: they had paid penalty enough for having broken the rules of the Club. She could carry her head high: not obtrusively high, but sufficiently! For, in effect they had surrendered Groby in order to live together and she had endured sprays of obloquy that seemed never to cease to splash over the garden hedges . . . in order to keep Christopher alive and sane!

No, she would have faced Mrs. de Bray Pape. But she would hardly, given Christopher's half-crazed condition, have kept herself from threatening Mrs. Pape with dreadful legal consequences if she touched Groby Great Tree. That would not have been jonnock. That would have been to interfere in the silent Northern struggle between the brothers. That she would never do, even to save Christopher's reason — unless she were jumped into it! . . . That Mark did not intend to interfere between Mrs. Pape and the tree she knew — for when she had read Mrs. Pape's letter to him he had signified as much to her by means of his eyes . . . Mark she loved and respected because he was a dear — and because he had backed her through thick and thin. Without him . . . There had been a moment on that dreadful night . . . She prayed God that she would not have to think again of that dreadful night . . . If she had to see Sylvia again she would go mad, and the child within her . . . Deep, deep within her the blight would fall on the little thread of brain!

Mrs. de Bray Pape, God be thanked, provided diversion for her mind. She was speaking French with an eccentricity that could not be ignored.

Valentine could see, without looking out of

the window, Marie Léonie's blank face and the equal blankness with which she must have indicated that she did not intend to understand. She imagined her standing, motionless, pinafored and unmerciful before the other lady who beneath the three-cornered hat was stuttering out:

'Lady Tietjens, mwaw Madam de Bray Pape desire coo-pay la arbre . . . '

Valentine could hear Marie Léonie's steely tones saying:

'On dit 'l'arbre,' Madame!'

And then the high voice of the little maid:

'Called us 'the pore' she did, your ladyship . . . Ast us why we could not take example!'

Then a voice, soft for these people, and with modulations:

'Sir Mark seems to be perspiring a great deal. I was so free as to wipe . . . '

Whilst, above, Valentine said: 'Oh Heaven!' Marie Léonie cried out: 'Mon Dieu!' and there was a rush of skirts and pinafore.

Marie Léonie was rushing past a white, breeched figure, saying:

'Vous, une étrangère, avez osé . . . '

A shining, red-cheeked boy was stumbling slightly from before her. He said, after her back:

'Mrs. Lowther's handkerchief is the smallest, softest . . . ' He added to the young woman in white: 'We'd better go away . . . Please let's go away . . . It's not sporting . . . ' A singularly familiar face; a singularly moving voice.

'For God's sake let us go away . . . '

Who said 'For God's sake!' like that — with staring blue eyes?

She was at the door frantically trying to twist the great iron key; the lock was of very old hammered iron work. The doctor ought to be telephoned to. He had said that if Mark had fever or profuse sweats he should be telephoned to at once. Marie Léonie would be with him; it was her, Valentine's, duty to telephone. The key would not turn; she hurt her hand in the effort. But part of her emotion was due to that bright-cheeked boy. Why should he have said that it was not sporting of them to be there? Why had he exclaimed for God's sake to go away? The key would not turn. It stayed solid, like a piece of the old lock . . . Who was the boy like? She rammed her shoulder against the unyielding door. She must not do that. She cried out.

From the window — she had gone to the window intending to tell the girl to set up a ladder for her, but it would be more sensible to tell her to telephone! — she could see Mrs. de Bray Pape. That lady was still haranguing the girl. And then on the path, beyond the lettuces and the newly sticked peas, arose a very tall figure. A very tall, thin, figure. Portentous. By some trick of the slope, figures there always appeared very tall . . . The figure appeared leisurely: almost hesitant. Like the apparition of the statue of the Commander in Don Juan, somehow. It appeared to be preoccupied with its glove: undoing its glove . . .

Very tall, but with too much slightness of the legs . . . A woman in hunting-breeches! Grey against the tall ash-stems of the spinney. You could not see her face because you were above her, in the window, and her head was bent down! In the name of God! . . .

There wafted over her a sense of the dreadful darkness in the old house at Grays Inn on that dreadful night . . . She must not think of that dreadful night because of little Chrissie deep within her. She felt as if she held the child covered in her arms, as if she were looking upwards, bending down over the child. Actually she was looking downwards . . . Then she had been looking upwards — up the dark stairs. At a marble statue, the white figure of a woman, the Nike . . . the Winged Victory. It is like that on the stairs of the Louvre. She must think of the Louvre, not Grays Inn. They were, in a Pompeian ante-room, Etruscan tombs, with guardians in uniform, their hands behind their backs. Strolling about as if they expected you to steal a tomb . . .

She had — they had — been staring up the stairs. The house had seemed unnaturally silent when they had entered. Unnaturally . . . How can you seem more silent than silent. But you *can*! They had seemed to tiptoe. She had, at least. Then light had shone above — coming from an opened door, above. In the light had been the white figure that had said it had cancer!

She must not think about these things!

Such rage and despair had swept over her as she had never before known. She cried to Christopher, dark, beside her, that the woman lied. She had not got cancer . . .

She must not think about these things.

The woman on the path — in grey riding-clothes — approached slowly. The head still bent down. Undoubtedly she had silk underthings beneath all that grey cloth . . . Well, *they* — Christopher and Valentine — gave her them.

It was queer how calm she was. That of course was Sylvia Tietjens. Let it be. She had fought for her man before and so she could again; the Russians should not have . . . The old jingle ran in her calm head . . .

But she was also desperately perturbed:

trembling at the thought of that dreadful night! Christopher had wanted to go with Sylvia after she had fallen downstairs. A good theatre fall, but not good enough. But she, Valentine, had shouted: No! He was never going with Sylvia again. *Finis Sylviae et magna* . . . . In the black night . . . Maroons had gone on firing. They could hear!

Well, she was calm. The sight of that figure was not going to hurt the tiny brain that worked deep within her womb. Nor the tiny limbs! She was going to slub the warm, soap-transfused flannel onto those little legs in the warm of the great hearth . . . Nine hams up that chimney! Chrissie looking up and laughing . . . That woman would never again do that! Not to a child of Christopher's. Not to any man's child, belike!

That had been Sylvia Tietjens' son! With a girl in white breeches! . . . Well, who was she to prevent a son's seeing his father? She felt on her arm the weight of her own son. With that there she could confront the world!

It was queer! That woman's face was all blurred . . . Blubberingly! The features swollen, the eyes red! . . . Ah, she had been thinking, looking at the garden and the stillness: 'If I had given Christopher that I should have kept him!' But she would never have kept him. Had she been the one woman in all the world he would never have looked at her. Not after he had seen her. Valentine Wannop!

Sylvia had looked up, contemplatively — as if into the very window. But she could not see into the window. She must have seen Mrs. de Bray Pape and the girl for it became apparent why she had taken off her glove. She now had a gold vanity box in her hand: looking in at the mirror and moving her right hand swiftly before her face . . . Remember: it was *we* who gave her that gold thing. Remember! Remember it hard!

Sudden anger came over her. That woman must never come into their house-place before whose hearth she was to bathe the little Chrissie! Never! Never! The place would be polluted. She knew, only by that, now she loathed and recoiled from that woman.

She was at the lock. The key turned . . . See what emotion at the thought of harm to your unborn child can do for you! Subconsciously her right hand had remembered how you pressed the key upwards when you made it turn . . . She must not run down the narrow stairs. The telephone was in a niche on the inner side of the great ingle. The room was dim: very long, very low. The Barker cabinet looked very rich with its green, yellow, and scarlet inlays. She was leaning sideways in the nook between the immense fireplace and the room wall, the telephone receiver at her ear. She looked down her long room — it opened into the dining-room, a great beam between. It was dark, gleaming, rich with old bees-waxed woods . . . Elle ne demandait pas mieux . . . the phrase of Marie Léonie occurred constantly to her mind . . . She did not ask better — if only the things were to be regarded as theirs! She looked into the distant future when things would spread out tranquilly before them. They would have a little money, a little peace. Things would spread out . . . like a plain seen from a hill. In the meantime they had to keep all on going . . . She did not in effect grumble at that . . . as long as strength and health held out.

The doctor — she pictured him, long, sandy and very pleasant, suffering too from an incurable disease and debts, life being like that! — the doctor asked cheerfully on the telephone how Mark was. She said she did not know. He was said to have been profusely sweating . . . Yes, it was possible that he might have been having a disagreeable interview. The doctor said:

'Tut! Tut! And yourself?' He had a Scotch accent, the sandy man . . . She suggested that he might bring along a bromide. He said: 'They've been bothering you. Don't let them!' She said she had been asleep — but they probably would. She added: 'Perhaps you would come quickly!' . . . Sister Anne! Sister Anne! For God's sake Sister Anne! If she could get a bromide into her it would pass like a dream.

It was passing like a dream. Perhaps the Virgin Mary exists . . . If she does not, we must invent her to look after mothers who can not . . . But she could! She, Valentine Wannop!

The light from the doorway that was open onto the garden was obscured. A highwayman in skirts with panniers stood in the room against the light. It said:

'You're the saleswoman, I guess. This is a most insanitary place and I hear you have no bath. Show me some things. In the Louie Kaators style.' It guessed that it was going to re-furnish Groby in Louie Kaators style. Did she, Valentine, as saleswoman suppose that They — her employers — would meet her in the expense. Mr. Pape had had serious losses in Miami. They must not suppose that the Papes could be bled white. This place ought to be pulled down as unfit for human habitation and a model workman's cottage built in its place. People who sold things to rich Americans in this country were sharks. She herself was descended spiritually from

Madame de Maintenon. It would be all different if Marie Antoinette had treated the Maintenon better, She, Mrs. de Bray Pape, would have the authority in the country that she ought to have. She had been told that she would be made to pay an immense sum for having cut down Groby Great Tree. Of course the side wall of the house had fallen in. These old houses could not stand up to modern inventions. She, Mrs. de Bray Pape, had employed the latest Australian form of tree-stump extractor — the Wee Whizz Bang . . . But did she, as saleswoman, doubtless more intimate with her employers than was necessary, considering the reputation of that establishment . . . did she consider . . .

Valentine's heart started. The light from the doorway was again obscured. Marie Léonie ran panting in. Sister Anne, in effect! She said: 'Le telephone! Vite!'

Valentine said:

'J'ai déjà telephoné . . . Le docteur sera ici dans quelques minutes . . . Je te prie de rester à côté de moi!' . . . 'I beg you to remain beside me!' Selfish! Selfish! But there was a child to be born . . . Anyhow Marie Léonie could not have got out of that door. It was blocked . . . Ah! . . .

Sylvia was looking down on Valentine. You could hardly see her face against the light . . .

Well, it did not amount to more than that . . .
She was looking down because she was so
tall; you could not see her face against the
light. Mrs. de Bray Pape was explaining what
spiritual descent from *grands seigneurs* did
for you . . .

Sylvia was bending her eyes on Valentine.
That was the phrase. She said to Mrs. de
Bray Pape:

'For God's sake hold your *damned* tongue.
Get out of here!'

Mrs. de Bray Pape had not understood.
For the matter of that neither did Valentine
take it in. A thin voice from a distance
thrilled:

'Mother! . . . Mo . . . ther!'

She — IT — for it was more like a statue
than a human being . . . Marvellous how she
had made her face up . . . Three minutes
before it had been all . . . be-blubbered! It
was flawless now — Dark-shadowed under
the eyes. And sorrowful. And tremendously
dignified. And *kind*! Damn! Damn! Damn!

It occurred to Valentine that this was only
the second time that she had seen that face.

Its stillness now was terrible!

What was she waiting for before she began
upon the Billingsgate they would both have to
use before they parted? For she, Valentine,
had her back against the wall. She heard

300

herself begin to say:

'You have spoilt . . . '

She could not continue. You cannot very well tell a person that their loathsomeness is so infectious as to spoil your baby's bathing place. It is not done!

Marie Léonie said in French to Mrs. de Bray Pape that Madame Tietjens did not require her presence. Mrs. de Bray Pape did not understand. It is difficult for a Maintenon to understand that her presence is not required.

The first time that she, Valentine, had seen that face — in Edith Ethel's drawing room, she had thought how kind — how blindingly kind it was. Those lips had approached her mother's cheeks and the tears had been in Valentine's eyes. It had said — that face of a statue — that it must kiss Mrs. Wannop for her kindness to Christopher. Damn it all, she might as well kiss her, Valentine now. But for her there would have been no Christopher.

*You must not say Damn it all. The war is over . . . Ah, but its backwashes, when would they be over?*

It said — that woman's voice was so perfectly expressionless that you could continue appropriately to call it 'it' — it said coldly to Mrs. de Bray Pape:

'You hear! The lady of the house does not

301

require your presence. Please go away.'

Mrs. de Bray Pape had been explaining that she intended refurnishing Groby in the Louis Quatorze style.

It occurred to Valentine that this position had its comicalities. Mrs. de Bray Pape did not know her, Valentine. Marie Léonie did not know who that figure was.

They could miss a good deal of the jam ... Jam to-morrow, jam yesterday ... Where was the jam? ... That figure had said 'The lady of the house.' Delicately. *Quelle delicatesse!*

But she did not appear denunciatory. She dropped sideways: pensive. Puzzled. As if at the ways of God. As if stricken by God and puzzled at his ways ... Well, she might be.

She caught at the telephone shelf. The child had moved within her. It wanted her to be called Mrs. Tietjens in its own house. This woman stood in the way. She could not give a father's name to the little thing. So he protested within her. Dark it was growing. Hold up there.

Someone was calling: 'Valentine!'

A boy's voice called:

'Mother! Mother!'

A soft voice said:

'Mrs. Tietjens!'

What things to say in her child's hearing!

302

. . . Mother! Mother! . . . Her mother was in Pontresina, complete with secretary in black alpaca . . . The Italian Alps!

Dark! . . . Marie Léonie said in her ear: 'Tiens toi debout, ma chérie!'

Dark, dark night; cold, cold snow — Harsh, Harsh, wind and lo! — Where shall we shepherds go, God's son to find?

Edith Ethel was reading from a letter to Mrs. de Bray Pape. She said: 'As an American of culture you will be interested . . . From the great poet!' . . . A gentleman held a top-hat in front of his face, as if he were in church. Thin, with dull eyes and a Jewish beard! Jews keep their hats on in church . . .

Apparently she, Valentine Wannop, was going to be denounced before the congregation! Did they bring a scarlet letter? . . . They were Puritans enough, she and Christopher. The voice of the man with the Jewish beard — Sylvia Tietjens had removed the letter from the fingers of Edith Ethel . . . Not much changed Edith Ethel! Face a *little* lined. And pale. And suddenly reduced to silence — the voice of the man with the beard said:

'After all! It does make a difference. He is virtually Tietjens of . . . ' He began to push his way backwards, outwards. A man trying to leave through the crowd at the church door.

303

He said to Valentine oddly interrogative:

'Mrs . . . eh Tietjens!' And then: 'Par*don*!' Attempting a French accent!

Edith Ethel remarked:

' wanted to say to Valentine: if I effect the sale personally I do not see that any commissions should be payable.'

Sylvia Tietjens said they could discuss that outside. Valentine was aware that, some time before a boy's voice had said: 'Mother, is this sporting?' It occurred to Valentine to wonder if it was sporting of people to call her 'Mrs. Tietjens' under Sylvia Tietjens' nose. Of course she had to be Mrs. Tietjens before the servants. She heard herself say:

'I am sorry Mr. Ruggles called me Mrs. Tietjens before you!'

The eyes of the statue were if possible doubly bent on her!

The bitter answer came to her as if from stiff lips:

'An the King will have my head I carena what he may do with my . . . '

It affected Valentine disagreeably — with a pang of jealousy. What it amounted to was that Sylvia said: 'You have my man, so you may as well have his name.' But by using a saying that Christopher used habitually — and that Mark had used habitually when he could speak — by using then a

304

Tietjens-family saying she asserted that she too had belonged to the Tietjens family, and, before Valentine, had been intimate with their sayings to the point of saturation.

That statue went on speaking.

It said:

'I wanted to get those people out . . . And to see . . . ' It spoke very slowly. Marmoreally. The flowers in the jug on the fald-stool needed more water. Marigolds. Orange . . . A woman is upset when her child moves within her. Sometimes more, sometimes less. She must have been very upset: there had been a lot of people in the room; she knew neither how they had come nor how they had gone. She said to Marie Léonie:

'Dr. Span is bringing some bromide . . . I can't find those . . . '

Marie Léonie was looking at that figure; her eyes stuck out of her head like Christopher's. She said, as still as a cat watching a mouse:

'Qui este elle? C'est bien la femme?'

It looked queerly like a pilgrim in a ballet, now, that figure against the light — the long legs slightly bent gave that effect. Actually this was the third time she had seen it — but in the dark house she had not really seen the face . . . The features had been contorted and thus not the real features: these were the real features. There was about that figure something timid. And noble. It said:

'Sporting! Michael said: 'Be sporting, mother!' . . . But sporting . . . ' It raised its hand as if to shake a fist at heaven. The hand struck the beam across the ceiling; that roof was so low. And dear! It said:

'It was Father Consett really . . . They can all, soon, call you Mrs. Tietjens. Before God, I came to drive those people out . . . But I wanted to see how it was you kept him . . . '

Sylvia Tietjens was keeping her head turned aside, drooping. Hiding a tendency to tears, no doubt. She said to the floor:

'I say again, as God hears me, I never thought to harm your child. His child . . . But any woman's . . . Not harm a child . . . I have a fine one, but I wanted another . . . with its littleness . . . It's the riding has done it . . . ' Someone sobbed!

She looked loweringly then at Valentine:

'It's Father Consett in heaven that has done this. Saint and martyr, desiring soft things! I can almost see his shadow across these walls now it's growing dark. You hung him: you did not even shoot him though I say you shot him to save my feelings . . . And it's you who will be going on through all the years . . . '

She bit into a small handkerchief that she

had in her hand, concealed. She said:

'Damn it, I'm playing pimp to Tietjens of Groby — leaving my husband to you! . . . '

Someone again sobbed.

It occurred to Valentine that Christopher had left those prints at old Hunt's sale in a jar on the field. They had not wanted the jar. Then Christopher had told a dealer called Hudnut that he could have that jar and some others against a little carting service . . . He would be tired, when he got back, Christopher. But he would have to go to Hudnut's, Gunning could not be trusted. They must not disappoint Lady Robinson . . .

Marie Léonie said:

'C'est lamentable qu'un seul homme puisse inspirer deux passions pareilles dans deux femmes . . . C'est le martyre de notre vie!'

Yes, it was lamentable that a man could inspire two such passions in two women. Marie Léonie went to look after Mark. Sylvia Tietjens was gone. They say joy never kills. She fell straight down onto the floor Lumpishly . . . It was lucky they had the Bussorah rug otherwise Chrissie . . . They had no money . . . Poor . . . poor . . .

# 4

Mark Tietjens had lain considering the satisfaction of a great night he had lately passed. Or perhaps not lately; at some time.

Lying out there in the black nights the sky seemed enormous. You could understand how somewhere heaven could be concealed in it. And tranquil at times. Then you felt the earth wheeling through infinity.

Night birds cried overhead: herons, ducks, swans even; the owls kept closer to the ground, beating along the hedgerows. Beasts became busy in the long grass. They rustled busily, then paused for long. No doubt a rabbit ran till it found an attractive plantain. Then it nibbled for a long time without audible movement. Now and then cattle lowed, or many lambs — frightened by a fox maybe . . .

But there would nevertheless be long silences . . . A stoat would get onto the track of the rabbit. They would run, run, run brushing through the long grass, then out into the short meadow and round and round, the rabbit squealing. Loudly at first.

In the dim illumination of his night-light

dormice would climb up the posts of his shelter. They would remain regarding him with beads of eyes. When the rabbits squealed they would hunch themselves together and shiver. They knew it meant S . . t . . o . . at — stoat! Their turn soon!

He despised himself a little for attending to these minutiae — as if one were talking down to a child . . . On his great night the whole cattle of the county had been struck with panic; you heard them crashing down through the hedges and miles down into the silent valleys.

No! He had never been one to waste his time and mind on small mammals and small birds . . . The Flora and Fauna of Blankshire! . . . Not for him. It was big movements interested him: 'wherein manifesteth itself the voice of God!' . . . Very likely that was true. Transport! Panic in cattle over whole counties. In people, over whole continents!

Once years — oh, years and years ago, when he had been aged twelve and on a visit to Grandfather he had taken a gun to Redcar Sands from Groby, over the moors, and with one shot he had brought down two terns, a sandpiper, and a herring gull. Grandfather had been so delighted with his prowess — though naturally the shot had been a fluke — that he had the things stuffed and there they were in Groby Nursery to this day. The herring gull stiff on a mossy rock; the sandpiper doing obeisance before it, the terns flying, one on each side. Probably that was the only memorial to him, Mark Tietjens, at Groby. The younger children had been wont to refer with awe to 'Mark's bag,' for long years afterwards. The painted background had been Bamborough Castle with lashings of foam and blue sky. It was a far cry from Redcar to Bamborough — but that was the only background the bird-stuffing chap in Middlesboro could paint for sea-birds. For larks and the like he had a cornfield in the Vale of York; for nightingales, poplar trees . . . Never heard that nightingales were particularly partial to poplars!

. . . Nightingales disturbed the majesty of great nights; for two months out of the year, more or less, according to the nature of the season. He wasn't decrying the beauty of their voices. Hearing them you felt like seeing a good horse win the St. Leger. No other things in the world could do it — just as there was no place in the world like Newmarket Heath on a breezy day . . . But they limited the night. It was true that nightingales deep down in the spinney near where Gunning's hut must be — say a quarter of a mile away — could make you think of great distance, echoing up through the deep woods. Woods dripping with dew beneath the moon . . . And air-raids not so long ago! The moon brought air-raids and its shining was discouraged . . . Yes, nightingales made you think of distance just as the night-jar for ever crepitating from twilight to dawn seemed to measure a fragment of eternity . . . But only fragments! The great night was itself eternity and the Infinite . . . The spirit of God walking on the firmament.

Cruel beggars, nightingales: they abused one another with distended throats all through the nights. Between the gusts of gales you could hear them shouting on — telling their sitting-hens that they — each one — were the devils of fellows, the other chap, down the hill by Gunning's hut, being a bedraggled, louse-eaten, braggart . . . Sex ferocity!

Gunning lived in a bottom, in a squatter's cottage, they said. With a thatch like Robinson Crusoe's bonnet. A wise-woman's cottage. He lived with the wise-woman, a chalk-white-faced slattern . . . And a grand-daughter of the wise-woman whom, because she had a cleft palate and only half a brain the parish, half out of commiseration, half for economy, had nominated mistress in the school up the hill. No one knew whether

Gunning slept with the wise-woman or the grand-daughter; for one or the other he had left his missus and Fittleworth had tanned his hide and taken his cottage from him. He thrashed them both impartially with a hunting thong every Saturday night — to teach them, and to remind them that for them he had lost his cottage and the ten bob a week Fittleworth allowed such hinds as had been in his service thirty years . . . Sex ferocity again!

And how shall I thy true love know
  from another one?
Oh, by his cockled hat and staff and by
  his sandalled shoon!

An undoubted pilgrim had suggested irresistibly the lines to him! . . . It was, naturally, that bitch Sylvia. Wet eyes she had! . . . Then some psychological crisis was going on inside her. Good for her.

Good for Val and Chris, possibly. There was no real knowing . . . Oh, but there was. Hear to that: the bitch-pack giving tongue! Heard ye ever the like to that, sirs. She had had Groby Great Tree torn down . . . But as God was her maker she would not tear another woman's child . . .

He felt himself begin to perspire . . . Well,

if Sylvia had come to that his, Mark's, occupation was gone. He would no longer have to go on willing against her; she would drop into the sea in the wake of their family vessel and be lost to view . . . But damn it, she must have suffered to be brought to that extreme . . . Poor bitch! Poor bitch! The riding had done it . . . She ran away, a handkerchief to her eyes.

He felt satisfaction and impatience. There was some place to which he desired to get back. But there were also things to be done: to be thought out . . . If God was beginning to temper the wind to these flayed lambs . . . Then . . . He could not remember what he wanted to think about . . . It was — no, not exasperating. Numb! He felt himself responsible for their happiness. He wanted them to go rubbing along, smooth with the rough, for many long, unmarked years . . . He wanted Marie Léonie to stay with Valentine until after her deliverance and then go to the Dower House at Groby. She was Lady Tietjens. She knew she was Lady Tietjens and she would like it. Besides she would be a thorn in the flesh of Mrs . . . He could not remember the name . . .

He wished that Christopher would get rid of his Jewish partner so as to addle a little brass. It was their failing as Tietjenses that they liked toadies. He himself had bitched all their lives by having that fellow Ruggles years ago sharing his rooms. Because he could not have borne to share with an equal and Ruggles was half Jew, half Scotchman. Christopher had had for toadies firstly Macmaster, a Scot, and then this American Jew. Otherwise he, Mark, was reconciled with things. Christopher no doubt was wise in his choice. He had achieved a position in which he might — with just a little more to it — anticipate jogging away to the end of time, leaving descendants to carry on the country without swank.

Ah . . . It came to his mind to remember, almost with pain. He had accepted nephew Mark as nephew Mark: a strong slip. A good boy . . . But there was the point . . . the point! The boy had the right sort of breeches . . . But if there were incest . . .

Crawling through a hedge after a rabbit was thinkable. Father had been in the churchyard to shoot rabbits to oblige the vicar. There was no doubt of that. He did not want rabbits . . . But supposing he had mis-hit a bunny and the little beast had been throwing gymnastics on the other side of the quickset? Father would have crawled through then rather than go all the way to the lych-gate and round. Decent men put their mis-hits out of their agony as soon as possible. Then there was motive. And as for not putting his gun out of action before crawling through the quickset . . . Many good, plucked men had died like that . . . *And father had grown absent-minded!* . . . There had been farmer Lowther had so died; and Pease of Lobhall; and Pease of Cullercoats. All good plucked farmers . . . Crawling through hedges rather than go round, and with their guns at full cock! And not absent-minded men . . . But he had remembered . . . just now, he had remembered that father had grown absent-minded. He would put a paper in one of his waistcoat pockets and fumble for it in all his other pockets a moment after; he would push his spectacles up onto his forehead and search all the room for them; he would place his knife and fork in his plate and whilst talking take another knife and fork from beside it and begin again to eat . . . Mark remembered that his father had done that twice during the last meal they had eaten together — whilst he, Mark, had been presenting the fellow Ruggles's account of Christopher's mis-deeds . . .

Then it need not be incumbent on him, Mark, to go up to his father in heaven and say: 'Hullo, sir. I understand you had a

315

daughter by the wife of your best friend, she being now with child by your son.' Rather ghostly to introduce yourself to the awful ghost of your father . . . Of course you would be a ghost yourself. Still, not, with your billycock hat, umbrella, and racing-glasses, an awful ghost! . . . And to say to your father: 'I understand that you committed suicide!'

Against the rules of the Club . . . For I consider it no grief to be going there where so many great men have preceded me. Sophocles that, wasn't it? So, on his authority it was a damn good club . . .

But he did not have to anticipate that *mauvais quart d'heure*! Dad quite obviously did not commit suicide. He wasn't the man to do so. So Valentine was not his daughter and there was no incest. It is all very well to say that you care little about incest. The Greeks made a hell of a tragic row about it . . . Certainly it was a weight off the chest. He had always been able to look Christopher in the eyes — but he would be able to do it better than ever now. Comfortably! It is uncomfortable to look a man in the eyes and think: You sleep between incestuous sheets.

That then was over. The worst of it rolled up together. No suicide. No incest. No by-blow at Groby . . . A Papist there . . . Though how you could be a Papist and a

316

Marxian-Communist passed his, Mark's comprehension . . . A Papist at Groby and Groby Great Tree down . . . The curse was perhaps off the family!

That was a superstitious way to look at it — but you must have a pattern to interpret things by. You can't really get your mind to work without it. The blacksmith said: By hammer and hand all art doth stand! . . . He, Mark Tietjens, for many years interpreted all life in terms of Transport . . . Transport be thou my God . . . A damn good God . . . And in the end, after a hell of a lot of thought and of work the epitaph of him, Mark Tietjens, ought by rights to be: *'Here lies one whose name was writ in sea-birds!'* As good an epitaph as another.

He must get it through to Christopher that Marie Léonie should have that case of stuffed birds with Bamborough and all, in her bedroom at Groby Dower House. It was the last permanent record of her man . . . But Christopher would know that . . .

It was coming back. A lot of things were coming back . . . He could see Redcar Sands running up towards Sunderland, grey, grey. Not so many factory chimnies then, working for him, Mark Tietjens! Not so many! And the sandpipers running in the thin of the tide, bowing as they ran; and the shovellers turning

317

over stones and the terns floating above the viscous sea . . .

But it was great nights to which he would not turn his attention; great black nights above the purple moors . . . Great black nights above the Edgeware Road where Marie Léonie lived . . . because, above the blaze of lights of the old Apollo's front, you had a sense of immense black spaces . . .

Who said he was perspiring a great deal? Well, he *was* perspiring!

Marie Léonie, young, was bending over him . . . Young, young, as he had first seen her on the stage of Covent Garden . . . In white! . . . Doing agreeable things to his face with a perfume like that of Heaven itself! . . . And laughing sideways as Marie Léonie had laughed when first he presented himself before her in his billycock hat and umbrella! . . . The fine, fair hair! The soft voice!

But this was silly . . . That was nephew Mark with his cherry-red face and staring eyes . . . And this was his light of love! . . . Naturally. Like uncle, like nephew. He would pick up with the same type of woman as his uncle. That made it certain that this was no by-blow! Pretty piece against the apple boughs!

He wanted great nights, then! — Young Mark, though, should not pick up with a woman older than himself. Christopher had done that and look!

Still, things were takking oop! . . . Do you remember the Yorkshireman who stood with his chin just out of the water on Ararat Top as Noah approached. And: 'It's boon to tak oop!' said the Yorkshireman . . . It's bound to clear up!

A great night, with room enough for Heaven to be hidden there from our not too perspicacious eyes . . . It was said that an earthquake shock imperceptible to our senses set those cattle and sheep and horses and pigs crashing through all the hedges of the county. And it was queer: before they had so started lowing and moving Mark was now ready to swear that he had heard a rushing sound. He probably had not! One could so easily self-deceive oneself! The cattle had been panicked because they had been sensible of the presence of the Almighty walking upon the firmament . . .

Damn it all: there were a lot of things coming back. He could have sworn he heard the voice of Ruggles say: 'After all he is virtually Tietjens of Groby!' . . . By no fault of yours, old cock! But now you will be cadging up to him . . . Now there speaks Edith Ethel Macmaster! A lot of voices passing behind his head. Damn it all, could they all be ghosts drifting before the wind! . . . Or damn it all, was he himself dead! . . . No, you were probably not profane when you were dead.

He would have given the world to sit up and turn his head round and see. Of course he could, but that would give the show away! He credited himself with being too cunning an old fox for that! To have thrown dust in their eyes for all these years! He could have chuckled!

Fittleworth seemed to have come down into the orchard. What the devil could Fittleworth want? It was like a pantomime. Fittleworth in effect was looking at him. He said:

'Hello, old bean . . . ' Marie Léonie was looking from beside his elbow. He said: 'I've driven all these goats out of your hen-roost . . . ' Good-looking fellow, Fittleworth. His Lola Vivaria had been a garden-peach. Died in child-birth. No doubt that was why he had troubled to come. Fittleworth said: Cammie said to give Mark her love for old time's sake. Her dear love! And as soon as he was well to bring her ladyship down.

Damn this sweat. With its beastly tickling he would grimace and give the show away. But he would like Marie Léonie to go to the Fittleworths'. Marie Léonie said something to Fittleworth.

'Yes, yes, me lady!' says Fittleworth. Damn it, he did look like a monkey as some people said . . . But if the monkeys we were descended from were as good-looking . . . Probably he had good-looking legs . . . How beautiful upon the mountains are the feet of them that bring good tidings to Zion! . . .

Fittleworth added earnestly and distinctly that his sister-in-law, Sylvia, *begged* Mark to understand that she had not sent that flock of idiots down here. Sylvia also said that she was going to divorce his, Mark's, brother and dissolve her marriage with the sanction of Rome . . . So they would all be a happy family down there, soon . . . Anything Cammie could do . . . And because of Mark's unforgettable services to the country . . .

Name was written in . . . Lettest thou thy servant . . . divorce in peace!

Marie Léonie begged Fittleworth to go away now. Fittleworth said he would, but joy never kills! So long, old . . . old friend! The clubs they had been in together! . . .

But one went to a far better Club than . . . His breathing was a little troublesome . . . It was darkish, then light again.

Christopher was at the foot of his bed. Holding a bicycle and a lump of wood. Aromatic wood, a chunk sawn from a tree.

His face was white; his eyes stuck out. Blue pebbles. He gazed at his brother and said:

'Half Groby wall is down. Your bedroom's wrecked. I found your case of sea-birds thrown on a rubble heap.'

It was as well that one's services were unforgettable!

Valentine was there, panting as if she had been running. She exclaimed to Christopher:

'You left the prints for Lady Robinson in a jar you gave to Hudnut the dealer. How could you? Oh, how could you? How are we going to feed and clothe a child if you do such things?'

He lifted his bicycle wearily round. You could see he was dreadfully weary, the poor devil. Mark almost said:

'Let him off, the poor devil's worn out!'

Heavily, like a dejected bulldog, Christopher made for the gate. As he went up the green path beyond the hedge, Valentine began to sob.

'How are we to live? How are we ever to live?'

'Now I must speak,' Mark said to himself. He said:

'Did ye ever hear tell o't' Yorkshireman . . . On Mount Ara . . . Ara . . . '

He had not spoken for so long. His tongue appeared to fill his mouth; his mouth to be twisted to one side. It was growing dark. He said:

'Put your ear close to my mouth . . . ' She cried out!

He whispered:

''Twas the mid o' the night and the
  barnies grat
And the mither beneath the mauld
  heard that.'

. . . 'An old song. My nurse sang it . . . Never thou let thy barnie weep for thy sharp tongue to thy goodman . . . A good man! . . . Groby Great Tree is down . . . '

He said: 'Hold my hand!'

She inserted her hand beneath the sheet and his hot hand closed on hers. Then it relaxed.

She nearly cried out for Marie Léonie.

The tall, sandy, much-liked doctor came through the gate.

She said:

'He spoke just now . . . It has been a torturing afternoon . . . Now I'm afraid . . . I'm afraid he's . . . '

The doctor reached his hand beneath the sheet, leaning down. He said:

'Go get you to bed . . . I will come and examine you . . . '

She said:

'Perhaps it would be best not to tell Lady Tietjens that he spoke . . . She would have liked to have his last words . . . But she did not need them as much as I.'

We do hope that you have enjoyed reading this large print book.

Did you know that all of our titles are available for purchase?

We publish a wide range of high quality large print books including:
**Romances, Mysteries, Classics**
**General Fiction**
**Non Fiction and Westerns**

Special interest titles available in large print are:
**The Little Oxford Dictionary**
**Music Book**
**Song Book**
**Hymn Book**
**Service Book**

Also available from us courtesy of Oxford University Press:
**Young Readers' Dictionary**
**(large print edition)**
**Young Readers' Thesaurus**
**(large print edition)**

For further information or a free brochure, please contact us at:
**Ulverscroft Large Print Books Ltd.,**
**The Green, Bradgate Road, Anstey,**
**Leicester, LE7 7FU, England.**
**Tel:** (00 44) 0116 236 4325
**Fax:** (00 44) 0116 234 0205

*Other titles published by*
*The House of Ulverscroft:*

## SOME DO NOT . . .

### Ford Madox Ford

Christopher Tietjens, quietly preoccupied with his disastrous marriage to the beautiful, faithless Sylvia, takes a diverting golfing weekend in the country at the suggestion of his friend Macmaster. This is to change the course of the brilliant mathematician's life, for it is here he meets suffragette Valentine Wannop. Despite their mutual attraction and affection however, Tietjens refuses to betray Sylvia as she has betrayed him. With the coming of the War, the world of sureties and moral codes that Tietjens has known, believed in and upheld is shattered — as is he . . .

# NO MORE PARADES

## Ford Madox Ford

Captain Christopher Tietjens endures cold, mud and air-raids in a French base camp, preoccupied with his crumbling marriage, and battling not the German forces but the nightmare bureaucracy of the British Army. Abandoned — so he supposes — by the heartless Sylvia, he is bombarded by insistent thoughts of Valentine Wannop, though his sense of honour forbids him from furthering their association beyond anything but chaste friendship. Then all is altered by the sudden appearance of Sylvia in France, for her machinations will throw everything into chaos . . .

# A MAN COULD STAND UP —

## Ford Madox Ford

Surrounded by the jubilation of Armistice Day, Valentine Wannop receives a telephone call which brings alarming news of her dear friend Christopher Tietjens. For whilst she strains to hear against the racket of celebratory firecrackers, Christopher's mind still echoes with the bombardments and horrors he endured in the hell of the Front. With trepidation, harbouring deep concerns over his mental equilibrium, the pacifist Valentine must seek out Christopher once more — but what will come of their reunion?